To Save His Baby
Judi Lind

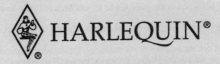

HARLEQUIN®

TORONTO • NEW YORK • LONDON
AMSTERDAM • PARIS • SYDNEY • HAMBURG
STOCKHOLM • ATHENS • TOKYO • MILAN • MADRID
PRAGUE • WARSAW • BUDAPEST • AUCKLAND

For my own special daughter,
Valerie, and the beautiful baby she and her hero
have brought into the world.

ISBN 0-373-22531-8

TO SAVE HIS BABY

Copyright © 1999 by Judith A. Lind

Visit us at www.romance.net

Printed in U.S.A.

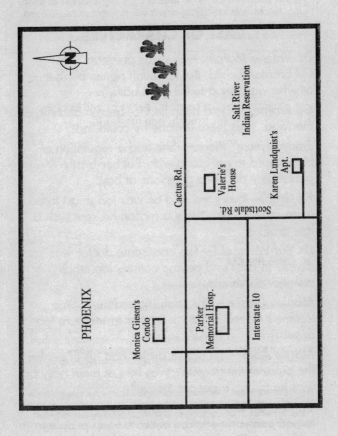

PHOENIX

Monica Giesen's Condo

Parker Memorial Hosp.

Interstate 10

Cactus Rd.

Scottsdale Rd.

Valerie's House

Karen Lundquist's Apt.

Salt River Indian Reservation

CAST OF CHARACTERS

Dr. Valerie Murphy—She was pregnant with Gil Branton's child. But he didn't remember her—or who was trying to kill them both.

Gil Branton—He'd been lied to, beaten and run off the road. Was there anyone he could trust?

Emily "Fierce" Pierce—She had a reputation of being hard to get along with. But her bristly personality did keep questions at bay.

Ed Grant—Everyone said he was too smart to be a mere orderly. Was there a reason he kept such a low profile?

Dr. Sid Weingold—The handsome doctor was deeply in debt and paying entirely too much attention to Valerie.

Monica Giesen—The sophisticated nurse was Valerie's trusted assistant. But her tastes were too expensive for a nurse's salary.

Martin Abel—The administrator had his finger on the pulse of the hospital. Was he just plain nosy or was he hiding a deeper motive?

Dr. Carl Bender—The arrogant young physician turned everyone off. The better to keep people from asking questions?

Marsha Ainslee—Her job offered access to all the records while providing the perfect cover-up. Why was she so helpful?

Ferdy Sanchez—The detective was everywhere. Was his investigation getting too close for comfort?

Chapter One

Tossing the single utilitarian blond braid over her shoulder, Valerie Murphy flopped into the battered avocado-green easy chair and lifted her feet onto the even more battered matching ottoman. Ohh. Relief shuddered through her weary body. This was the first time she'd been off her feet in what—seven hours?

Fortunately the Lundquist birth had been simple and swift because the Diaz delivery had been touch-and-go for a while, draining Valerie's physical and mental strength. Bringing a healthy and much-wanted baby into the world was euphoric, but tending to a pair of mothers in labor at the same time had nearly wiped her out.

She offered a quick but sincere prayer that the city of Phoenix would remain baby-free long enough for her to down a revitalizing dose of coffee. Fingers mentally crossed, she raised the steaming mug to her lips.

The doctors' lounge door swung open and the charge nurse stepped in, her broad face flushed. "Oh, thank God you're still here!"

"I'm not." Valerie shook her head. "You don't see me. I'm gone."

"Sorry, Doctor, but we have a situation. Twelve seri-

ous and twenty non-life threatening injuries on their way.
All available MDs needed in ER.''

Valerie groaned. A "situation" was the hospital code
word for a disaster. "What happened?"

"Sandstorm. Eighty-car pileup on Interstate 10. Gotta
round up the others." The door swung closed behind the
nurse's ample backside.

An eighty-car collision? The number was staggering.
Rogue windstorms were legendary in the Phoenix area.
Sudden swirling gusts swept across the desert, ushering
in a blinding curtain of sand. Valerie had seen cars that
had been caught in windstorms, their paint scoured down
to bare metal by the whipping sand.

She shuddered, imagining the carnage that might result
when drivers hurtling down the freeway were suddenly
blinded by that opaque wall of raging desert sand.

Valerie gulped the scalding brew, hoping the caffeine
would kick in by the time she reached the emergency
ward. Instinctively brushing her hand across the surgical
scrubs that used to bag around her middle, she sighed in
resignation. It was going to be a long night. She rose to
her feet and rubbed the small of her aching back.

As she made her way from the physicians' lounge to
the elevator, her own natural adrenaline took command
and she was fully alert when she bumped open the stainless-steel door to the emergency department.

The white-tiled space looked like the staging area for
a major battle. Pink-, blue- and green-uniformed staff
choked the hallways. Nurses stocked supplementary
crash carts while orderlies shoved additional beds and
gurneys into every available nook and cranny.

Snapping on a pair of sterile latex gloves, Valerie reported to the head nurse who was directing medical personnel into the appropriate cubicles.

"What have we got?" she shouted over the din.

Emily Pierce, night charge nurse of the ER and known throughout the hospital as Fierce Pierce, shoved a chart in Val's hand and led her into treatment room six. "You tell me, Doc. Ambulances are on the way with most of the collision victims. In the meantime, we just received a John Doe, probably homeless, approximately thirty-five to forty, although who can tell with all that fur growing on his face?"

Valerie ignored the nurse's aside and waited for her to continue. Fierce Pierce might be flippant, irreverent and even disdainful of some of the physicians who rotated through the ward, but she was the best triage nurse in the hospital, maybe even the city.

Without skipping a beat, Nurse Pierce rattled off the unknown patient's vital statistics. Valerie glanced at the bloody, inert man lying on the gurney. His features were obscured by a three-day growth of beard and a tangle of darker hair around his face. His clothing, blue T-shirt and jeans, were caked with filth and torn or slashed in several places. Dark-red blood oozed from every rent in the fabric.

"You say he wasn't involved in the pileup?" Valerie asked.

Pierce shook her mop of unkempt red hair. "Nope. He was found by a beat cop in the alley behind Frisco's." Frisco's was a notorious biker bar on the outskirts of town. "Unconscious, dehydrated and in shock. Mr. Doe apparently ticked off one or more of the bikers, resulting in massive trauma to the head and torso, probably the result of a tire iron."

Approaching the gurney, Valerie flicked on her penlight and raised the patient's eyelids. His pupils were equal and reactive; still, because the victim had lost consciousness, she couldn't rule out concussion. "Call neuro, tell them to get somebody down here for a consult."

Pierce noted the orders on the patient's chart while another nurse picked up the intercom phone and made the request.

Assessing the most obvious wounds on the cruelly beaten man, Valerie ordered X rays, then cut open his shirt to palpate his abdomen. Although bruises were already coloring the mystery man's stomach, there was no evidence of internal bleeding.

In fact, his well-defined stomach muscles were exceptionally supple. But his entire torso was splotched with ugly red welts and abrasions.

Her previous rotation in the trauma unit had been a deciding factor in Valerie's decision to specialize in obstetrics. She'd found it nearly impossible to separate herself from the incredible brutalities human beings inflicted on one another. Where was the sport in a gang of roughnecks, armed with chains, knives and tire irons, nearly beating the life out of a helpless and unarmed man?

Her heart ached for the stranger lying unconscious on the gurney.

She raised her stethoscope to his chest and was pleased to find his heartbeat strong and steady, despite the severity of his injuries. Her trained eye scanned his chest, with its mat of dark hair. His flesh was firm, his biceps and pectorals taut and developed. This man didn't live on the streets. The shape he was in was excellent. A robbery victim?

"Any ID?" she asked.

Fierce Pierce shook her head. "Not that we've found. Maybe the responding officers found something. Grant, go check with those two cops out front. Or the paramedics if they're still around. See if anyone found any personal effects for our John Doe.''

The orderly nodded and hurried to do her bidding. She'd worked with him before when he'd been assigned to obstetrics. In Valerie's opinion, Ed Grant was too sharp and too intuitive to waste his talents as an orderly. She made a mental note to talk to him again about applying for nursing school.

Reaching for John Doe's wrist, she took his pulse again, satisfied that he was stabilized and out of immediate danger. Until the two specialists she'd requested arrived, and X rays were taken and read, there wasn't much Valerie could do except treat his cuts and bruises.

While the nurse fetched gauze and antiseptic, Valerie continued to stare at her patient, feeling an eerie kinship with him. The slope of his wide shoulders seemed almost familiar. Since she knew precious few men who weren't on the hospital staff, and John Doe certainly wasn't someone she encountered frequently, she wondered if he might be the husband of one of the nurses. No wedding ring adorned his long slender finger, but that didn't mean he wasn't married.

There was no way to tell how long he'd been lying unconscious in that alley, but surely someone was looking for him.

"Is something wrong, Doctor?" Fierce Pierce stood at her elbow, holding a basin filled with sterile cleansing solution.

Valerie jerked free of her daydream, aware of her encroaching feelings of attachment to this nameless man. *Stay detached, Doctor,* she warned herself. She shouldn't have to be reminded that emotional detachment was the key to survival.

But his medical background could be vitally important

to his treatment, she rationalized. Except for his unkempt appearance, she might have thought he was a businessman who'd been mugged. She shook her head, dismissing her first impression. He was too lean, too exceptionally muscular for a sedentary businessman.

One bruise, high on the left side of his chest, almost at his left shoulder, was more deeply colored than the others. Valerie dabbed a piece of antiseptic gauze with alcohol and gently rubbed the area. Most of the discoloration was oil and tar residue from the alley, but *something* was hidden by the grime. A birthmark? Tattoo? She continued wiping until the marking on his skin was readily apparent.

A tattoo. The small all-too-familiar tattoo of a hawk's head—the noble symbol of strength and perseverance. Her hand stilled and a curious dryness scourged her throat. No…it couldn't be. Not him. Her gaze flew to his face, his features suddenly completely recognizable beneath the dirt and heavy stubble.

As the realization began to sink in, Valerie's mouth watered and her stomach clenched in protest. She was going to be sick.

A pink-uniformed technician rattled into the room, pulling a portable X ray machine behind him. "Make way, folks. The king of cameras, the baron of bones, is here to photograph the body parts of Mr.—" He broke off and glanced at a paper he'd had tucked under his arm. "Mr. Doe, is it? Well, Mr. Doe, we're gonna make you famous."

Normally Valerie enjoyed the man's perpetual good mood and harmless banter. Not today. She barely noted his presence.

As Valerie instinctively backed away from the patient so the technician could position the film plates, Fierce

Pierce touched her shoulder. "You never said—do we wait for the attending neuro or find a backup?"

Valerie stared at the nurse as if seeing her for the first time. "Wh-what? What did you say?"

"Are you okay, Doc? You look kinda pale."

Valerie waved aside her comment. The nausea was rising in her gorge, blocking her voice.

Taking her silence as a denial, Pierce waved the patient chart like a flag. "Yoo-hoo, Dr. Murphy. The patient— John Doe? What do you want me to do about a neurological consult since the attending is delayed for another twenty minutes?"

Valerie stared at the unconscious man lying in his own blood. She peeled off the sterile gloves with a loud snap and dropped them into the hazardous-waste container. Her stomach roiled with acid and she feared she might faint. Turning on her heel, she ran for the hall, pausing in the open doorway. "You can let the bastard die for all I care."

STOPPING AT THE WATER COOLER, Valerie gulped three cups of cool liquid in a futile attempt to quench the fire in her stomach. Why now? After nearly four months, why had Gil Branton returned to Phoenix? And why did he have to end up in *her* treatment room?

Valerie's head jerked upright. *Yeah, Doctor,* your *treatment room.* Your *responsibility.* A chill of shame washed over her for fleeing from her patient, even though he'd been stabilized. Because no matter how she felt about Gil Branton, and there'd been times she'd wished she could beat him senseless herself, it was her sworn duty to treat his injuries and watch out for his well-being as long as he was under her care.

So where's that famous objectivity, Dr. Murphy?

She crumpled the paper cup and dropped it into the trash receptacle. Straightening her back, she drew in a deep breath for courage and laid a calming hand across her stomach. Calling on her medical training to see her through this ordeal, she willed the memory of Gil Branton and what he'd done to her back into the hidden recesses of her mind. Back into the box where she'd kept those painful images hidden for the past four months.

Pasting a smile on her face, she flipped her braid over her shoulder and marched back into the treatment room.

THE HAZY RED CURTAIN of pain lifted slightly and Gil risked opening one eye. The dazzling white from the tiled walls and floor almost blinded him and he closed the eye in defense. That brief peek had been enough, though. That white light wasn't the welcoming glow of heaven. He wasn't dead. He was lying on a gurney in a hospital. An emergency room, he guessed, judging from the movement around him.

He wondered briefly if he was going to die. Seemed kind of a shame to give in now after what he'd been through these past months. Still, thoughts of a pain-free peace of death weren't altogether disheartening. There wasn't much in his life left to look forward to, he thought, except more pain.

There wasn't much in his life, period. What he could recall of it, anyway. For the thousandth time in the past four months, Gil clenched his eyes and tried to will a fragment of memory into his consciousness. He knew *who* he was—but only because others had told him. Just as they'd informed him of his occupation and the fact that he was a loner, with no family and few friends.

But who was he—inside—and why had he led such a solitary existence? And, dear God, why did he instinctively *know* that he'd lost something incredibly precious when he'd lost his memory?

Gil turned slightly and felt a searing jolt of pain down his side. His slight moan captured the attention of a blue-suited nurse and she bustled to his side.

"Hey, Bearded Wonder, have we decided to come back and join the living?"

Gil grunted. "Why don't *we* dispense a couple c.c.'s of morphine? And water."

Fierce Pierce reached for a chart on the foot of his bed. "I'll have to check with the doctor about your pain meds, Mr. Branton, but I think we can manage the water."

He grabbed her arm, unexplained panic rippling along his spine. "How did you know my name?"

She pulled loose from his grasp, and an instant later, the sweet relief of an ice cube slid across his cracked lips. "Vee hafe our methods. Vee know everysink."

Her manner was teasing, and although his memory was fuzzy and specific details unaccountably elusive, Gil remembered enough to be afraid. If he'd been recognized, he had to leave. Now.

Before he could question the nurse further, she moved away, along with the sliver of consciousness he'd been holding on to. Gil slipped back into blessed sleep.

Sometime later—a minute? a week?—he felt a gentle touch on his shoulder and his eyes fluttered open. The large red-headed nurse was at his side again, a tumbler of water in her hand.

Gil licked his lips in anticipation of the quenching liquid and tried to sit up. Another pain-racked groan escaped his lips. "What the hell did you people do to me? *Beat* my ribs back into place?"

The nurse chuckled as she deftly slipped a supporting hand behind his back. "Doctor said you'd be a terrible patient. But don't give me a hard time,'' she warned. ''Remember, I have the power of the Fleet enema on my side.''

She raised the flexible straw to his lips and he sucked the water into his parched throat. Gil drank deeply until she pulled the glass from his greedy mouth. "Enough now. I just put some happy juice into your IV, so you should rest comfortably for a while. Nightie night.''

Unable to form a cohesive reply, he shuddered back onto the rock-hard pillow and closed his eyes.

MIDNIGHT. ALL THE ACCIDENT victims had finally been treated and hospitalized or released. Incredibly only a single fatality resulted from the myriad of crushed vehicles. Valerie leaned against the wall and drank in the silence. She could go home now. And sleep. Forget this night.

She had the next three days off. Three whole days away from the clinic. Away from birth, death and this hospital.

Away from Gil Branton.

By the time she returned on Thursday, he should be discharged. She'd never have to see him again.

But she'd also never know why he'd abandoned her.

Not that it mattered, she reasoned, gathering her personal items from her locker. She'd picked up the pieces of her life and moved on. She didn't need Gil or his lousy excuses. She was finished with him. Done. Over it.

Except it wasn't over. For Valerie, their brief history would never be over.

The price she would pay for loving Gil Branton was going to be extracted for a very long time.

She tugged her braid over her shoulder onto her chest to make room for her backpack, then wound the braid into a knot on the back of her head and pinned it into place. Gil had always loved her long hair.

Who cared what he liked? Maybe she'd cut it off. A short pixie style would be easier to care for.

She strode out of the physicians' lounge and headed for the exit nearest the staff parking lot. Why was she thinking about Gil, anyway? As far as she was concerned, he probably deserved the beating. Guilt rippled through her. No, he didn't deserve that beating. No one did. Not even a lying, perfidious, leave-you-all-but-at-the-altar jerk like Gil.

Why had he been so badly beaten? Obviously he was the victim of a robbery, but what was he doing near that biker bar in the first place?

She bumped the exterior door open with her hip and pulled her keys out of her pocket. "Night, Pete," she called to the security guard who patrolled the parking lot.

Well, for the next three days, she could put Gil out of her mind. He was stabilized and receiving excellent medical care. Nothing more for her to worry about. Besides, she had her own future and her own problems to sort out.

As she slid behind the wheel of her Celica, Valerie glanced up at the imposing hospital structure. Automatically her gaze lifted to the fifth floor. Most of the lights were out; the patients in the fifth-floor ward, Gil's ward, were sleeping peacefully. She'd done her duty to her patient. She could go home with a clear conscience.

But not an easy heart.

Despite her protests to the contrary, Valerie had to know the truth. Why had Gil dumped her so callously? Hadn't she at least deserved a phone call? A last meal?

If she didn't get an explanation, Valerie knew she would never be fully free of him, nor of the shell of cynicism she'd erected around her heart. She'd never be able to trust again, and that would be her loss, not Gil Branton's.

Filled with determination, yet sick with the thought of facing him, she slid out from behind the wheel and headed back for the hospital entrance.

Minutes later she was on the fifth floor and making her way quietly down the hall. The ward was eerily silent; only the mechanical whoosh of an occasional respirator broke the stillness. The ward lights had been dimmed and the temperature was cool, almost chilly. Like a morgue, she thought, then shivered in surprise that her thoughts had become so morbid. She'd served her share of night duty and never felt the creeps before. She was giving in to the uneasiness of facing Gil, transferring the blame for her uneasiness to the dim wards of a sleeping hospital.

Although she moved slowly, her footsteps nonetheless eventually led her to Gil's bedside. Pausing beside the privacy curtain surrounding his bed, she steeled herself for the coming confrontation.

It took a moment for her eyes to adjust to the near darkness. The venetian blinds, which were set between two layers of glass in the unopenable windows, were closed tightly. Not even moonlight penetrated the darkness.

Once she'd gained her night vision, she padded around the bed and stood near his head. Gil was sleeping, so peacefully that she hesitated to awaken him. His dark lashes lay against his cheeks. Valerie's fingertip brushed the stubble of his salt-and-pepper beard.

How she'd loved this man once.

How she hated him now.

Summoning all the anger, all the hurt and all the self-doubts his desertion had caused, she forced her heart back into its stainless-steel casing. "Gil?"

He stirred slightly, but didn't awake.

"Gil." She poked his shoulder with a fingertip. "It's me, Valerie. Time to wake up and face the music. Gil!"

The dark lashes fluttered and he opened his eyes. Those lovely melting chocolate-brown eyes she'd once trusted and adored. Those duplicitous brown eyes.

His hand reached out and clutched hers tightly, like a drowning man clinging to a life raft. "Honey, is that—" He broke off and licked his parched lips.

Despite her hatred for this man, her medical training and physician's heart refused to let him suffer. She reached for the carafe by his bed. Empty. Stifling a sigh, she whispered, "I'll get you some water. Then we'll talk."

Pulling her hand from his disconcerting grasp, she gathered up his carafe and empty glass and headed for the adjoining bathroom. To protect him from the bright fluorescence, she closed the bathroom door before turning on the light.

Adjusting the cold-water flow to a trickle, she glanced into the mirror. She was startled by her reflection. Her mouth was drawn tight, and her eyebrows were knotted in a ferocious frown. She looked like an unhappy bitter woman.

She laughed wryly. Wasn't that what she'd become? A woman who no longer found any joy in life? When Gil had jilted her, he'd taken a part of her—her vibrancy, her humor—with him. Now she was going to take it back.

Returning to the task at hand, she filled the plastic carafe and rinsed out his tumbler and straw. She switched off the light and allowed her vision to readjust to the darkness before she swung open the bathroom door.

She halted after taking only a couple of steps, shocked into place by the sight of a man leaning over Gil's bed. A part of her registered that something was very wrong, but she was too startled to pay it heed.

"Hello," she called softly, not wanting to startle the person who was attending to Gil. "I'm Dr. Murphy. I treated your patient in the ER and stopped in to see—"

The man beside the bed whirled around, stared at her for a moment, then bolted for the door.

"I'm sorry, I didn't mean to—" Before she could complete the sentence, he pushed past her, almost knocking her down in his mad race to escape. Never looking behind, he disappeared into the corridor, leaving the door open wide.

Shaking her head in wonder, Valerie moved to the door to close it. The conversation she intended to have with Gil was better done in private. Her hand still clutching the water pitcher, she glanced down the corridor just in time to see the man dash through the steel fire door into the stairwell.

"Wait!" she called. "Why are you..." Her voice trailed off and she leaned against the doorjamb for support. At that moment she knew what her instincts had been trying to tell her all along. That man had been dressed in jeans and a dark T-shirt. No uniform. No hospital identification badge.

Sudden fear clutched her heart and she darted back to Gil's bedside. He was thrashing in the bed, his fingers clutching his throat as he gasped for breath.

Chapter Two

Valerie set the carafe on the nightstand and flipped on the overhead light. Reflexively Gil turned from the harsh glare and she grabbed his head between her strong hands. Was he choking? A reaction to his meds?

Like a cornered cougar, he instinctively fought her. Not wanting to take the precious seconds to find the call button and summon help, Valerie leaped onto the narrow bed and put one leg over his torso to stifle his thrashing. When he'd quieted somewhat, she tilted his chin. His airway seemed clear and from the way he was gulping air, nothing was lodged in his lungs.

She yanked down the sheet and scanned his torso. No welts or hives indicative of anaphylactic shock from an allergic reaction. Grabbing her penlight from her backpack, she opened his mouth and checked his airway. Clear. No swollen tissues. Nothing obvious was obstructing his breathing. But *something* was wrong. "Gil! Calm down. You're okay."

He waved a dismissive hand and continued to suck in oxygen rapidly, like a drowning victim who'd been plucked from the ocean at the last possible moment.

He stared at her as if he'd never seen her before.

"Gil? What's wrong? You're hyperventilating." Had

he been surprised, even frightened, by the man who'd been in the room? She'd never imagined Gil to be the panicky type. But then, had she ever really known him?

After a few moments his breathing slowed and she thought he'd gone back to sleep. When she started to leave the room to let him rest, his hand clamped around her wrist.

"No! Don't leave."

She settled back down on the edge of the bed. Despite her bitterness toward the man lying on the bed, she none-theless felt a splinter of compassion. As if they were act-ing independently of her will, her fingertips smoothed the rumpled dark hair from his forehead. "Go to sleep, Gil. I'll stay."

He shook his head and forced out halting words. "No. Can't stay. They'll…kill me."

"What?"

"That man…tried to…" Gil didn't finish, but he pointed to the floor beside the bed.

She glanced down and was startled to discover a pillow beside her foot. Gil was tired, delirious. He must have pushed it off the bed while thrashing about. Her gaze traveled back to his dark head. The pillow was beneath it.

But it was on the floor, so how…?

Valerie's gaze darted across the room to the vacant bed. Where a pillow should have been was glaringly empty. Even as her mind put the pieces together, she could scarcely believe the finished picture. In his present condition, hooked to IVs, tubes and myriad machinery, there was no way Gil could have managed to cross the room and get that pillow. Yet there it was on the floor beside his bed, quietly telling a horrible truth.

Like a sleepwalker, she bent over and retrieved it, still

not believing what must have transpired. "That man, who was he?"

Ignoring her question, Gil struggled to sit up. "You have to help me, Doctor. He'll be back. Believe me, these people never quit."

Apparently exhausted from the effort of speaking, he sank back down on the bed.

"Who, Gil? Who are these people and why would they want to kill you? Talk to me!"

His dark eyes, their whites shot with broken blood vessels, searched her face. The haunted face that stared at her now barely resembled the man she'd known a few short months ago. The man who'd left her without a word of farewell. "No time," he whispered. "Either get me out of here or…or I'll be…dead by morning."

Valerie reached for the bedside phone. "All right. I'll get security."

Her hand was stilled by Gil's laugh. A harsh sound that mocked her suggestion. "Security guard? That man was a pro. Your…rent-a-cops…would be as effective as preschoolers. We…have to get out of here."

Her hand still on the receiver, Valerie nodded. "The police, then. If there's anything to your story, they'll put a guard on your room."

Again that ugly laugh. Once more Gil struggled to sit upright, and this time he managed it. "Don't you understand? That man was a hired killer. And you saw him." His voice was measurably stronger, as if his strength were buoyed by the dangerous situation. "The cops are no match for a…hit man."

"Who? Who's after you?" She wanted to grab his shoulders and shake the truth out of him, for despite her anger, he'd somehow convinced her that his life—and possibly hers—was in danger.

In a move powered by sheer will, Gil managed to swing his legs over the edge of the bed. "Move," he muttered, reaching for the stainless-steel cart that held the vinyl bags containing intravenous fluids.

Valerie grabbed his hand and moved the cart. "No! You need that medication. I'll help you, Gil. Just as soon as you tell me what's going on. You owe me that much." She almost choked on the bile filling her throat at the oblique reference to how much he'd hurt her.

"Why? Why do I owe you?"

Her heart felt as if it were covered with a shell of ice. Valerie stared into his eyes, seeing no warmth. Not even any recognition. "You don't even know who I am, do you?"

His gaze raked her features. "Sure, you're the doctor from the ER. So, are you going to help me or not?"

Without waiting for a reply, he ineffectively pushed her from the cart, and wobbled to his feet. He stood for a moment, visibly corralling his strength. His voice was nearly normal when he stepped away from the bed. "The less you know, Doc, the safer we'll both be. Just get my clothes and put me into a cab. Once I'm gone, I don't think he'll come after you. He doesn't even know your name."

He took another step and almost fell on his face.

She grabbed his shoulders as he sagged against her. "Look at you—you can hardly stand. How do you expect to defend yourself against a man you tell me even the police can't stop? You're not making sense, Gil. Now get back into bed."

Turning his shaggy head, he stared into her eyes. "Then move me. Hide me. Now."

Valerie started to argue, to repeat that the only correct medical course was for him to remain in bed. But he was so agitated, his fear so real it was almost palpable, that she found herself wavering. Had the man really tried to smother Gil with the pillow?

How had he even known how to find him? Once she'd discovered who it was behind several days' growth of stubble, she'd been too shaken to reveal his identity to anyone other than Fierce Pierce. He was still listed on the hospital rolls as John Doe. And it was hospital policy not to release any information on a John Doe without police authority.

Something was dreadfully wrong.

Fully aware that she might be putting her job—even her life—on the line for a man who'd betrayed her, Valerie nonetheless knew she had no choice. No matter how badly Gil had treated her, she couldn't abdicate her moral responsibility. She couldn't stand idly by while another attempt was made on his life.

Putting her hands on his shoulders, she gently tipped him back onto the bed. "Stay here. I'll find another room."

She jerked her gaze away from the painfully raw emotion she saw reflected in his, and ran from the room.

As Valerie made her way down the deserted corridor, she reflected how different the atmosphere seemed tonight. How many hundred times had she traversed empty hospital hallways late at night? Never before had she felt this sense of isolation.

Her rubber-soled shoes were soundless in the eerily quiet ward. No quiet murmur of gossiping nurses reached her ears, no muted buzz of televisions or whispers of worried visitors. As she passed the partially open doors to the patients' rooms, the only sound was the occasional hum of life-sustaining machinery. She rounded the corner and the empty nurses' station was in sight.

Her heart sank. She'd expected the night nurse to be back from her rounds by now and felt oddly discomfited that the station was still unattended.

As Valerie approached the horseshoe-shaped nurses' station, bedecked with wilting flowers left by departing patients and draped with thank-you cards and cartoons inspired by hospital humor, she felt her equilibrium returning. Down the hall, the murmur of the night nurse's voice was calming.

Surrounded by the familiar accoutrements of her profession, Valerie felt her confidence surging. She stepped behind the desk and scanned the chart on the white erasable ink board hanging on the wall. The patients on the ward were listed in alphabetical order, along with their room numbers. Any special information was encoded on a small block beside their name.

Valerie's eyes flew down the list, Addams, Barber, Chavez, Criswell... No Branton. What was going on? Then she remembered that his identity was still unknown to the hospital computer. She glanced farther down the chart. Criswell, Delacruz, Doe. There he was. Doe, J.

When the authorities had heard a fragmented account of Gil's beating outside the biker bar, the hospital had been instructed not to allow visitors until he was questioned further by the Phoenix police.

The charge nurse's voice was louder now and Valerie was suddenly reminded that her intended course of action might not be in keeping with hospital policy. Valerie's domain was normally OB/GYN, so technically, now that Gil was no longer in ER, he wasn't her patient. The resident in charge of his case might not appreciate Valerie's interference.

But if Gil was truly in jeopardy, moving him was the only viable solution. Still, it might be better if her covert actions weren't witnessed. She quickly scanned the board for an empty room. Herschel in 533-A had been discharged earlier that evening. Like all the rooms on this floor, 533 was a double, but with any luck... No, 533-B was vacant, as well. Right across the hall. Easy enough for Valerie to manage his transfer without assistance.

She quickly changed the notation by Gil's name so the nurse wouldn't be blamed for any resulting foul-up, then raced back toward Gil's room. Just outside his door, she was assailed by a disquieting thought. What if the man had merely been the night janitor or someone who'd entered the wrong room? A hospital employee might take the stairs, instead of the elevator. What if Gil was delusional and she, supposedly a clear-thinking professional, had bought into his delusion?

Remembering the unexplained pillow, Valerie shook her head. If someone meant to harm him, she was doing the right thing. If Gil was, in fact, delusional, easing his fears might calm him. She could arrange for a psych consult in the morning.

Certain now that she'd made the right decision, she hurried into his room—and stopped when she saw his empty bed. Intravenous tubing dangled uselessly from the stainless-steel poles that held the medication pouches.

My God, had the killer returned during her absence? Drawing in a deep breath, she bit her lip and scanned the floor around the bed, looking for Gil's lifeless body.

Not so much as a dust bunny lurked on the gleaming floor.

Then, a slight sound, like the whisper of fabric, skittered into her awareness. She straightened and turned, acutely aware of a looming presence behind her.

Her heart hammering against her rib cage, she lifted her gaze to the hulking figure. "Gil!" Relief flooded through her only to turn to anger. "What are you doing out of bed? Your IVs!"

He shrugged in the darkness. "I was afraid you wouldn't come back. Alone."

Those brief words eloquently bespoke the fear, confusion and sense of aloneness that radiated from him. What had happened to him during these past months when he was missing? His injuries from the beating accounted for some of his mental confusion, but what about this paranoia? The Gil she'd known had been confident and intelligent, and exhibited no signs of mental illness.

Sometimes, she thought ruefully, even the paranoid are being watched.

For the very first time, Valerie questioned her own reaction to Gil's disappearance. Why had she so swiftly leaped to the conclusion that he'd jilted her? What if…what if something truly horrible had happened to him and she'd never even tried to find him?

Gulping back the scalding tears that were forming at the back of her throat, she closed her mind to the possibility that she'd been terribly wrong and grabbed Gil's arm. "Hurry up, then. Let's get you moved."

ALTHOUGH GIL HADN'T BEEN at all sure the beautiful doctor would help him, he had to admit that she'd moved quickly once she'd made the decision. In truth, her agreeing to move him to another room had taken him by surprise. He vaguely remembered her as the physician who'd treated him in the ER. Even then, she'd looked familiar. And oddly trustworthy.

Later, though, when he'd glanced at her name tag, he realized why she seemed so interested in him. After all, according to his notes, Dr. Valerie Murphy had been the focus of his investigation several months before.

Could this woman with the face of an angel truly hide a soul capable of the vile crime he'd been investigating? Why was he so willing to trust her now?

Because he had no one else.

His memory was patchy at best, but by using his extensive case notes, Gil had been able to reconstruct at least part of the events of the past several months. He'd come to Phoenix in an undercover capacity to ferret out the ringleader of a stolen baby operation. It was while following a lead to Los Angeles that his car had been run off a cliff. Now, he was back in Phoenix, and once again Valerie Murphy was at the center of the investigation.

Gil twisted in the bed and slammed his bruised knuckles into the pillow. Why the hell couldn't he just remember? In the wreckage of his splintered memory, nothing could be trusted. The very instincts he'd depended on all his life were now faulty, suspect. But if he relied purely on logic and his case file notes, Valerie Murphy was a desperate criminal quite capable of murder.

Still, if she'd recognized him, why call in the hired dogs to finish him off when she could have easily slipped a lethal dosage into his IV line? It would have been much easier to simply let him expire in the ER than to have a hired thug skulking through the halls. Nothing in this convoluted nightmare-without-end made any sense.

His ears picked up at a muted sound near the door.

His eyes, now acclimated to the darkness, scanned the room. Valerie had fallen asleep in the straight-back plastic visitor's chair. Her neck was crooked and she looked miserably uncomfortable. Casting the sheet aside, Gil started to slide out of bed, thinking to tuck his own pillow behind her neck.

At the sudden movement, a team of Clydesdales seemed to gallop through his skull. He sagged back on the bed and leaned against the headboard while he waited for the pain to ease.

After a few seconds the gallop slowed to a trot and he opened his eyes.

Then, another sound in the hallway sliced through the residual pain. Moving slowly, he eased to his feet. He listened intently, then exhaled his breath when the hallway remained silent. Valerie slept on.

In her sleep she looked soft. Vulnerable. Innocent. And very touchable.

He reached for the pillow, surprised at the tension radiating through his shoulders. Tension that was oddly lessened when he moved closer to the dozing woman. His prime suspect.

Gently lifting her head, he slipped the pillow behind her neck. Her eyes fluttered open. "What time is it?"

Gil marveled at the way she awoke fully alert, her wits immediately engaged. These days, more times than not, he awoke groggy, filled with confusion, jagged memories and a choking sense of danger. He glanced at the wall clock. "Two-fifteen."

She nodded and stretched. Her arms flexed above her head, tightening her sweater against her body, outlining her full breasts and slightly rounded tummy. An enticing earth mother, he thought. Sensual and inviting. Gil had to remind himself that he couldn't afford to let his guard down with this woman. His very life might depend on his vigilance.

Yet her natural and seemingly innocent movement was stirring and provocative. His groin tightened in automatic response to her physical pull.

She rubbed her cheeks with her knuckles, blew a golden strand of hair from her mouth and looked up at him, her eyes luminous in the soft moonlight. "Why aren't you sleeping? You need to build your strength."

He shrugged, ignoring that jab of pain that accompanied the movement. "I guess that twelve-hour catnap refreshed me. Besides, I—"

He broke off when she raised her hand, signaling for silence. Sensing that she'd heard the same sound that had woken him, he held his breath and craned his neck. Wordlessly they both listened intently for a repeat of the stealthy noise. Motioning her to remain still, Gil inched toward the door.

His hand was on the knob when he felt Valerie's warm breath on the back of his neck. She was standing so close behind him that the heat off her body scorched his shoulders. He tensed, unaccountably annoyed by her obvious willingness to plunge into the dangerous situation. Did she think the assassin would demur because she was a woman or a doctor? Or did she have another more sinister reason for believing she was safe?

Gil turned and jabbed his finger toward the guest chair, giving her an agitated glare. *Stay over there where it's safe,* he silently implored.

Either she couldn't see his expression in the darkness or she chose to ignore him, because her strong hand grasped his shoulder. She clamped down, firmly enough to sting his bruised muscles, and motioned him aside. "Move!" she hissed.

She was right of course. If the killer spotted Valerie, he wouldn't necessarily be alerted, but if he saw him...

Gingerly rubbing his sore shoulder, he stepped aside. Valerie crept to the door, opening it a scant inch. Leaning over her shoulder, Gil felt her back muscles tense, then a sharp intake of breath just before she closed the door and collapsed against it.

Gil grabbed her wrist, pulling her into the tiny adjoining bathroom. Closing the door to assure they wouldn't be overheard, he pressed his mouth against her ear. "You saw him?"

"Yes."

"What was he doing?"

"G-going back into your room."

Gil hesitated for a moment, then nodded decisively. "Where'd you hide my clothes? I've got to get out of here."

As he moved toward the door, she tugged at his flimsy cotton nightgown, causing a breeze to chill his backside. "You can't go out there!" Urgency was harsh in her whispered voice. "He...he had a gun."

"All the more reason for me to hit the road, Doc. Now are you going to tell me where my clothes are, or do I have to take yours?" A concept Gil wouldn't mind exploring further under different circumstances.

She shook her head. "Your clothes are nothing but bloody rags. We had to cut them off you."

"Then I hope the candy stripers aren't going to be shocked by the sight of my bare butt, 'cause I'm getting out of here!"

"Wait a minute. I'll find you something." She slipped out of the confined space.

Although Gil feared she would telephone hospital security or try to apprehend the gunman by herself he had no choice but to let her go. When he heard the door to the hall close behind her, though, he was almost overcome by a sense of...loss. As if the room had been fuller, more complete, with her in it.

Moments later she was back. She tossed his Reeboks and a pair of green surgical scrubs at him, saying, "The shoes were in the bottom of the nightstand. Hurry. I'll see what he's up to. By now he knows you aren't in your old room.''

She disappeared again and Gil leaned against the bathroom wall while he donned the trousers. It took three tries to fasten the drawstring waist.

This unaccustomed weakness was ticking him off. Even without his memory, Gil knew he'd spent the first thirty-five years of his life in excellent physical condition. Able to meet any challenge. Until that ''accident'' four months ago.

Since his release from the Los Angeles hospital, he'd worked like a fiend to recover his strength. Then, today, those bikers had wiped out all his progress with a few well-placed blows from coiled chains. How in hell was he supposed to protect the sexy doctor? In his present condition he couldn't protect himself against a kitten.

By the time he'd managed to get his clothes on and his bare feet thrust into his Reeboks, Valerie was back.

''He knows you're gone,'' she said softly. ''He's checking the rooms on the other side of the hall. He'll be here in no time!''

Gil drove his fingers into his hair as he tried to think of a plan, a way to get them out of this trap. But he was still fuzzy, a combination of the punches he'd taken and the drugs the hospital had dripped into his veins. ''We need a diversion. Something to distract him so we can get away.''

''What about calling 911? If we reported an armed man loose in the hospital, the police would be here in force within minutes.''

''Not soon enough,'' Gil responded.

''We have to do something! We can't just wait here until he finds us.''

''I'm thinking, I'm thinking.'' The hospital windows

didn't open, so they were out as potential escape routes. And only a single door led into the corridor. "Where's the nearest fire escape?"

"The end of the hall," she said. "Six or eight rooms away."

"Okay. When he goes into the next room, we'll make a run for it."

Valerie tossed her head. "Not enough time. You couldn't run ten feet. But I think I have an idea."

"What?"

"Just tie your shoes and wait by the door for the signal." Once more she darted out of the tiny bathroom.

"Wait! What signal?"

She didn't reply and an instant later, a wedge of light sliced the darkened room as Valerie opened the door to the hall.

Chapter Three

Valerie poked her head out the door and jerked it back as the man stepped out into the hallway again, his gun glimmering beneath the overhead light. Taking deep breaths to calm her pounding heart, she inched the door open and watched.

With a quick glance behind him, the man hoisted his weapon and tiptoed down the hall to the next room. Valerie counted the seconds he was in the room. "One-one thousand. Two-one thousand. Three…"

Twenty-two seconds later he reappeared, twisting his head right and left, looking for any sudden motion, any break in the routine, before checking the next room.

Twenty-two seconds.

All the time she had to save their lives.

When the shadowy figure disappeared into the next room, Valerie stepped out into the hall and scanned the bare walls, looking for the object she knew shouldn't be far away. There! Four doors down.

Between her and the killer.

Could she make it there and back in twenty-two brief seconds? If he spotted her, Valerie was under no illusions that he would hesitate to stop her from calling for help. Permanently.

She had no choice. It was the only chance they had.

Once again the killer, farther away this time, reappeared in the dim hallway and looked around. He quickly covered the few feet to the next room. Only one more room on that side of the hall, then he'd turn and head back in their direction. Once he started working his way toward them, her odds of success would be cut even more.

Her hand trembling on the cold doorknob, Valerie held her breath and waited. Like clockwork, the killer furtively reentered the hallway, scanned the area and methodically went about his business.

The instant he disappeared into the last patient room on the opposite side, she raced out the door and ran. One-one thousand. Two-one thousand. Three...

Four seconds to reach the fire-alarm fixture mounted on the wall. Another precious six seconds to read the instructions printed on the front. Eleven-one thousand. Twelve... Valerie snapped open the glass-fronted plate shielding the unit. Thirteen-one thousand. Pulled the handle. Fourteen-one thousand.

She jumped reflexively as a shriek, wild and penetrating as a banshee's wail, reverberated in the quiet. Clutching her ears against the piercing siren, she darted back down the hall. No sense counting the seconds any longer. That shrill noise would cause comatose patients to leap from their beds and spill into the corridor.

She had to get back to the room and out of sight before the killer made it into the hall.

The next few seconds were a blur of noise and chaos as bells pinged and apprehensive patients called out in confusion. Guilt stabbed her for frightening people who needed uninterrupted rest to aid in their recovery. Fortunately, she thought as she pulled open Gil's door and slipped inside, no cardiac patients were housed on this ward, so at least she wouldn't be responsible for someone expiring of heart failure. Unless her own pulsing heart burst.

With Gil hovering over her shoulder, they peeked out the door as the normally quiet hospital exploded into pandemonium. Nurses, orderlies and patients poured into the hall as emergency procedures for evacuation were set into instant motion.

Hospital administration had been diligent in conducting fire- and catastrophe-response drills. Valerie knew the well-trained staff would have the entire floor evacuated in less than five minutes. If Gil was right in his assertion that the killer was a professional, he'd take even less time to figure out the alarm was a ruse. Once the floor was vacated, he'd have free rein to conduct a quick—and deadly—search.

They had to use the cover of the crowded hallway to make their escape. "Okay, stay close to me and we'll blend in long enough to reach the lobby," she said as she opened the door.

Valerie had taken one step into the hall when she spotted him.

The dark-clothed executioner, with a suspicious bulge beneath the thin jacket he carried, was moving toward a group of patients being hustled toward the nurses' station. Valerie saw his head bob as he inspected each patient, anticipating finding his prey.

She ducked back inside just as he swung around. Dear God, had he spotted her?

Holding her hand against her thudding heart, she whispered, "Scratch plan A."

"What's plan B?"

"I haven't the foggiest."

Gil flipped on the overhead light. The bright fluorescent glare stung their eyes as the shrieking alarm singed their senses. Valerie had the sensation that the end of the world was rapidly approaching. She hugged her waist in a protective gesture to still her trembling hands.

Gil was moving about the room, opening drawers and cabinets. "Help me find something to use as a weapon. He won't be expecting me to take the offense. It's our only chance."

Valerie shuddered, remembering the huge gun she'd glimpsed in the killer's hand. No, they wouldn't disarm that man with iodine and a scalpel. But maybe they could outwit him.

Opening a supply cupboard filled with the implements needed to change surgical dressings, she grabbed a roll of gauze and adhesive tape. "Get back on the bed. Quick!"

"But—"

"Don't argue. Just do it!"

Gil stared at her for a second, then complied wordlessly. Valerie put the dangling intravenous tubes into his hand and tucked the sheets up under his chin. "Hold on to those tubes so it looks like the IVs are connected."

She ripped open the protective plastic covering from the gauze roll and quickly swathed Gil's face, leaving small openings for his eyes, nose and mouth. She plastered the makeshift mask into place with the adhesive strips and smeared Betadine on his bandaged temple. At a distance the red antiseptic solution would pass for blood.

"Okay, if you hear me speak to anyone, just groan like you're in labor. Got it?"

He grunted. "Don't know much about being in labor,

Doc, but I imagine I can do a fair imitation of a man in pain.''

Valerie cringed. He'd been acting so…normal the past half hour that she'd completely forgotten the savage beating he'd sustained only hours before. Since he'd disconnected the IV pain-relief medication, no doubt Gil was feeling the effects of his injuries. She couldn't allow herself the luxury of counting on him to help if they were stopped by the gunman.

They probably only had another minute or so before the entire floor was emptied. It was now or never.

Gritting her teeth, she set the pneumatic latch over the door so it would remain open and wheeled Gil into the corridor. She started to the right, toward the elevators, then stopped abruptly. The elevators were programmed not to run during a fire. Only a single elevator was kept operational to aid in evacuating patients who weren't ambulatory. It would be jammed with people, and no doubt the killer would be scanning every individual who entered.

Abruptly she reversed her direction and headed toward the emergency stairwell. ''Hope you can manage the stairs,'' she muttered.

Gil groaned a response. She wondered if he was acting or if his pain was worsening. She wheeled the narrow bed around the corner and paused at the entrance to the stairs. Glancing over her shoulder to make certain they hadn't been spotted, she whipped back the sheet and helped Gil to his feet.

With the sounds of the evacuation fading with each passing second, they hadn't a moment to spare. She slipped a steadying arm around Gil's back and draped his arm across her shoulder. He stiffened. ''I can walk,'' he muttered.

"Not very well. Whose help do you want? Mine or the killer's?" She knew she sounded snappish and authoritarian, but precious seconds were being sacrificed to Gil's male ego.

As if he understood, he nodded mutely behind the haphazard gauze mask and they started forward.

Valerie couldn't count the times she'd taken this route as a shortcut between the floors as she hurried from the delivery room to the nursery or to the patients' ward. Often, she'd whistle or hum, then laugh at the way the sounds echoed through the cavernous space. Tonight, though, there was nothing friendly about the forlorn concrete enclosure. An image flitted through her mind of two small mice trapped in a concrete maze as a hungry cat stalked their progress.

They rounded the landing and passed the third floor.

She wasn't sure how much of the hospital would be affected by the alarm she'd raised and figured the lobby, or even the basement, might be their best hope of escaping unnoticed.

Second floor. Gil's breathing quickened with each step. Valerie recalled the X ray results: two hairline fractures on his ribs. Still, he didn't utter a word of protest, nor did he slow his pace.

First floor. Lobby.

"Is this our stop?" he asked hopefully.

She hesitated. "I...I'm not sure. He *could* still be upstairs. Or he could have been sent down to the lobby with everyone else. What do you think?"

Gil leaned over the steel railing. "Did you know there are twenty-six stairs between each floor?"

She gave him a sharp glance. The bandages had come loose near his mouth and she saw the moisture pooling above his upper lip. This was too much exertion for a man in his condition. She reached for the lobby door and his warm hand enveloped hers.

"Let's play it safe, Doc. The basement's only twenty-six steps away."

"Are you sure?"

Suddenly a steel fire door clanged somewhere above them.

They both glanced up. The killer? Probably a fireman or another hospital employee taking a shortcut. But they couldn't take the chance. Wordlessly she eased the lobby door closed and they started down. More slowly this time, as if they'd made a silent pact to make as little noise as possible.

Valerie smiled ruefully. They'd always been in tune with each other—mentally, emotionally and physically. Until Gil had unceremoniously dumped her.

She opened the basement-level door and they emerged into a deserted hallway deep in the bowels of the vast hospital. Another sharp sound in the stairwell. Whoever was behind them was still clomping down the steps. They had to find a place to hide. Fast.

Unlike most of the hospital, there were no public facilities in the basement. No unlocked doors. Supply rooms, laundry facilities and laboratories hid behind numbered but unmarked panels. The first three had standard key lock mechanisms, denoting nonmedical use. Any room a physician might want to enter was fitted with an electronic lock for which a computer card and access code were required. Valerie had such a card, but no keys for the other rooms that were not within her normal realm.

Again a loud clang overhead hurried their pace. Fortunately the fourth door they tried had an electronic lock. Fumbling in her pocket, Valerie jammed the card into the slot and keyed in her numerical sequence. She had no idea if she was cleared for access to this room and held her breath until the green light flashed and the door swung open.

She grabbed Gil around the waist and ushered him inside ahead of her. Behind them another crash of a steel door slamming in the hallway—this time louder. Closer.

The room was dark and she didn't dare risk turning on the overhead light for fear a sliver would show beneath the door and give away their location. Her hip bumped an empty gurney and she gratefully eased her arm from beneath Gil's and lowered him onto the portable bed.

"Are you okay?" she whispered.

"Hunky-dory," he said with only a hint of breathlessness. "Look, Doc, I'll be fine here. Why don't you go on back upstairs with the others?"

"Where it's safe?"

"Whatever. This is my problem, Doc. There's no need for you to get involved."

"I'm already involved. And stop calling me Doc." She rummaged in her backpack for her penlight. "Makes me sound like I ought to have sideburns and suspenders."

"Sorry, Ms. Doc."

Recognizing his feeble attempt to lighten their situation with a bit of humor, she smiled slightly and flicked on the flashlight. They were in a small anteroom, with a few filing cabinets, two desks and a pair of uncomfortable-looking armchairs. The gurney was against a bare wall. From the numerous gouges and marks on the pale green surface, she knew gurneys were often parked in this spot. The room seemed vaguely familiar.

Then the flickering beam caught a double door behind the desks. Valerie darted across the room and was surprised to discover she needed her key card to open this second door. Still, it would be another barrier between them and the killer.

She punched in her access code and opened the security door. Her flashlight beam played across the room, exposing shiny steel tables, a concrete floor, banks of large filing cabinets and several deep porcelain sinks. Now she knew why the anteroom looked familiar. They were in the pathology department.

More commonly known as the morgue.

GIL COULD TELL from her crestfallen expression that she was disappointed by whatever was on the other side of those double doors. Her shoulders slumped and when she turned around, she sagged against the wall.

"What's wrong?"

She slapped the penlight rhythmically in her palm, causing the beam to flash drunkenly across the ceiling. "Dead end. No way out."

Gil rubbed his side, where behind the constricting bandages his ribs throbbed painfully. "So we wait him out here."

Even as he spoke, the noises in the stairwell grew in intensity. Whoever was following them was apparently testing every door on his way down, clearing each floor before continuing his inexorable search. The man was patient and methodical, as well as armed. They were trapped like canaries in a cage. And the "puddy-tat" was slinking ever closer.

Gil's jaw clenched. He was the worst kind of jackass. This wasn't Valerie Murphy's fight, and he should have sent her back to the safety of the lobby while she had the chance. Now, judging by the escalating noise level, the killer was between them and the first floor. There was truly no way out.

"What's behind those doors?" he asked.

"The autopsy room."

Although he had no specific memory of ever watching an autopsy, Gil knew he must have at some point in his law-enforcement career. In his mind's eye, he could picture the layout: widely spaced tables of gleaming stainless steel, hoses, knives, saws and other evil-looking equipment neatly stacked on metal shelves. Drawers for cadaver storage and sometimes—

The final steel door separating the basement from the staircase crashed open. The killer was in the basement.

"Get that door open again," Gil whispered urgently, then outlined his rudimentary plan while Valerie manipulated the electronic lock.

She propped the door open with her foot, and Gil painfully wheeled the empty gurney through the opening. When they were safely in the autopsy suite, she flicked on the overhead lights long enough for them to get their bearings.

As he'd hoped, a wide stainless-steel door was set in the wall on the opposite end of the room. A walk-in cooler where bodies could be stored until the pathologist finished his procedures. He hoped they didn't already have a full house.

With Valerie's help, he wheeled the gurney to the cooler and grabbed a couple of folded sheets from a stack on a shelf near the door. The gurney barely fit inside and Gil clambered onto it while she ran back to turn off the lights. His heart pounding, he could hear the faint sounds of the gunman trying to get in the outer door.

Valerie's breath frosted in the air when she swung open the cooler door. An instant later, they were plunged into frigid darkness.

And the killer was in the morgue's reception room.

Chapter Four

Gil's heart crashed like thunder.

Fear was a powerful emotion, he acknowledged, but it wasn't fear of the unseen gunman that convulsed his breath from his lungs. It was Valerie's body crushed against his that forced him to inhale with exquisite slowness.

He didn't understand this woman. The emotion that flashed so clearly in her blue eyes vacillated from cold and distant—even venomous—to a superheated fire that singed his very soul.

If only he could remember what had happened during his previous stay in Phoenix. That he and the lovely Dr. Murphy shared a history of some kind was indisputable; but his damnable memory with its gaping holes left him with more questions than answers. Who, exactly, was Valerie Murphy? What was her role in this puzzle that had nearly cost him his life?

He had to admit her resourcefulness was something. After slamming the door to the walk-in cooler, she had jockeyed his gurney between several other carts loaded with draped bodies. Parking Gil at the very rear of the refrigerated space, she yanked his shoes and socks from his feet and tied a cardboard tag around his big toe. Then, tucking his Reeboks between his ankles, she clambered atop his prone body and tugged a sheet over their heads, leaving his bare feet exposed.

With any luck their pursuer would glance at their lumpy silhouette and mistake them for a very fat, very dead, person. But Gil's luck had run out four months ago; he wasn't counting on a miracle now.

A slight noise infiltrated their chilly cell. Was the assassin even now inching across the morgue toward them? Despite their hazardous situation, he had a hard time focusing on the encroaching peril. His attention was absorbed by Valerie's heartbeat drumming through her breast. By the rainwater scent of her hair against his face. The warmth of her thighs pressing against his.

Whatever she'd meant to him four months ago—friend or foe—he felt strongly tied to this woman who was risking her life for him. If anything happened to her, he'd never forgive himself.

Gil bit his lip to break the hypnotic hold of her nearness.

Then another stealthy sound brought their immediate danger into sharp focus.

His fingers instinctively tightened around her back, pulling her firmly against him as if the small gesture would protect her.

Creak!

The sound of the door opening between the reception area and the morgue penetrated the cooler's insulated walls. Valerie's body stiffened and Gil pressed his lips against her hair, as if to reassure her. He didn't know how, but he would protect her from the stalker if it took his last breath.

"How did that guy get inside?" Gil whispered in exasperation. "You had to use a key card."

''I don't know. Maybe it's not him. Maybe it's the janitor, or security, or—'' She broke off as the soft tap-tap of leather-soled shoes echoed like the wings of death circling overhead.

Closer and closer still.

A sudden rush of warm air warned him that the killer had invaded the refrigerated cubicle. Gil poised his tender muscles, ready to pounce if he came too close. The element of surprise was his only advantage.

Gooseflesh rippled up his back as his every instinct went on full alert. The footsteps faltered, slowed, then paused as if the man was listening for an alien sound; then he took another tentative step.

A sheet rustled a few feet away and Gil realized he was checking each cadaver. Thorough. Professional. They didn't stand a chance.

Moving with infinite slowness, Gil started easing from beneath Valerie's soft form. He had to be ready the moment the man approached. The fake toe tag wasn't going to fool this guy; he was an obvious pro.

Another step. The killer was only inches away; Gil could feel the heat of his body on his bare feet. The toe tag tickled against the sole of his foot as the man grasped the sheet covering their bodies.

Gil tensed, ready to shove Valerie aside when a man's voice suddenly called from the outer room, breaking the taut silence.

''Hey! Who's back there?''

The man in the cooler spat out an expletive and ran from the room, his feet slapping the concrete floor.

''What are you doing in here?'' The newcomer's voice reverberated throughout the cavernous space. ''Let me see your ident—''

The man's voice broke off abruptly, followed by a loud metallic crash.

A moment later dead silence claimed the morgue.

Pushing Valerie's warm body from his, Gil struggled to his feet. He draped an arm around her trembling shoulders and tugged her toward the door. "Come on. We've got to get out of here while we have the chance."

"You don't think he'll be back?"

Gil shrugged, then realized she probably couldn't see the gesture in the dim light filtering from the autopsy suite. "He seems pretty determined to me. I'd say it's a good bet he's still hanging around."

"Why? Why does that man want to kill you?"

"Damned if I know."

"Don't insult my intelligence!" She wrenched away and stood facing him, her fists jammed against her hips. "I'm not a fool, Gil. That man isn't a homicidal maniac running through the halls shooting anyone he meets. He's after you personally. And I'm not lifting another finger to help you unless you tell me why."

Frustrated by the fallibility of his sporadic memory, he gnawed on his upper lip. He couldn't give her an answer because he didn't know it himself. "You've got to trust me. Just a little longer. Please."

He reached for her arm and tried to urge her toward the door.

Valerie planted her feet, refusing to budge. "This is insane, Gil. We have to phone the police. That man has a gun!"

The logic of her words slammed him like a forty-pound hammer. She was right. Getting Valerie out of this mess had to be his first priority; the case would have to wait. The only way he could ensure her safety was to enlist the help of the Phoenix Police Department. He didn't have a cover story ready for the locals, but he'd wing it.

"All right." He squeezed her shoulder. "Let's get to a phone."

"Promise?" She cocked her head, her distrust obvious.

Her imploring tone made him feel oddly guilty, as if he had abused her faith before. "Yeah, I promise. Now let's get a move on."

He took two steps and staggered against a cart already occupied by a blue-sheeted corpse.

"You don't have any business being out of bed," Valerie snapped as she put her arm around his waist for support. Her gentle touch belied the harshness of her words.

"I'll be fine, Doc. Where's the nearest phone?"

"There should be one in the reception area," she said as they made their way back into the morgue. Someone had turned on the overhead lighting and the fluorescent brightness made him lift a hand to shield his eyes.

"We should have called for help in the first place, instead of trying to handle this alone," she said. "I'm sure the police will post a guard outside your room un- til— Oh, my God!"

He looked up and followed the path of her horrified gaze.

A man wearing the grayish-blue uniform of hospital security was draped, facedown, across an autopsy table. Blood dripped and pooled in a crimson lake.

Valerie raced across the room and gave the man a cur- sory examination. Her face was white with shock when she looked up. "He's been shot!"

Wrapping his arms around his abdomen to protect his throbbing rib cage, Gil hobbled around the metal tables bolted to the floor to join her. Acutely aware of his bare feet on the cold tile, he helped wrestle the unconscious guard onto his back. Valerie peeled off her cotton jacket to stanch the blood flowing from the gaping hole in the man's chest. Her quick fingers sought his pulse.

"He's still alive! Go into the reception room and pick up the white phone on the wall. Press zero—that'll connect you to the hospital paging system. Tell them we need a trauma team in the basement stat. Tell the operator we've got a code. That's important. Got it?"

"Trauma team, code, stat. Got it."

Sweat streaming down his face from the effort of forcing his injured body to hurry, Gil ignored his own pain and did Valerie's bidding. After repeating the message twice for the disbelieving hospital operator, he returned to the autopsy room.

"What can I do to help?"

Valerie was straddling the man's prone body, pressing his chest in a rhythmic motion. "Go wait in the hall to direct the trauma team."

He felt like a small boy who had been given a meaningless task to get him out of the way. Still, he knew his fractured ribs wouldn't allow him to perform CPR. He glanced at the ominously gray face of the security guard, feeling helpless and responsible. But there wasn't a damned thing he could do about it.

Except track down the assassin—and whoever hired him.

He'd put those bastards safely behind bars if it was the last thing he ever did.

AN HOUR LATER word filtered down from the operating room that the injured security guard was in critical but stable condition.

Valerie heaved a grateful sigh and sank into the plastic

chair. It seemed like half of Phoenix was crowded into the morgue reception room. Just as the guard was being hustled off to surgery, the Phoenix PD, Maricopa County Sheriff's Department and hospital security had invaded the morgue in force. Pandemonium reigned as conflicting commands and questions were barked from every direction.

Within moments, however, a pecking order was established and a detective from the Phoenix PD took command.

Detective Ferdy Sanchez was short and compact, reminding Valerie of a fire hydrant. His dark simian face was pleasantly ugly, but his sharp black eyes missed nothing. After ushering everyone into the hall, he called for a crime-scene unit, thanked the deputies and hospital security force for their prompt response and dismissed everyone except his own officers.

Then he turned his unflinching gaze on Valerie and Gil.

"Ya know, hospitals are just full of surprises. I had an uncle once who went into the hospital down in Nogales for a broken leg. He came out dead. Blood clot. Now we've got shooters in the morgue, drumming up business for ya. Another surprise. And they say police work is exciting. So, Dr. Murphy, suppose you tell me about all the excitement."

Her brain, her instincts, her entire life history shouted at her to confess the whole story to this officer. Dump it in Gil's lap where it belonged and let him explain. But her heart, her damned betraying heart, urged her to keep his confidence.

"There was a fire alarm," she said, "and I was trying to get my patient, Mr. Branton, to safety. We, uh, didn't think we should use the elevator, so we took the stairs."

"Smart move." Sanchez took a battered notepad from inside his jacket and scribbled a note. "So I guess you lost track of what floor you were on and missed the lobby, ending up in the basement, instead? Makes sense."

Valerie nodded mutely. Gil had edged to the background, as if by fading from view he'd disappear from the policeman's memory.

Sanchez tapped his ballpoint against his lower teeth. "Now let's see if I got this straight. You think the building's on fire so you flee, right?"

"Yes."

"And you accidently overshoot the lobby and end up in the cellar, right?"

Not wanting to lie, Valerie smiled vaguely.

"So how'd you come to end up in the morgue? Seems to me a prudent person would have left the building."

Valerie licked her lips. "Someone was following us, so we hid."

"Aha!" He smacked his forehead with the heel of his hand. "Well, it's all clear to me now. You're in the middle of an evacuation and someone's behind you on the stairs. 'Course you'd assume it was somebody with a gun intent on popping you and your patient. So naturally you'd duck into the morgue to hide out."

Sanchez grinned broadly and she gave him another vague smile in return.

In a flash the jocular light disappeared from his dark eyes, replaced by an intense stare that bored straight through her. "Cut the crap, Doc. I'd ground my four-year-old if he couldn't gimme a better story than that one."

When Gil called her Doc, it had the sweet ring of an endearment. Sanchez made it sound like an accusation.

The elevator door pinged open, saving her from the necessity of inventing a new lie. Martin Abel, the hospital administrator, stepped out quickly, followed by Fierce Pierce and Ed Grant, the orderly who'd assisted her in the ER.

Relieved by the sight of familiar faces, Valerie rushed to greet them. "What are you guys still doing here? You should have been home hours ago."

"We were," Pierce said. "I hate to be the one to break the news, Valerie, but you've been in this hospital over twenty-four hours."

Disbelief was quickly replaced by realization, followed quickly by bone-numbing fatigue. She'd already put in a twelve-hour stretch when she'd been summoned to the ER yesterday afternoon.

Pierce poked a fiery red curl behind her ear. "We were just coming back on shift when we heard what happened down here. Are you all right?"

"Do you mind?" Martin Abel snapped, pushing past the others. "Dr. Murphy, what happened down here? I heard someone was shot. Should I phone the legal staff?"

Valerie almost laughed. Like most bean counters, Abel wasn't worried about anyone being actually injured, just whether or not it was going to cost money.

Before she could respond to his callous query, Sanchez wedged between them. "I hate to break up this little reunion, but this *is* a police investigation. So if you're not directly involved in this incident, I'd suggest you folks head on back to your stations."

Abel puffed up like a blowfish. "Excuse me, Sergeant, but—"

"Detective."

"What?"

"Detective, not Sergeant. Sanchez. And you would be?"

The administrator handed Sanchez an embossed business card and explained the importance of his being fully informed of all aspects of the investigation.

"A helluva plan, Mr. Abel. Sir. Why don't we just carry this little talk up to your office where we can have some privacy? Think your staff could rustle up coffee? I could use that caffeine kick right now, even though the missus says I need to wean myself off it. Says I'm hyper, if you can imagine that. Now where'd you say your office was? The top floor, I imagine."

Valerie stuffed her knuckle into her mouth to keep from laughing. She'd never seen anyone wrest control from Martin Abel, but Ferdy Sanchez had the situation well in hand. After giving last-minute instructions to his assistant, Sanchez shooed the ER crew back upstairs and waited for the next elevator to transport the rest up to Abel's office.

When Sanchez had comfortably settled himself behind Abel's desk, he turned his attention on Gil. Valerie twisted in her seat to watch Gil's face.

"Mr. Branton, is it?"

"That's right."

"I understand you were brought into the emergency room last night, the victim of a violent assault."

"Yes."

He fished a paper out of his pocket, unfolded it and scanned the fine print. "The report done by the sheriff's office says you got into a tussle with some mean-spirited bikers, that right?"

"Yes."

"Not real talkative, are you, Mr. Branton?"

"Just trying to answer your questions, Detective."

As if unable to abdicate control for even another moment, the hospital administrator jumped up and strode behind his desk. Pointing a shaking finger at Gil, he rasped, "I remember you! You're that accountant sent by the FDA to audit our pharmaceutical accounts."

When Gil didn't respond to his claim, Martin Abel turned excitedly to the detective. "I always thought there was something strange about him. He disappeared, you know. Hung around the hospital, poking his nose into everyone's business for weeks, then poof! One morning he doesn't show up. No goodbye or even thanks for a great time! If you ask me, the man's a fraud."

As if exhausted by his tirade, he propped a hip on the corner of the desk. Taking a crisp white handkerchief from his pocket, he mopped his forehead. He fingered the lock of hair he kept swirled over his pate in a losing effort to conceal his baldness.

Raising his chin triumphantly, he turned to Detective Sanchez.

"This man should be arrested immediately!"

The bulldog of a detective swiveled back in Abel's chair. "On what grounds, sir?"

"Wh-why of…of causing trouble, setting off a false fire alarm."

Sanchez raised an eyebrow. "Did you set off that fire alarm, Mr. Branton?"

"No."

"Can't arrest a man for something he didn't do, sir."

Quivering with rage, Abel turned his wrath on Valerie. "It's her fault. She never should have gone along with this man's crazy scheme and moved him from his hospital bed. It's negligence at best, medical malfeasance at worst!"

Martin Abel was a small man in every way, Valerie

thought. His slight stature seemed to diminish his own opinion of his worth. He was always on a rampage, railing at someone. She'd never had any personal conflict with him, but plenty of the junior staff complained of petty clashes with him.

Taking a deep breath to calm the waves of indignation boiling inside, she managed a quiet and, she thought, calm tone. "Martin, I realize you're upset, but before you accuse me of malpractice again, I suggest you think about the ramifications of such an action. I promise you, I will sue you for libel."

"Slander," Sanchez interjected.

"Pardon?"

"Slander. Libel is if he *writes* falsehoods about you. Slander is if he defames you in front of other people."

"Now see here, Officer—"

"Mr. Abel," the detective interrupted, "I think your personnel concerns can wait. Right now, you have a patient who was chased through *your* hospital by an armed man, who, I might add, is still on the loose, thereby endangering even more patients in *your* hospital. So if you'd just have a seat over there while I interrogate the victim..."

Clearly unaccustomed to being ordered about in his own office, Abel grumbled but complied. When he'd slumped back against the cushions of the sofa, the detective glanced at his notes.

"Now, where were we?" He picked up his pen and rapped his lower teeth for a full ten seconds. "Ah, yes, Mr. Branton. I believe you were getting ready to tell me what happened."

"At the biker bar?"

"Yeah. And later, as well. I'd like to hear how an

armed man came to stalk you in the hospital. Do you live here in the Valley, Mr. Branton?''

"No. At least, not permanently. I've been here on, uh, temporary duty off and on for the past several months.''

"Temporary duty. Are you with the military?''

"No. I, uh, haven't been working lately. I was involved in a…accident in Los Angeles.''

Sanchez cocked his head and scratched his chin. "You seem to be accident-prone, Mr. Branton. So after your…accident, you came back to Phoenix, is that right?''

"Yes.''

"When was that?''

"Yesterday. No, the day before.''

The detective's eyebrows raised and he leaned back in the chair, calmly assessing Gil. "Didn't take you long to find trouble, did it?''

"I guess not.''

Martin Abel rose to his feet and tossed a sofa cushion onto the floor. "This is just a waste of time! Why aren't you out searching the grounds for the gunman? I don't see how all these questions are going to help, Detective.''

"I guess that's why I'm the policeman and you're not,'' Sanchez calmly responded.

"I shall be speaking to your superiors later today,'' Abel threatened as he sank back onto the couch.

Ignoring his outburst, Sanchez picked up his pen and scrawled something in his notebook. "What did you argue with those fellas about, Mr. Branton? The bikers, I mean.''

Gil shrugged. "I don't recall.'' He rubbed the white bandage taped to his temple. "Guess they smacked me pretty good.''

"I guess so.'' Sanchez nodded slowly. "Let's leave

that for now. So you came to the hospital. When was the first time you realized you were in danger?''

Valerie's mind wandered as Gil picked up the story from when she'd entered his room and discovered a man trying to suffocate him. That he was holding back information was obvious. But how much and why? Why not just tell the truth and ask for police protection? That was what an innocent person would do.

Did his unwillingness to involve the authorities mean Gil was guilty of more than a conveniently forgetful memory?

A knock on the door dragged her back to the present. She looked up as a uniformed officer stepped in. Sanchez beckoned silently and the patrolman approached the desk and murmured something in his ear.

When the officer departed, Sanchez rose to his feet. ''They've gathered up five men who were in the building, but don't work here. Let's go downstairs and see if you recognize any of them.''

Silently the trio trooped behind the detective. The five men were being detained in the chapel on the first floor. Valerie had expected a more formal lineup, but instead, they were ushered into the small room where the potential suspects occupied the first pew.

''All right, gentlemen, could you stand up, please?'' The young patrolman gestured to the men.

When the quintet stood, Gil and Valerie were directed to walk in front of them. ''Take your time,'' Sanchez admonished. ''If you need to see a profile or would like them to speak, we can do that.''

Valerie felt the curious gazes of the five men follow her as she silently marched past them.

All five fit the general description of the man who'd tried to kill them. One even had a striking resemblance to the killer. But when she looked into his eyes, this man lacked the reptilian coldness that had emanated from the hit man.

She waited until Gil had traced her footsteps, then they turned to Sanchez.

"Recognize anybody?"

"Nope," Gil said.

"No, I didn't, either," Valerie said. "Look, Detective, I'm out on my feet and I need to get my patient back into bed."

Sanchez's mobile eyebrows raised northward again. "Your patient? Aren't you an OB—a baby doctor?" He gave Gil an evil grin. "Not making scientific history, are ya, Mr. Branton?"

Gil's eyes rolled in disgust at the feeble joke.

"Since I'm the one who disconnected Mr. Branton's intravenous fluids and removed him from his hospital bed, he's my responsibility until I get him back under the care of his attending physician. That makes him my patient. For the moment."

She knew she was stretching the truth, but she was bone weary and mentally exhausted. She had to get home and rest so she could sort out this mess.

She had to get away from Gil Branton.

Sanchez expelled a frustrated sigh. "All right, folks, thanks for your cooperation." He turned to the young patrolman. "Make sure you have names, addresses and phone numbers, then let 'em go."

"Yes, sir."

The detective made for the exit of the chapel, Martin Abel, Gil and Valerie on his heels. Sanchez paused in the doorway. "Make sure you double-check their drivers' licenses," he called to the patrolman.

When they were back in the wide corridor outside the

chapel, Sanchez looked at Gil. "You sure you didn't recognize any of those men?"

"I'm sure."

He hooked a thumb toward the chapel. "When Officer Carpenter finishes with them, give him an address and phone number where we can reach you. And nobody leaves town, got it?"

Valerie nodded numbly as Gil went back into the chapel. She started to follow, but Sanchez grabbed her sleeve.

"I hope you know what you're doing, Doc. This guy smells like trouble. Big trouble."

She swallowed a mirthless laugh. The policeman wasn't telling her anything she didn't already know. Didn't *bitterly* know. "Thank you for your concern, Detective, but there's no need. Mr. Branton is my temporary patient. Nothing more."

"Yeah, sure." He started back toward the elevator bank, then turned and gave her a final caution. "If this thing goes sour, you could lose more than your license, Doc. You could lose your life."

After he stepped into the elevator and disappeared behind the sliding doors, her hand settled on her abdomen as she stood for a long moment contemplating his warning. Sanchez was right; she had more important things to do than protect Gil Branton.

She couldn't believe the man she'd known so intimately could be involved in criminal activity, but what other explanation could there be? It was time to find out.

A strand of hair had come loose from her braid. She threaded it back into place. Gil was going to give her some answers right now.

Straightening her shoulders, she strode into the chapel. The young officer was the only occupant of the small room. He tossed aside the magazine he was skimming. "I still need your home address, phone and beeper numbers, Dr. Murphy."

"Where's Gil?"

"Pardon?"

"My patient, the man whose information you just took down. Where is he?"

The patrolman shrugged and thumbed at a nearly hidden door beside the altar. "He went out that way. Why? Anything wrong?"

"Everything!" She turned and headed for the corridor.

"Wait, Dr. Murphy! I need your information."

"Get it from personnel," she said as she ran out the door. Her eyes scanned the nearly deserted lobby area. One of the janitors ran his buffer with slow patience across the expanse of polished tile. A lone figure, probably the relative of someone in surgery or intensive care, was stretched out on a sofa, a newspaper over his face.

Her heart leaped when she spotted a tall, dark-haired man hurrying toward the entrance. "Wait!" she called, and rushed across the polished floor.

The man obediently paused and glanced over his shoulder.

"Oh. Never mind," she said. "Sorry."

The man who had seemed so familiar was one of those in the impromptu lineup. Probably a policeman or relative of an inpatient.

Where could Gil have disappeared to so quickly?

She spent another five minutes looking behind columns and watching the men's room door, but no sign of Gil.

Finally, except for the sleeping man and a blue-haired woman in the pale pink uniform of a volunteer shuffling some papers behind the information desk, the lobby was empty.

Gil Branton had disappeared.

Chapter Five

Disheartened, Valerie trudged toward the elevator. She wanted nothing more than to crawl into her nice cozy bed and sleep the rest of the month. Except her keys were in the backpack she'd forgotten in Martin Abel's office. And she should stop by the woman's clinic, adjacent to the hospital, just to make sure everything was on track since she was going to be off the next four—make that three—days.

She was already well into the first day of her much-needed mini-vacation. Because of the complexity of scheduling, this lovely four-day-off period only happened every six weeks or so.

The elevator arrived and she stepped into the cab, nodding to a pair of white-coated colleagues. At the next stop Dr. Sidney Weingold stepped aboard. Sidney was a fellow OB/GYN specialist who was also Valerie's personal physician. And a good friend.

"Val! I just heard you were involved in a bit of a commotion earlier."

"Hi, Sid. Yeah, a lunatic set off the fire alarms on the fifth floor and chased me and a patient into the morgue. A security guard was injured."

The elevator paused and after giving Valerie a curious glance, the other two doctors disembarked.

"That's incredible!" Sid said. "You weren't hurt, were you?"

"No, I'm fine. Just shaken up."

He nodded. "You look a little pale. Why don't you stop by my office later and I'll give you a quick once-over?"

The elevator stopped again and Sid stepped out. She pressed the button to keep the door open. "I can fit you in around ten," he said.

She smiled and shook her head. "By ten I hope I'm home getting some serious snooze time. I'm fine, Sid, really."

"Okay," he said doubtfully, "but if you have any problems, don't hesitate to phone. Here or at home."

"I will. Thanks." She released the hold button and the door slid closed.

Sid Weingold was the prize catch of Parker Memorial Hospital. Tall, thick wavy brown hair and honey-brown eyes. Probably filthy rich, judging from his life-style. And a nice guy. Two-thirds of the single women on staff were madly in love with him.

For a while it had seemed as if his and Valerie's friendship was going to develop into something deeper. Then Gil Branton had come into her life and old reliable Sid was quickly forgotten.

She should have stuck with Sid, she thought ruefully as the elevator continued its ride to the administrative level. With any luck, no one else she knew would come aboard and expect conversation. She was too tired to form words.

Her mental and physical reserves were totally depleted. All she wanted was sleep. She could kick Gil's butt for dragging her into this mess. Come to think of it, she could kick his butt for several reasons. Was that why she felt so churlish and out of sorts? Because Gil had deprived her of the opportunity to ream him out?

The hospital was starting to come alive, she noted as the elevator stopped at each floor, disgorging and picking up new passengers. She murmured an occasional greeting, but by the time she reached the sixth-floor administration level, she was blessedly alone.

The office staff kept different hours than the medical personnel, and so the sixth-floor corridor was still dim and deserted as she trod silently down the plush carpet to Martin Abel's office. With any luck, the pompous hospital administrator would still be downstairs irritating the police. Maybe she could just sneak in, grab her backpack and be on her way without encountering a soul.

Luck, however, turned out to be elusive. As she approached the spacious anteroom where his secretary generally kept the hoi polloi at bay, the sound of voices wafted out of Abel's office. Although she couldn't make out more than an occasional word, the tone of the half-heard conversation was heated.

Courtesy demanded that Valerie backtrack and wait discreetly until the encounter was over. But courtesy didn't have an aching back and swollen feet. Drawing a deep breath, she rapped sharply on the burled mahogany door.

"Come in!"

She turned the ornate brass handle and poked her head into the sumptuous office. Abel was standing behind his desk, scowling down at a man seated in front of him. She could only see the back of the man's head, but tension sparked between them like a live wire. "Sorry for the interruption, but I left my backpack—"

"It doesn't matter," Abel interjected. "We were finished, anyway."

The other man rose and leaned forward. Speaking so softly Valerie wasn't certain she'd heard him correctly, the man intoned, "We're finished. For now."

He turned and took two steps in her direction. Ed Grant! Mild shock waves rippled through her. She couldn't imagine two more unlikely combatants than the head of the hospital and an orderly.

Ed nodded tersely, his lean jaw locked so tightly she could almost see his teeth grinding. "Dr. Murphy."

"Ed."

He brushed past her, bumping noisily against a chair in the reception area.

Lifting her gaze, Valerie stared at the administrator. A man who would remain pale after a two-week Hawaiian vacation, Abel's skin looked bleached white. His lips were compressed and his left eye blinked furiously.

"What was it you wanted?"

She eased into the office and pointed to the denim bag lying beside the sofa. "My backpack. I forgot it earlier."

"Ah."

She'd grabbed it and almost made it back to the door when his voice stopped her. "Did they find the intruder?"

It took her a second to realize he was referring to the gunman. Somehow the tension rippling through the air in Abel's walnut-paneled office seemed more treacherous than a would-be killer stalking the halls. "No, I don't think they found him."

He nodded slowly. "No doubt the man made his escape before the authorities even arrived on the scene."

"Probably."

"Did the detective get all his questions answered?"

Abel picked up a paper from his desk and crushed it into a ball. "I had to leave. A, um, personnel matter."

She couldn't conceive of a personnel matter involving a lowly orderly that would take precedence over an armed gunman loose in the hospital, but she kept her opinion to herself. "I believe Detective Sanchez is still in the building. Would you like me to page him for you?"

He stared at the crushed paper in his hand as if seeing it for the first time. "What? Oh. No, that's all right. I'm going back downstairs. I'll find him. Was there anything else you needed, Doctor?"

Valerie slung her backpack over her shoulder. "No, thank you."

"Well, go home and get some sleep. You're beginning your four-off rotation, aren't you?"

"Yes," she said, startled that he would know her schedule.

"Try to put this dreadful situation behind you. Let the police sort it out."

"Of course." Although she was clearly being dismissed, Valerie hesitated in the doorway. A multitude of questions bubbled in her mind, but he was already shuffling through a stack of folders.

With a shrug she stepped into the reception area and turned to pull the door closed behind her. Abel was staring at her with the intensity of a black widow eyeing a nice juicy fly.

VALERIE SAT in the hospital cafeteria and scooped out the last spoonful of cherry-vanilla yogurt from the carton. Her hands were still trembling. The encounter in Abel's office had unnerved her, although for the life of her, she couldn't say why.

During the elevator ride down to the cafeteria, she'd thought about his intent stare. Then she'd recalled Emily Pierce once confiding that Abel was very nearsighted but too vain to wear his glasses. If she hadn't been so exhausted and overwrought, she might have realized sooner that his disconcerting gaze was merely the result of myopia.

It was Gil's fault for making her feel so paranoid. The calamity that had followed him into the hospital was an isolated occurrence, not an elaborate conspiracy involving respected members of the hospital staff.

Once she had some food in her stomach, Valerie calmed down enough to realize the absurdity of her apprehension. Ed Grant must have been called on the carpet for some minor infraction. No doubt that sort of thing happened every day. During her own brief interchange with him, Martin Abel had certainly been gracious enough. Still, she couldn't forget that tic in his eyelid, that raw edge in his voice and his predatory stare. Like a chipped and rusty razor blade being dragged across a pane of glass.

Or was her imagination working overtime?

She crushed the yogurt container and dabbed her lips with a stiff paper napkin and picked up the banana she'd purchased. She started to peel it but realized she was no longer hungry. In fact, a mild wave of nausea warned her that her overtaxed system wouldn't tolerate another morsel.

Damn Gil Branton, anyway.

Everything was his fault. Once again he'd burst into her life, then disappeared, leaving her to deal with the aftermath. She had to face the truth; the man was bad news. She'd been stupid to let her guard down again.

Disgusted with her own naiveté, she stuffed the banana

into her backpack and shoved the empty yogurt container into the trash. She just wished she could stuff Gil into an equally confining container. Out of sight and definitely out of mind.

Although she was off duty and desperately needed sleep, Valerie decided to make a quick stop at the WomanCare clinic before going home. The clinic was her baby. She'd hounded, harassed, begged and pleaded for nearly two years before Parker Memorial Hospital had come through with the necessary funding for the crucial facility.

Like every major metropolitan area, Phoenix had its share of working poor and indigent women who couldn't afford basic health care. Unfortunately these were the same women who most needed the services and counseling of competent medical practitioners.

Monica Giesen, the physician's assistant who ran the clinic under Valerie's careful supervision, bustled out of an examining room carrying a stainless-steel basin of instruments to be sterilized. "Oh, good morning, Dr. Murphy. We didn't expect you in today."

Valerie raised a fingertip to her lips. "Shh. I'm not here. You didn't see me."

"See who?" Monica responded conspiratorially.

"Anything going on?"

"The usual. Except we've had a lot of bigwigs through this morning."

"Bigwigs?"

"Yeah. Abel and a couple of his henchmen were nosing around when I came in. Then, just a few minutes ago, Merriwether Parker-hyphen-Lathrop herself graced us with a visit. Wonder what's up?"

Valerie shrugged. "I can't imagine. They're probably considering raising our funding."

Monica raised a manicured fingertip in a disbelieving gesture and laughed. "Yeah, right. You really ought to do stand-up comedy. Raise our funding—that's a good one."

They chatted for a moment, then Valerie, assured the clinic was in good hands, headed for the exit.

A blast of air, hot enough to bake a soufflé, slammed into her, and she quickly retrieved her sunglasses. Ah, Phoenix in August. A furnace would be cooler.

But look at the benefits of the blazing desert heat, she thought as she slipped behind the wheel of her Celica and opened the windows to allow some of the built-up heat to escape. She always lost weight in the summer. Too hot to eat and, besides, her favorite Cherry Garcia ice cream always melted before she could get it home, so she swore off when the temperature soared.

The Celica finally started to cool down about the time Valerie turned onto Chaparral Road, in Scottsdale, a suburb of Phoenix. For the next three days she was banning all serious thoughts—especially the troubling ones about Gil Branton. Three days of pure relaxation and hedonistic living. She intended to doze away the mornings. Nibble on rolled tacos with guacamole for lunch and spend her evenings lolling by the pool.

She pulled into her drive and smiled despite herself. The low-slung adobe was the first home of her own and she loved every square foot of the unimposing structure. Xeroscape plantings of native cacti and succulents gave the graveled front yard a splash of color. As did the deep-turquoise front door that she'd adorned with a *ristra* of bright red chile peppers.

Intending to park the Celica in the garage, she flicked the remote. When the door opened, she growled in exasperation. She'd left her mountain bike in the middle of the floor, instead of hanging it back on the rack where it belonged.

Faced with the decision of moving the bike now or dealing with the boiling-hot interior of her car later, she opted for the latter and left the Celica in the drive. Frowning at the bike that didn't have the decency to put itself away, she closed the automatic door behind her, savoring the sudden drop in temperature.

Not wanting to track the reddish earth onto her new off-white Berber carpet, she kicked off her shoes. Since the garage opened into the laundry room, she stripped and dropped her sweaty clothing into the hamper.

She padded naked into the bedroom where she dumped her denim bag on the dresser while planning her agenda for the rest of the day. A huge glass of ice water, her vitamins, take the phone off the hook and collapse into bed. Tonight, if she woke up at all, she'd order in pizza and watch a schmaltzy old movie.

Right now, though, she felt like she could drink a full gallon of ice water. Remembering that she'd stashed a banana in her backpack, she retrieved it before starting for the kitchen. A nice banana shake with yogurt and wheatgerm would be perfect for lunch, after some sleep.

Feeling somewhat wanton strolling through the house completely nude, she smiled, remembering a remark Gil had once made. He said she only wore clothes as a shield against her true erotic nature. But she wasn't going to think about Gil. She was going to concentrate on the cool *saltillo* tile floors caressing her bare feet while the whir of the evaporative air conditioner chilled the atmosphere. The house was dim and peaceful, her sanctuary.

As she walked past the open living room, furnished with *equipale* leather furniture and Navajo rugs, she blinked against the glare of bright sunlight. She must have forgotten to close the blinds when she left yesterday. If her evaporative cooler had to compete with the boiling Phoenix sun, her electric bill would soon equal the national debt. She had to remember to close those blinds on her way back to the bedroom.

Continuing toward the kitchen, her senses suddenly went on full alert. She took three more steps before she realized what had raised her hackles. A reddish footprint on her off-white carpet.

She paused, trying to recall if a repairman or friend had been in the house recently. But, no, yesterday was her cleaning day. Maria had been busily running the vacuum when Valerie had left for the hospital. So how did that rather large footprint appear on her newly vacuumed rug?

Valerie was suddenly acutely aware of the fact that she was completely naked, armed only with a banana. What if the maker of that print was still in her house? The print was pointed toward the kitchen so she began to slowly backtrack, an inch at a time, her mind frantically working.

There had to be a logical solution. Maybe Maria had come back into the house for some reason and tracked the carpeting herself? No, the answer was immediate. That print was much too large to be made by a tiny woman like Maria.

Her eyes flitting from one shadowy corner to the next, Valerie continued pacing backward toward the bedroom. She had often heard that the human mind took odd turns under stress. All she could think about was being caught in the buff, and the fact that the banana she clutched so tightly in her fist would be too badly bruised to eat.

Really bright, Murphy. Let's not worry about taking a burglar by surprise and getting shot, but heaven forbid he should see you naked. The illogic almost made her laugh.

She backed into the bright slice of sunlight that told her she was approaching the archway that opened into the living room. If Maria hadn't returned the cordless phone to the stand in the den, it was sitting on an end table.

Relief washed through her. A few more steps and she could call for help. The Scottsdale police were reputed to be prompt in responding. Help would be here in a matter of minutes. And there was a chenille throw draped over the arm of the sofa. Help and covering were only a few feet away.

She turned to step down into the sunken living room when she caught a movement out of the corner of her eye.

The motion had been faint, but enough for her conscious mind to register. Valerie had no pets. Someone was definitely in her house. One intruder in the living room and another in the kitchen? And she was trapped like a plucked chicken between them.

Her heart thrummed like an Apache war drum, and blood rushed, hot and furious, through her veins. Her knees threatened to buckle even as she willed her feet to move. To get out of that shaft of brilliant sunlight. Now that the living room was out, the nearest telephone extension was in the tiny alcove built into the wall just a few feet on the other side of the archway. If she could somehow reach the phone, dial 911 before...

Fearing her heart was going to explode, Valerie tiptoed toward the alcove. For a moment she thought she would make it, then a huge shadow fell across the gleaming tile.

Her legs wobbling uncontrollably, she glanced into the living room. Less than three feet away, a large masculine form stood silhouetted against the light flooding in from the front window. As if sensing her presence, he started to turn.

Valerie didn't know whether to scream or to faint. She brandished the banana like a sword, her left arm wrapped protectively across her naked body.

She had to think. There was a way out of this. There had to be. She couldn't let this man hurt her. Naked and cut off from the telephone, she'd never felt more helpless in her life.

After working in medicine for so many years, particularly in obstetrics, she'd grown used to the sight of the unclothed human form. If you'd asked her ten minutes ago, she would have insisted that she had no qualms about nudity. Now she couldn't imagine anything worse than that man turning around and catching her so exposed.

That irrational fear gave her a burst of fool's courage.

Knowing now that she would never make it to the phone unnoticed, she boldly stepped down into the sunken living room and jammed the end of the banana in his back.

"Make one move and I'll shoot."

Chapter Six

"Is that a banana in your hand, or am I just glad to see you?"

"Gil!"

When he heard the now badly bruised fruit hit the floor with a dull thud, he slowly turned to face her. He couldn't stop the smile that tugged at his lips. It hadn't been a dream, after all. Valerie really was standing before him, deliciously, delightfully nude.

While waiting for her return from the hospital, he'd fallen asleep in her comfy denim easy chair. The muted whisper of her footfall had awakened him, but a glance in the mirror over the mantel almost convinced him he'd lucked into a pleasant dream.

Dimly aware of the croak in his voice, he murmured, "It's really great to see you, Doc."

Following his gaze, she looked down as if only now becoming aware of her nudity. "Oh!"

Moving faster than he would have believed possible for a woman just coming off a double shift, she darted across the room. Jerking the Southwestern-patterned afghan from the sofa, she wrapped it around herself like a toga, depriving him of the delectable view.

''Aw, Doc, you didn't have to get dressed on my account.''

She whirled around, her eyes hard and glittering like shards of steel. ''What the hell are you doing in my house? Why did you run away again? How did you get in here? You have exactly five seconds to convince me not to phone the police and have your keister thrown in jail.''

''Five seconds, huh?'' He couldn't blame her for being angry. Hell, in her place, he would have tossed his butt out first and asked questions later. Much later. Speeding up his response before she made good on her threat, he ticked off his answers on his fingers. He decided not to mention that he'd snagged her address from his notes. He didn't know where this case was headed. He only knew it revolved around Valerie. ''One—I didn't know where else to go. Two—if that hit man was still hanging around the hospital, I didn't want him to see us leaving together. Three—the spare key you leave under the barrel cactus.''

A surreptitious glance at her scowling visage confirmed that his explanations hadn't made much impact. Although he wanted nothing more than to hang around in hopes of another tantalizing peek under that afghan, he strove to keep his mind on the very serious situation. ''And four—although it wasn't really a question—we're both in a helluva lot of trouble, and frankly I don't expect the cavalry to come charging up to save our hides. It's just us, Doc.''

''Trouble? *I'm* not in any trouble—although disaster trails after you like a pet dog. How did you know?''

Gil shook his head. Granted, that beating he'd taken had scrambled his brains for a while, but he'd totally lost the thread of her logic. ''Know what?''

''The key. I have more than two dozen potted plants

on the patio, how did you know the house key was under the barrel cactus? Has your amnesia been miraculously cured? Or was that just another act, another game for your amusement?''

He frowned. Now that he thought about it, he realized that he hadn't consciously searched for her spare key. Some…instinct had prodded him to lift that particular clay pot. As if he'd *known* it would be there.

The faintest flicker of a memory danced through his mind. He'd flopped into that soft denim easy chair before. A memory of Valerie curled up at his feet, her golden hair loose and flowing across his knees. Then, like a watercolor dissolving in the rain, the image melted away and he was left with that black nothingness. "Bits and pieces, Doc. Just bits and pieces.''

To his surprise, she dropped the subject. She seemed afraid to delve too deeply, more willing to let the monster that must have been their past slumber on.

"Your time is up, Gil. Out or I phone the police.''

From studying his case notes, he knew he'd been operating undercover before he'd left Phoenix, and that at one point Valerie Murphy had been his prime suspect. Surely he'd been mistaken. The woman who had taken a terrible risk with her own career by moving him without authority and saved his life by covering his body with her own couldn't be the woman responsible for the heinous crime he'd been investigating.

"Please,'' he said, "let me explain. Then if you still want to throw me out, I'll go peacefully.''

His breath tightened as she cinched the blanket around the swell of her breasts. "Why should I listen? Why should I believe a word you say? You've lied to me from the moment we met.''

Although he couldn't recall specific incidents, Gil

knew that he'd gone undercover several times in the past. He also knew, without actual remembering, that he'd never considered how his subterfuge would affect others. Pretending, lying, fabricating were all in a day's work for an FBI operative. He felt slightly shamed seeing himself through the eyes of a civilian, a real person who still valued honesty.

"If you'll fix me a cup of coffee, I'll tell you the truth. At least, as much as I know."

She stared at him for a long hard moment. "It shouldn't take too long to hear what little truth you seem capable of telling. But fix your own coffee. I'm going to put some clothes on."

Turning on her heel, she took two brisk steps, then paused and whirled to face him. "Where'd you get those clothes?"

He glanced down at the T-shirt and jeans he'd traded for the too-short surgical scrubs.

While he'd waited for Valerie to come home, he'd strolled through her house, trying to get a sense of who she was, what she cared about. Whether there was a man in her life. Unfortunately he'd found pretty good evidence that she wasn't celibate. A razor and aftershave in the bathroom, a half-used box of condoms in the bedside table and a few items of masculine clothing hanging neatly at the end of her closet.

Apparently the boyfriend was about his size.

Still, he was only in her home on sufferance, and if she discovered he'd been snooping... "These clothes?"

"Yes. Those."

"I, uh...found them."

She held up a hand. "Don't bother. I haven't believed your last dozen lies, no sense adding another."

Then, still clutching the afghan to her, she strode down the hallway.

Ten minutes later Gil poured them each a mug of dark Java roast, his favorite. Valerie stirred two packets of sweetener into her mug and added a healthy dollop of nondairy creamer.

"You're ruining a perfectly good cup of coffee."

"So you tell me every time."

He did? One more puzzle piece snapped into place. He'd known where she kept her spare house key and used to razz her about how she took her coffee. In his shadowy past she'd been more than a suspect. Had they become friends? At the very least, they must have been cordial acquaintances.

A sudden intuition clutched him and refused to let go. One of them had wanted more than friendship. The way Valerie was acting, all prickly and full of venom, he had to guess she'd wanted more from their relationship than he had been able or willing to give.

He searched her face, looking for a sign, confirmation, that his gut feeling was right. Her expression was devoid of emotion. If they had evolved beyond friendship, would she withhold that knowledge now? Wouldn't her face reveal the truth?

Bad deduction, Branton. This woman isn't pining for you. She just wants you gone.

She sipped at her adulterated brew. "You're back on the clock, Gil. Five minutes. And I want the truth. I deserve at least that much."

Was it his imagination or did her voice catch a little at the end? "Okay," he said. "But this is in the strictest confidence. You have to promise not to reveal anything I tell you."

She tossed her head. Her pale hair, crimped from hours

of confinement in her waist-length braid, fell across her face. "You're just going to have to trust *me* for a change. I'm not making any more promises to you."

The raw pain revealed by the harshness of her tone jammed another piece of the puzzle firmly into place. Their relationship had been a close one. And he'd hurt her. Badly.

He shoved this new painful knowledge deep down. He couldn't afford to have his focus diverted. Right now he had to concentrate on solving this case, free them both from the danger that stalked them, then he'd try to patch up the remnants of his past. Somehow he'd make amends to her. If they both lived long enough.

Taking a deep swallow of the hot strong coffee, he nodded. "Okay. Guess I'll just have to rely on your discretion."

"Four minutes."

"The amnesia and my name aren't fake. Everything else was."

Her head jerked up. Color leeched from her skin and she clutched the mug like a lifeline. "Three minutes," she whispered.

"Everything that I remember, anyway. I'm a field operative for the FBI."

She avoided his eyes while she sipped at her coffee. "Yeah, and I'm Michelle Pfeiffer's body double."

Gil reached into his hip pocket and tossed the slim black leather folder containing his photo ID and silver shield onto the table.

She hesitated, then picked it up. After studying it intently, she tossed it back. "Okay, you're a fed. If that badge isn't as phony as everything else you've told me. Go on with your tale, Special Agent Branton."

Ignoring her sarcasm, he tucked the folder back into

his jeans pocket. "Six months ago I was assigned to go undercover as a governmental bean counter conducting an audit."

"At Parker Memorial? Where we met."

"That's right. I needed a cover that would give me access to hospital records. As well as employee records of the staff."

"I see. And what were you hoping to find?"

Gil hesitated. Now they were at the heart of the matter. Could he trust her or not? If he confided in her and she was even peripherally involved, it would blow the entire operation. Months of investigation and untold taxpayer dollars right down the proverbial porcelain fixture.

She looked up pointedly at the kitchen wall clock. "Two minutes."

He scanned her face for long moments, searching for some sign of guile or subterfuge.

"One minute left."

He glanced behind him at the wall clock she'd been watching. It was Southwestern kitsch: a purple coyote howling at a vivid yellow sun. The sun's rays were the hour marks. Another flash of lucid memory—Valerie laughing with delight when she'd opened the package. He'd given her that clock for Christmas. Once upon a time he'd made her happy.

Closing his mind to caution, Gil started his story. "I was sent to crack a fake adoption scam."

She frowned. "What's that got to do with Parker Memorial?"

"There was a strong connection. In the year before I came to Phoenix, four infants disappeared."

"Here in the Valley? I don't remember hearing about anything like that on the news."

"It was never made public. Actually the bureau didn't

get involved until the fourth one. In fact, I don't think the disappearances were even tied together by the local authorities until then.''

''What!''

He wiped a coffee mustache from his lip with his forefinger. ''You can't blame them. Whoever is behind this scam is slick. The babies were chosen very carefully. And they weren't taken from the hospital—that would have brought the law down on their heads with the first disappearance. No, our kidnapper waited until the babies were a week or so old and well removed from the hospital.''

''So how did you connect them?''

''Our computers are set to give printouts of certain patterns. For one thing, all the stolen infants were born at Parker Memorial Hospital. Secondly, they were all born to women who were likely to leave the area immediately after giving birth, or of a 'type' that wouldn't necessarily be believed if they reported their babies were stolen from their cribs.''

''What do you mean?''

''When the babies of very young unstable mothers disappear, the authorities are more likely to look at her as a suspect rather than a victim.''

Valerie nodded. ''I see that kind of prejudice every day in our WomanCare clinic. Women who are devalued because of social class, poverty or even youthfulness.''

''Yeah. And whoever is behind this scam is well aware of that fact. One stolen infant was the child of a teenage runaway. Two were born to single mothers who lived on the outskirts, not part of the city proper. The last baby belonged to a Prescott woman, but she came to Phoenix for the birth because they expected complications.''

Shoving her hair out of her face, Valerie leaned forward and studied him intently. "I...I had a patient like that a few months ago. Natalie...Natalie Brown? Brennan? No, Brewer! Natalie Brewer."

"That's right."

"Oh, no! You mean her baby was taken? How awful. She and her husband had tried for years to conceive. Hers was a change-of-life miracle baby. Her only chance. Oh, please say you got her baby back for her."

Gil avoided her hopeful gaze as he sipped the last of his coffee. "No. None of the infants have been recovered. Not yet, anyway."

Unshed tears glimmered in her eyes. "But...but I don't understand. Why kidnap children from women who were obviously unable to pay the ransom?"

Gil got up and fetched the coffeepot. When Valerie covered her mug with her hand and shook her head, he poured the dregs of the glass carafe into his own mug. "No ransom notes were ever received."

"Then why?"

He swung the chair around and straddled it. "You're in obstetrics. You know how many desperate childless couples are out there. Too many of them are willing to sell their very souls for a healthy baby. We think those infants were sold to the highest bidder."

"That's terrible!" She propped her elbow on the table and cupped her head in her hand. "But how do they get away with it? I mean, every birth is registered. Babies are issued social security numbers. They can't start school without shot records and birth certificates."

Gil nodded his agreement. "That's why we're pretty sure that someone in the medical community is involved. Possibly—probably a doctor."

"A doctor! No, I can't believe that!"

He laughed wryly. "Come on, Val, you're not that

naive. You can't seriously believe there are no greedy or unethical physicians.''

"Of course there are, but...most of my colleagues went into medicine to save lives, not destroy them."

"I don't doubt that, but all it takes is one bad apple. At any rate, someone with the knowledge and clearance to issue phony birth certificates is certainly involved. These babies are 'adopted' by wealthy couples. I understand the going black-market rate for a healthy Caucasian infant is upwards of a quarter million dollars. Four missing babies is a cool million-dollar profit—tax free. A doctor who can be blackmailed, say, one with a drug problem, may convince himself that he can do an awful lot of good with a million dollars.''

She nodded slowly. "Unfortunately, abuse of prescription narcotics is at an all-time high in our profession right now." She rose and carried her mug to the sink. From the way she was worrying her upper lip, Gil could tell she was processing this plethora of unpleasant information.

She picked up a sponge and absentmindedly wiped the spotless table. "All right, you have me hooked. I can understand why you had to go undercover, why you didn't tell me the truth. At first. But later, after you'd..." She hesitated, as if searching for a word. "After you got to know me better, why didn't you confide in me?"

Gil shrugged. "I don't know." He tapped his temple with his index finger. "Except for bits and pieces, everything that happened before my alleged accident is all a blur." That much was the truth, but only part of it. Confiding in Dr. Murphy would have been a severe breach of duty. Even if he'd been sleeping with her. Which, of course, he hadn't been. Not even amnesia could rob him of a memory that delicious, he was certain.

Rising from the table, she carried her half-empty mug to the sink and ran water into it. Gil could see the tension in her posture as she stood staring out the narrow kitchen window.

When she'd rinsed the cup a full two minutes, she finally turned off the flow of water and turned to face him. Her expression was closed, unfathomable. Gil waited. His gut told him that her next few words would affect both their lives.

She pulled a dish towel from its holder and slowly wiped her fingertips. "And that's it? The truth?"

"Every word."

"I'm still confused about one detail." She nibbled her upper lip, a habit he knew meant she was deep in thought. "You told me you had to go to Los Angeles on business and…and you never came back."

He nodded, glad for the opportunity to finally address what she obviously perceived as his desertion. "That's right. We had a tip that the babies were being transported out of state, to California. I made a trip to the field office in Los Angeles to request their help in running records' checks. Adoption records are sealed in most states, so I needed some friendly muscle to gain access to those files."

"Did you find what you were looking for?"

Gil unconsciously rubbed the raw abrasion on his temple. How many days, weeks, had he lain in a hospital bed with a constant headache? The physical pain had been bad enough, but the mental emptiness, the confusion and sense of impending peril had nearly pushed him over the brink. Even now, recalling the accident and the agonizing weeks that followed, caused his head to throb.

"No," he said finally. "I didn't find anything. Someone ran my car off Topanga Canyon before I had the chance to talk with the Special Agent in Charge there.''

Holding his breath at the overwhelming memory of a broken windshield, his mangled shoulder, crushed ribs, flashing lights, screaming sirens and being raced to the operating room, Gil finally looked up. Valerie was staring at him, her eyes wide and gentle. She tossed the towel aside and crossed the few feet that separated them.

She placed her hand on his shoulder in a calming gesture. ''And that's when you contracted traumatic amnesia?''

He rubbed his temple, where the dark hair had grown back in a silvery color. ''Yeah. I had something called an intracranial hematoma. They said I had brain surgery a few days after the accident. I don't remember much after my car went off the cliff. It's like that single memory—the truck hitting my fender—is all I clearly know. Almost my entire life before, and the first days after, the accident are gone. Only a few fragments of memory are left to drive me crazy.''

''I...I was very worried. I didn't know where to look. I called dozens of hotels and every hospital.''

Valerie Murphy was a strong but proud woman, he sensed. It must have cost her a lot to admit the extent of her search for him. ''They cut some of my clothes off at the scene of the accident. I guess my wallet wasn't recovered until someone from the towing company found it several days later. I was John Doe for a while.''

''That's becoming a habit. You're listed as John Doe at Parker Memorial, as well.''

''Thanks to you, Doc.''

She laughed. The first real laugh he'd seen since his return. ''I just didn't want to admit that I knew you. You were pretty disreputable-looking when they brought you in.''

He grinned in appreciation of her small joke. ''You can't look like a *GQ* cover model when you've been rumbling with drunken bikers.''

She sobered. ''It's a wonder you didn't die. That beating you took so soon after a serious head injury could easily have been fatal. It certainly accounts for why your amnesia isn't receding more quickly.''

''It accounts for this miserable headache, too. You have any aspirin?''

She nodded and moved to a cupboard on one side of the sink. A few seconds later she handed him a glass of water and two tablets. ''Here, this should help.''

''Thanks.'' He swallowed the pills. ''Listen, Doc, would it be pushing your hospitality too much to ask for the use of your bed for a couple hours? Just for a nap,'' he amended quickly at her quirked eyebrow.

She drew in a deep breath and held it for several seconds before slowly releasing it. ''I guess not. But there's one thing I still don't understand.''

''Only one? Hell, I've got an entire lifetime that I either don't remember or can't make sense of.''

''That's what I mean. If your amnesia is almost total, why do you know so much about the adoption ring and the trip to Los Angeles?''

''I don't really remember those events as much as having reconstructed them. Apparently I'm a note-taking, report-filing, rigidly structured kind of guy. Once they found my ID and discovered I'm a federal agent, we started rebuilding my past. I'd filed computerized reports of my findings in Washington and had tons of case notes on a laptop computer that survived the crash.''

He polished off the dregs of the now-cold coffee and

carried his mug to the sink. "I don't have any real memory of why I went to Los Angeles, only what I've pieced together. I don't know who knew I was there and ran my car off the road. But the evidence eventually confirmed my partial recollection that my little rental had been 'nudged' several times by a dark-green Ford pickup. One of those big jobs."

"And that's everything? You've left nothing out?"

Valerie's actions during the past thirty hours had just about convinced him of her innocence. Just about. But years of law enforcement had taught him to play his cards close to his chest. There was no real reason to confide that one of those infants had been delivered by her colleague, Dr. Sidney Weingold.

The other three had been delivered by Valerie herself.

He feigned a yawn and discovered that the night's activities had finally caught up with him. He was exhausted. "Can we wrap up the twenty-questions session for now? I'm whipped."

She snatched up his water glass and slammed it on the counter near the sink. "Heaven forbid I should inconvenience you with my silly questions, Agent Branton. By all means, let's make your comfort our number-one priority!"

With a final scorching glare, she stormed out of the kitchen.

Valerie Murphy's hot button rode very close to the surface, he reflected. Every time he was on the brink of accepting her innocence, some tiny comment set off a spark of anger. If she had no connection to this adoption scam and wasn't reacting to fear of exposure, why the barely controlled hostility?

Trailing her down the hall, Gil vowed to get some much-needed sleep, then find another safe house. If Valerie was involved in the kidnapping ring, he wasn't safe in her home. At least not for long. Even if she was just a good Samaritan, she could be endangered purely by her association with him.

Either way, his best chance of keeping them both alive was for him to get as far away as possible from the lovely Dr. Murphy.

Chapter Seven

Valerie stood over the bed watching him sleep.

When he'd been talking earlier in the kitchen, she'd found herself almost believing him. His explanation had been very convincing. Now that she was free from the allure of his smooth voice and beguiling eyes, doubt assailed her.

Once before she'd believed him. She'd been a fool then and she'd be a bigger fool now to fall for the wild tales of a man who admittedly made his living through deceit.

A stolen-baby ring in Phoenix? Unbelievable.

As head of obstetrics at one of the city's major hospitals, surely she would have been informed. Security precautions would have been tightened; patients would have been warned. If someone at Parker Memorial was a suspect or if the hospital was in any way implicated, the administrators would have been notified.

And Martin Abel would have been all over her like grease on a deep-fried *chimichanga*.

Besides, if Gil's story was true, why hadn't he confided in her? Granted, their intimate relationship had been of short duration, but it had been special. He'd said he loved her. So how could he have kept such potentially devastating information from her?

She looked down at his face, once so loved, now so distrusted. For a man who professed such concern for the well-being of those missing infants, he'd dumped her with the responsibility of their own unborn child.

Valerie sighed. That was unfair and she knew it. Gil didn't know about her pregnancy.

He hadn't stuck around long enough for her to tell him.

Out of habit—not concern, she assured herself—she tugged the sheet up over his bare shoulder. Her fingertip skimmed the hawk's-head tattoo. She'd once likened him to the raptor etched into his skin: proud, valiant and fiercely independent. Was he also a sly predator like the red-tailed hawks that flew over the desert landscape, seeking out and destroying unwary victims who had the misfortune to cross his path?

What would his reaction be if she told him about the child? Would he bolt and run again? Or would he grudgingly allow the responsibility of parenthood to clip his wings?

Could she bear either response?

She sighed and slipped out of the cool bedroom.

ALONE ON VALERIE'S king-size bed, Gil tossed and turned. His "nap" had extended to several hours, and the sun was already sinking in a brilliant display of purple and fuchsia when he opened his eyes and stared out the deep-set narrow window.

The window faced west and although the air conditioner whirred incessantly, the room felt warm. Close. Lately he was hot all the time. As if all the unresolved questions whirling through his mind were funneled into energy that kept his body superheated.

Despite his rest, Gil was still on edge, tired. Those elusive memories that perforated his sleep and pummeled him with their intensity made him feel like a punch-drunk fighter boxing shadows in the dark.

All the unanswered questions. Poking, probing, prodding and persistent questions. Why had he gone to Los Angeles? Had he found something in the hospital files he'd been looking through? Something, perhaps, that incriminated Valerie?

After his release from the hospital, Gil had returned to Phoenix in an effort to retrace his steps. But due to his lengthy unexplained absence, the hospital had terminated his staff privileges, depriving him of access to those all-important records.

He could have gone to Martin Abel and revealed his true identity and mission, he supposed. But Abel was a political animal, clawing his way through the administrative ranks, and Gil couldn't be certain of the man's loyalty. If exposing Gil's cover would gain him brownie points, Abel wouldn't hesitate.

So Gil had contrived an altercation in a bar, knowing that severe bruises and contusions could gain him entrée into the hospital. His opponents, however, had been far more diligent in their punishment than he'd counted on. He'd landed in intensive care, instead of a cushy bed on the general ward.

Even that feeble plan had backfired when he and Valerie were forced to flee Parker Memorial. His investigation was well and truly stalled.

Unless...unless he could talk Valerie into helping him.

He sat up as an idea took hold.

True, earlier he'd made a mental vow to clear out as soon as he'd rested. But she had access to the hospital computer, including dial-in privileges. With her help, he could hack into medical records and maybe find some common denominator, something that would point him in the right direction.

It was his only chance. The only chance those heart-broken parents had of ever seeing their children again.

He rolled out of bed and headed for the small en suite bathroom. Splashing cold water on his face, he slicked back his unruly hair with his fingers and thought about the best approach to take with Val.

How could he convince her that an illegal tap into hospital records was justified? Appeal to her sense of justice? Or her concern for her patients? Another choice would be to exploit her soft spot for babies.

Shame shuddered through him as he realized he was once again prepared to use her for his own purposes. Without concern for the consequences she might suffer.

But those children had to be found. And those heartless criminals had to be stopped. No matter the cost to Valerie's feelings and career. Or to his own integrity.

Filled with determination and a sense of hope that had eluded him for weeks, Gil was grinning when he sauntered into the kitchen. One look at Valerie's pain-racked face stopped him in his tracks.

"What's wrong? Has something happened?"

She shifted on her chair, avoiding his eyes. "I guess you could say that."

Gil sank into the opposite chair and studied her face. So lovely yet so thin, with hollows and shadows that bespoke a woman who was suffering. "What's wrong?" he asked gently, reaching for her hand.

She snatched her hand back like she'd been stung by a deadly scorpion. Lifting her chin, she pinned him with the cold almost hate-filled gaze he'd come to expect.

"This kidnapping ring. Is that why you slept with me? To get information?"

Gil was stunned speechless. He and Valerie? Intimate? While she was a suspect? No, he couldn't have been so stupid. So unprofessional. But even as he denied the accusation, he knew it to be true.

Although his memory was still fuzzy, ephemeral at best, he could vividly recall the sweet scent of her golden hair against his face. The luxurious texture of her skin beneath his hands. The taste of her flesh on his tongue.

No wonder she hated him.

At this moment he hated himself.

Was this what the job had done to him? Allowed his single-minded quest for truth to turn him into a cold calculating bastard who'd use anyone to achieve his goal? Had his arrest record become more important than his integrity?

He hated to believe it of himself, but the stark bitterness of Valerie's words was proof enough.

"I...I didn't know we'd been together," he said. "If I hurt you, I'm truly sorry."

"Hurt me?" She laughed, dry and mirthlessly. "A person can survive hurt, Gil. It's even reputedly good for character growth. But you used me, left me with..." She hesitated.

"With what?" he asked, not sure he wanted to hear the answer.

"With everyone at the hospital asking questions, expecting me to have the answers. Everyone knew about us."

She didn't verbalize the mortification she must have felt when her colleagues wondered why the auditor she had been dating suddenly disappeared. But he could feel her shame, her bruised pride, radiating from every pore.

But it wasn't all his fault. Surely she could see that. "I explained what happened," he said. "You can't hold me responsible for an attempt on my life that left me in the hospital for weeks. That's not fair."

She leaned forward, eyes glittering with rage. "What wasn't fair was your lying to me. You became involved with me under false pretenses. If I'd known the truth, Gil, I would have had some place to look when you disappeared. I could have called the FBI, and maybe you wouldn't have lain as a John Doe patient without any friends or family around for weeks. I would have *known!*"

"Val, I can't say a thing to justify my actions, because I just don't remember." Actually it was pretty clear that he hadn't taken her into his confidence because she was still under suspicion. But to tell her that now would only make matters worse.

She leaped to her feet and shoved the chair under the table. Hands clenched tightly over the wooden chair back, she spoke softly, "That's because there is no justification for your actions. You used me."

There it was, the bald unadorned truth.

"Val, sit down. Please. Let me explain."

"I don't want more lies. I want you to leave. And stay out of my life."

He rose and rounded the table to stand in front of her. He wanted badly to take her in his arms, to kiss away all the suffering he'd caused. Yet instinct warned him to keep his distance, to appeal to her logic and give her emotions time to heal. "Please," he whispered, "I need your help."

"No. Use someone else. I'm finished."

"There is no one else, Val. These monsters have to be stopped and I can't do it alone."

"It's not my problem. Find someone else."

Gil shook his head. How could he convince her? He couldn't blame her for her flat refusal, but he desperately needed her help. Suddenly he knew the key. He had to take her completely into his confidence, tell her everything. For a woman with her principles, only the truth would do. "It is your problem too, Val."

She crossed her arms over her chest. "How do you figure that?"

"There's more that I haven't told you."

"Imagine that." Sarcasm flowed hot and thick over her soft voice.

"Look, why don't you go lie down and get some sleep?" he said. "We'll talk later."

"No, let's get it over with. Besides," she said, her voice softening, "I slept on the sofa. I'm fine."

"Okay." He motioned to the table. "Then, sit back down. Please. I'll tell you everything. I promise."

She held up a hand as if to stop the flow of his words. "I'll listen, Gil. But do me a favor? Don't make any more promises. They aren't worth the breath it takes you to make them."

Abruptly turning her back, she pulled out her chair. Sitting with her arms still folded in a protective manner, she waited for him to take his place across from her. "Okay, Gil, I'm listening. What new fairy tale do you have for me now?"

Ignoring her scorn, he plunged ahead. "Everything I told you about the stolen-baby ring is the truth. There are just a few...details I've left out."

"For instance?"

"Most of the missing babies were born to young single mothers or disadvantaged women with several offspring already at home. Women who wouldn't necessarily be believed when they reported their babies were kid-napped.''

"You already told me that."

"Yeah, but what I didn't tell you is that every one of those mothers is fair-skinned, with light hair and blue eyes. Apparently the kidnappers are only interested in specific physical traits."

He glanced up as Valerie gasped sharply. "What is it? What's wrong?"

"N-nothing. Only…that seems so cold-blooded. So heartless.''

Gil was a bit taken aback by her words. Was she implying that the abduction of fair-skinned babies was somehow worse than it would have been had the babies been Hispanic or black? "Stealing any newborn seems pretty merciless to me."

"That's not what I meant. It only made those missing infants seem…more real somehow. To hear them described so precisely, I mean."

He nodded. The whole unsavory mess had abruptly become real to Valerie. Gone beyond abstract numbers to real humans with real heartaches. Her sudden pallor was simple revulsion against the inhumane criminals who stole helpless babies from their cribs.

"Yeah, our perp is not only selective," he said, "but must have a chunk of ice where his heart should be."

She tilted her head, her expression more quizzical now than hostile. "You said earlier that this was my problem. What did you mean?"

Gil explained that she'd been the physician of record for three of the four births.

Valerie sat back in her chair, her face bland as she processed the information. "So I'm a suspect?"

He blew out a breath. He'd opted for the truth, so he

"Yes, of course. I often make notes to my patients' charts from home. Why?"

"Because the answer is in those records. When are you due back at the hospital?"

"Not until Tuesday. This is my four-off rotation."

"Good! That's perfect. If you'll trust me with your computer and access code, I can spend the weekend poring over the charts of the four mothers."

"What about me? What can I do to help?"

"Take these few days off and go to a hotel. Get some rest. You deserve it."

Her eyes widened. "Wait a minute. I'm supposed to be the helpless little woman who lounges by the pool while the big bad *special* agent rides in on his white charger and saves my professional reputation?"

"This is no time to carry the banner for your equality, Val. Two attempts have already been made on my life."

"So maybe *you* should hide out by the pool."

"Ha-ha. Val, if you get in the way, this vicious criminal won't hesitate to kill you to save his own skin."

Valerie closed her eyes and considered her options. Gil was right—this was dangerous. And she had her baby's welfare to look out for, not just her own.

She should just give him her identification code and pack a suitcase. Head out for a fancy resort like The Buttes and work on her tan. But she couldn't do that. No matter what was at stake, she had to be involved. Had to be a part of uncovering the culprit.

Valerie thought about the description of the mothers Gil had given her. Blond, fair-skinned single women. She herself fit that profile. If they didn't stop these kidnappers, would her baby also "disappear"? She couldn't take the chance.

Besides, she needed to know if Gil was finally telling

might as well give her all of it. "Yeah, I think so, at least according to the reports I filed with Washington. But you weren't the only one," he hastened to add.

"I'm glad to hear it." Her tone was icy again.

In a last-ditch effort to gain her cooperation, Gil reached across the table and grasped her hand. To his surprise, she didn't pull away. "Look, Val, I'm a pretty dedicated investigator, but I'm not completely unscrupulous. If we were...lovers, then I must have cleared you. I must have."

"Are you trying to convince me or yourself?"

"Both."

Her tense expression softened perceptibly. "That actually had the ring of truth, Agent Branton. You'd better watch yourself or it could become a habit."

"That's Special Agent Branton," he quipped, and was rewarded with a smile.

While she seemed receptive, he plunged on with the background facts he'd accumulated. "I'm convinced of your innocence, Val, but the evidence is still open to interpretation. Only someone with access to medical records could have pulled this thing off. How else could the kidnapper have ascertained the dates of birth, babies' health and coloration? Not to mention the mothers' home addresses. If it wasn't you, the physician of record three of the four cases, then the answer is pretty obvious."

She nodded. "Someone on the staff of the Woman clinic."

"Precisely."

They were both quiet as they pondered the impl of his words. Finally Valerie broke the silence. do you want me to do?"

"You have a portable computer? With a mo

her the truth. All of it. She had to know how far she could trust him. Only then could she make the decision whether to tell him about the child she carried. The one she'd conceived during that last night of wild unbridled passion.

Her decision made, she spoke firmly. "No. I need to know for myself that we've done everything right. You're accusing one of my co-workers of a vile crime, Gil. Someone I trust. I have to be involved."

"I can't put you in danger, don't you understand?"

"You don't have any choice. You need me far more than I need you."

Her heart cringed the moment she said the words. *If only that were true.* If only Gil needed her half as much as she needed him.

If she was going to work with him, though, she had to keep her feelings under control. Maintain the professional armor she donned whenever she walked into the hospital. Striving for a dispassionate tone, she asked, "Now, what exactly do you hope to uncover in the hospital records?"

"I want to see if I can find a pattern of treatment. A lab tech who drew blood from each of those women, or something like that."

"I don't know what that would tell you. A phlebotomist probably draws blood from a hundred patients a day. And blood is drawn from expectant mothers on almost every visit. It wouldn't be a big coincidence for a particular tech to draw blood from each of the four in question."

"Whew. That makes it harder."

"A perfect example of why you need my involvement. I know hospital routine, as well as every person employed in the WomanCare clinic. Besides, it's my computer and my access code."

Realizing he was defeated, Gil gave a half grin. "If we don't play by your rules, you're going to take your football and go home, is that it?"

"You got it. There's just one minor glitch, though."

"What's that?"

"My laptop computer is in the shop. I'll have to use the one at the hospital." She glanced at the coyote clock. "It's too late tonight—I only had a few hours' sleep. I'm bushed."

She filled a tall glass with ice water and shook some pills from a container into her palm. After swallowing them, she licked her lips. "I'll be right back."

He wandered around the kitchen, examining a shelf of cookbooks, most devoted to healthy—cardboard, in his opinion—food. A moment later Valerie strode back into the room, a stack of neatly folded bed linen in her arms.

"Make yourself comfortable," she said, "on the couch."

He took the sheets and pillow. Sleeping alone on a lumpy sofa didn't sound all that inviting. Still, he guessed he should consider himself lucky that she hadn't ejected him completely, leaving him to slumber on the porch among her many pots of cacti.

Giving him a brief, and somewhat insincere, smile, she paused on her way out of the kitchen. "First thing in the morning I'll go to the office and see what my limited computer skills turn up."

"But I can't go with you during the day. Too many people milling around. Obviously the kidnapper knows who I am."

"Then I'll just have to go alone. No one will be suspicious of me going into the office to do some paperwork. Heaven knows, that's how I spend most of my free time."

"What am I supposed to do while you're gone?"

Valerie laughed aloud. Gil sounded like a petulant child who'd just learned he couldn't go shopping with Mommy. "I guess you'll just have to lie by the pool. Work on your tan."

Chapter Eight

Leaving a grumpy Gil alone at her house, Valerie backed the Celica out of the driveway. Her mind wouldn't let go of the remarkable string of incidents that accompanied his sudden appearance in her life. She'd lived quietly prior to Gil Branton, no danger, intrigue or confounding puzzles.

Since Gil had first come into her world, the contrast was bewildering.

Even as a child she'd been pensive and nurturing. She was only eight when she had first patched up a Barbie doll after her little brother Mike popped its leg off. From that moment on, Valerie knew she wanted to be a healer. In high school, when her girlfriends were going ga-ga over boys, Valerie spent her weekends poring through *Gray's Anatomy*.

College, and later med school, required total commitment and dedication to her studies. Oh, there had been that first heart-stopping romance with a guy in his third year of veterinary medicine. But when he'd graduated and left the state, she'd been too swamped with her own studies to engage in more than the most casual of relationships.

Med school was quickly followed by her residency,

then an OB/GYN position had opened at Parker Memorial and she'd been busy building her career. Two years ago she'd enjoyed a brief fling with a surgeon who, it turned out, was too enamored with himself to ever find anyone else as fascinating.

So when Gil had waltzed into her life with his lazy smile, thatch of ink-dark hair and devilish sense of humor, she'd been bowled over. He was the first man she'd ever truly loved. The first man who had broken her heart.

Now he was back. What was she going to do about him? Or about her own perfidious heart?

Although her mind was focused on her problems, she drove in a kind of autopilot mode, scarcely noticing when she approached her exit from the freeway. The new off-ramp was steeply banked, so she stepped on the brake as she entered the curve.

Her shiny red Celica didn't slow down.

Slightly alarmed at the mushy-feeling pedal, she pressed harder, then pumped the brakes. Still no response.

Don't panic, she told herself, as she reached for the gearshift. She could slow the car by downshifting. But she had picked up too much speed. The car couldn't make the sharp turn.

Truly frightened now, she yanked on the emergency brake. The brakes screeched and the acrid scent of burning rubber filled the air. Although the little car tried valiantly to hold on to the asphalt, it spun out of control.

Valerie stared at the crazily spinning scenery. It was like watching a slow-motion sequence in an action film with too many car crashes. Too many rotations to be real. But this was no movie stunt. Helpless, all she could do was watch as the car continued its inexorable spin toward a concrete stanchion.

The baby! she thought, as pure instinct guided her actions. She let go of the wheel, clutched her arms over her stomach to protect her unborn child.

A millisecond later a tremendous crash rattled her teeth. She bit through her lip as her head smacked against the dashboard. The scream of ripping metal filled her ears. The Celica had lost its duel with the concrete pylon.

Then darkness, a compassionate friend, took her from the pain and terror.

THE NEXT HOUR was a blur of flashing lights, intrusive voices and agony as Valerie floated in and out of consciousness. Heavy punishing pain hammered at her head, her face, her chest.

She was dimly aware of men with loud voices and gentle hands loading her into an ambulance. A frantic bumpy ride at breakneck speed. Then, sure professional hands transported her to a cold room with blinding white light overhead. The antiseptic smell of alcohol and the more subtle coppery scent of blood scourged her nostrils.

"My God, it's Dr. Murphy!"

The voice was muted, ethereal, as if coming from another galaxy.

"You know her?" The male voice was sharp, staccato in its delivery.

"Yes, she's chief baby catcher."

"Here? At Parker Memorial?" the masculine voice grilled. "Good. Call up her chart."

Through the soggy gauze curtain shielding her awareness, Valerie had a faint understanding that they were referring to the computerized medical chart kept on all medical personnel. Although the information it contained was scant, it did list emergency contacts and pharmaceutical allergies.

The frenetic activity softened to a muted hum as she felt herself drifting away again. Then someone bumped the bed and she moaned as a painful spasm shuddered through her body.

Something sharp pricked her arm and Valerie tried to call out, to tell them not to give her drugs for fear of injuring her baby, but someone slapped an oxygen mask over her face and the opportunity was lost.

Sweet semidarkness alternated with hard-edged cognizance as she floated above herself, gliding on a sea of pain. Although at times the agony was unbearable, she fought to stay awake. She had to find her voice, make someone understand about the precious cargo she was carrying.

A firm masculine voice ordered X rays and Valerie ripped the oxygen mask off her face. "No! No...no X rays." Her voice was a barely discernible croak and she wondered if anyone had heard. Horror filled her as she realized that she had miraculously survived the accident, but now faced the very grave danger of losing or harming her child due to medical ignorance of her condition. She'd been a fool not to inform the Human Resources Department and put this pregnancy in her record.

She'd been too proud to admit that with all her training and experience, her birth-control methods had failed her. Worse, that the father of her child had abandoned her.

After years of counseling unwed mothers, Valerie feared her co-workers would treat the news of *her* unplanned pregnancy with snickering and embarrassed pity, so she'd kept the news to herself. If something happened to her baby because of her stupid pride, it would be all her fault.

Then a staunch female figure, clad in the pale blue scrubs of an ER nurse, approached her bed. "Dr. Murphy? Can you hear me? It's Emily Pierce. The nurse said you refused the C-spine series the doctor ordered. You could have serious internal injuries.''

''No. No X rays,'' she gasped between bursts of pain. ''First trimester.''

Even through the pain and drug-induced fog, Valerie heard the nurse's sharp intake of breath. But Fierce Pierce quickly recovered her professional composure. ''Dr. Murphy, are you saying you're pregnant?''

Valerie licked her dry lips and nodded. ''Yes. Get Sidney. Dr. Weingold. He…he's my OB.''

''Right away, Doctor.''

Pierce bustled away and Valerie was left in relative peace.

After a while the pain receded slightly, and she was fairly alert when Pierce returned accompanied by Monica Giesen, the physician's assistant from the WomanCare clinic. As Pierce started swabbing at a section of Valerie's scalp behind her left ear, Monica patted her hand. ''Oh, Val, are you all right?''

''Other…than a rotten headache…I think I'll live.''

''I, er, understand you wanted a consult from Dr. Weingold?'' Monica's tone was faintly accusatory.

Valerie realized her assistant's feelings were hurt because she hadn't taken the woman into her confidence. Fear of intimacy, on any level, had long been a problem of Valerie's. Only once had she hurled caution aside and given herself completely to another person, and that had cost her dearly.

''I'm…sorry I didn't…tell you, Monica,'' she said slowly, pausing frequently to draw a tortured breath. She hoped no ribs were broken. She could imagine the pain of Lamaze breathing techniques with cracked or badly bruised ribs. "I...wasn't...sure yet how I was...going to resolve...the situation."

Her professional demeanor now firmly back in place, Monica again patted her hand soothingly. Monica Giesen was the glamour queen of the hospital and was always cognizant of the danger of being judged by her looks rather than her skills. Sometimes the result was an over-zealousness, a yearning for perfection that she never quite reached.

"I'm sure you would have talked to me when the time was right. Anyway, Dr. Weingold is in the middle of a difficult delivery and can't get away just now."

Valerie was crestfallen. Although she could read the signs herself, she didn't want to rely on her own judgment. She needed a valued colleague's reassurance that the fetus had survived the accident unscathed.

"Dr. Weingold suggested we call Carl Bender, so I did. He should be here momentarily."

"Thanks, Monica. I appreciate it."

"Anything else I can do?"

"No, nothing. Thanks."

"Sure I can't call someone for you?"

Inexplicably the only person she wanted to talk to right now was Gil. And he was stuck at her house without a car.

As if reading her thoughts, Monica leaned down and whispered in her ear. "I heard Gil Branton was back in town. Don't you want me to call him?"

Valerie hesitated. She couldn't deny how badly she yearned to have Gil at her side but...even though she kinda-sorta believed his story, she couldn't get involved with that man again. Once burned... "No, I—" She broke off as lanky Carl Bender strolled into the treatment room.

"Nurse, perhaps you could give us some privacy," he snapped at Monica without bothering to look at her. "And have someone set up for a sonagram."

Monica rolled her eyes at his lack of courtesy and pulled the curtain around Valerie's bed. "Yes, Doctor."

"Monica!" Valerie called out to her retreating back. "Maybe you could make that call, after all. To my house. Don't...don't ask him to come. Just...just tell him what happened."

Monica winked over the doctor's shoulder. "Now you're talking, girl."

"Thanks for all—"

"Dr. Murphy," Carl Bender interrupted. "If you could give me your attention?"

She dutifully turned her gaze to the young physician and answered his questions as he dispassionately took her medical history and grilled her on details of the accident.

Carl Bender had the reputation of being a fine diagnostician, but sorely lacking in social skills. Several patients had complained of his shortage of warmth, and Valerie had been intending to have a private discussion with him regarding his bedside manner.

Now she had the opportunity to observe his methods firsthand.

When she'd answered all his questions, Dr. Bender conducted a thorough, if brusque, examination. Then he turned on the sonagram machine and pressed the wand into her abdomen. She tried to peek at the screen, but he twisted the monitor so the image was hidden from her view.

She knew he was simply trying to protect her in case the prognosis was poor, but she was nonetheless irritated by his failure to recognize her professional standing. Finally he snapped the machine off and turned to face her.

After once more checking her heart sounds, he draped his stethoscope around his neck. "I'd say you were pretty lucky, all things considered. The fetus seems to be intact and except for a few contusions, you don't appear any the worse for wear."

"Thank you, Carl. I was just concerned."

"Mmm. Well, as I said, everything seems okay. I am a bit concerned that you might have cracked a rib, but we can't chance an X ray, so we'll tape you up to keep them immobilized just in case."

She unconsciously rubbed the sore spot just under her left breast. "Not a bad idea."

He took the necessary bindings from the drawer and tore open the plastic wrapping. With quick measured motions, he wound the elastic bandage tightly around her upper abdomen, binding her bruised ribs into place. "There," he said, when he'd fastened the bandage and replaced her hospital gown. "That should hold you. I want you to rest here awhile, make sure you remain stable."

She breathed slowly and shallowly. "Whew. I had no idea the wrapping would be so tight."

"Not much point in doing it otherwise, Dr. Murphy," he uttered in a censorious tone.

"I understand that, Dr. Bender. I was merely commenting on the discomfort—much as a patient might do. You have dealt with patients, haven't you? You know, those creatures who expect concern, maybe even compassion?"

Bender had the grace to look embarrassed. "Sorry, I wasn't thinking. As I said, everything seems to check out okay. You might want to make an appointment with your regular OB as a follow-up."

"I will."

"All right, then." Nodding tersely, he yanked open the curtains and left the treatment room.

About an hour later, Monica Giesen returned. "Sorry to take so long. Message delivered."

It took Valerie a moment to realize that Monica was referring to having phoned Gil. Despite the tight, almost pinching sensation of the rib binding, Valerie smiled. She felt like a schoolgirl waiting to hear if little Bobby really liked her. "So what did he say?"

"He's a man of few words, honey. But I got the distinct impression when he hung up the phone before I was finished talking that he was flying out the door even as we spoke."

These drugs must be really good, Valerie thought as a sense of smug satisfaction flooded her insides.

"So what's the verdict?" Monica poked Valerie's arm to gain her attention. "I didn't notice any glee on Callous Carl's face, so apparently everything checked out okay."

Valerie gave her a conspiratorial grin. "Not exactly a warm 'n' fuzzy people person, is he?"

"For all the rapport he has with his patients, he should have been a pathologist."

"Or a urologist." Valerie laughed. She normally wouldn't joke at the expense of another staff member, but the misnomered Dr. Bender was so rigid and unbending, and she was so relieved to be alive, that Valerie let her professional standards relax just a fraction.

"Or a proctologist!" Monica hooted in appreciation of her own one-upmanship.

The joke ended abruptly when Valerie glanced up and saw an irate-looking Carl Bender standing behind Monica. Embarrassed at having been caught poking fun at the prudish resident, she gave Monica a sharp glance. "Dr. Bender, I didn't see you come back in."

"I think that's fairly obvious. Sorry to interrupt your little joke with the staff, Doctor, but I thought I would give you the results of the blood work."

He tossed a computerized printout onto the bed and stalked out of the room without another word. Chastened, Valerie picked up the paper. As she'd hoped, all the chemical components of her blood sample were within the normal limits.

Relief flooded her. Any remaining chagrin about her banter with Monica Geisen faded into oblivion. The austere Dr. Bender was well overdue for a reality check. It was time to celebrate, and there was only one person with whom she wanted to share her good news.

As if on cue, Gil raced into the treatment room. "That cab took forever!"

Dark hair disheveled as if he'd run from her house, he elbowed past Monica and grabbed Valerie's hand. Despite his agitated state, as evidenced by his pasty color and heavy breathing, his voice was calm and soothing. "Sweetie, are you all right?"

Unaccountably, tears stung her eyelids. "I'm fine," she managed to say without blubbering.

"Guess you won't be needing me anymore," Monica murmured as she made a discreet exit.

"Bye, and thanks," Valerie called over Gil's shoulder, never taking her gaze from his concerned face.

Slipping his hands beneath her back, he scooped her into his arms. She snuggled, feeling safe and comforted in his grasp, wanting the moment to last forever. She'd forgotten how desperately she'd once yearned for his touch. His hands on her skin had become as necessary to her as breathing. She sighed, luxuriating in the joy of again finding her breath, her life.

If only for these few moments.

Gil smoothed back a strand of hair from her forehead and pressed his lips there. "I was so worried. What happened?"

"I...I'm not sure. My brakes went out."

He leaned back, his face contorted with a scowl. "Your brakes? Just went out? Without any warning?"

She shrugged. "They were fine when I drove home yesterday. Boy, am I going to give my mechanic a piece of my mind. I just had a complete checkup last week and he said everything was fine."

She wouldn't have believed it possible, but even more color leeched from Gil's face, with its motley array of cuts and bruises. His voice, though, was tough and unyielding. "And he specifically checked your brakes?"

"Of course. Every ten thousand miles I have a complete tune-up. They check the brakes, hoses—all that stuff. I hate car trouble, so I try to keep my car in perfect working order."

He nodded slowly. Yes, that fit perfectly with her personality. Thorough, cautious and always meticulous. Except, he thought with a clear flash of remembered pleasure, except in certain unguarded moments when she was unfettered and wild. Rare moments he'd been privileged to enjoy. Hot steamy moments that he suddenly missed as though he'd lost a vital part of himself.

Right now, though, he had to put his own pleasure aside and get her out of this hospital. Get her somewhere safe. Until her car was thoroughly checked over and pronounced clean by the auto-evidence techs, they had to go on the assumption that someone had tampered with her brakes.

He didn't know why the kidnappers had suddenly targeted Valerie; he only knew he'd dragged her into this mess and it was his responsibility to keep her safe. A job he'd botched so far.

Holding her trembling hand in his, he asked, "You ready to get sprung from this joint, or do you have to hang around for some reason?"

She shook her head. "No, as far as I know I've been released."

He tugged at her hand. "Then let's go. We'll take a taxi over to a car-rental company. Uncle Sam will foot the bill."

"I'm sure my insurance covers rental cars in case of an accident, but—" she pointed down to her ill-fitting hospital gown "—I think a change of clothes might be in order before we go traipsing across town."

Trailing a long lingering glance down the length of her gown, taking his time as he enjoyed her bare legs, he said, "I don't know, Doc, that little frock you're wearing might get us a hell of a discount on the rental car."

"It can also get me arrested, considering the, er, open-air effect in the back."

He waggled his eyebrows in a mock leer. "I know I'm a strong advocate of your wearing that gown home. In this Phoenix heat you might be glad of the air-conditioning."

"I'd be glad if you'd get out of here so I can get dressed," she said severely, although they both knew it was only bluster.

For the first time since his return, Valerie seemed relaxed and free of the terrible antipathy she'd harbored toward him. Maybe, just maybe, he thought, there was still a chance they could recapture whatever they'd had in the past.

Chapter Nine

Getting away from the hospital proved more complicated than Gil had anticipated. The rib bindings made it difficult for Valerie to bend, so he was helping tie her sneakers, when another white-coated physician rushed into the room.

"Valerie! I came as quickly as I could."

"Oh, Sid, thanks for coming. Carl Bender gave me a pretty thorough examination, but I'll feel better once you've confirmed his diagnosis."

Glancing pointedly at Gil, Sidney Weingold said, "Mr. Branton, I'd heard you'd come back. Are you involved in all this?"

"All what?" Gil asked as he straightened and glanced at the doctor's name tag. He wasn't ready to admit to anyone else the extent of his memory loss. Weingold. Weingold. Why was that name so familiar?

"This used to be an orderly institution. First you show up in the ER, beaten up by a gang of bikers, I understand. Then Dr. Murphy is chased through the hospital by an armed gunman, and this morning her brakes mysteriously fail on the freeway!"

"Wait, Sid." Valerie held up her hand to stem the flow of rhetoric. "There's nothing mysterious about my brakes going out. Mechanical devices simply break from time to time. There's no reason to believe these incidents are connected."

She turned to Gil, as if waiting for his confirmation.

Unable to grant her even this small consolation, he turned away and studied an evil-looking metal implement soaking in an alcohol solution.

The atmosphere in the small examining room was suddenly tense. There was a long awkward silence.

Finally Sid coughed. "Well, yes, I see. At any rate, Mr. Branton, perhaps you could wait in the reception area while I give Dr. Murphy a brief examination."

Gil shrugged. He thought she'd already been checked over by at least half a dozen medics, but maybe physicians were like cops in that they rallied around when one of their own was in jeopardy.

"This shouldn't take long," Valerie said.

"No problem. I'll be waiting by the information desk." He nodded at Weingold and made his way into the crowded ER corridor. It was hard to believe that only yesterday he himself had been wheeled through these congested hallways. The full contingent of personnel trained to handle bodily trauma had been put into force on his behalf. He'd come close, too damned close, to dying.

And for what? The job?

How much longer could he fool himself into believing that everything he'd given up and all the risks he'd taken on meant anything in the overall scheme of life? With or without Special Agent Branton on the job, men would still commit desperate acts, criminals would be apprehended, jails would be overcrowded so that the already short sentences would be cut even more. Those unrehabilitated felons would appear back on the streets and the entire cycle would start again.

Idealistic young men, as Gil had once been, were slowly chewed up by the inept system. All too soon they became bitter cynical men without homes, families or even the vague satisfaction of having accomplished their career goals.

Why did he stay?

He dropped onto a hard sofa, done in kind of a pinky tweed fabric. Throughout the hospital, that same pinky color—Valerie had called it taupe—was interspersed with turquoise and terra-cotta. Very chichi Southwestern. Supposed to be soothing colors for the patients and their visitors. As if any color scheme could override the sense of fear and pain that permeated any hospital.

Grabbing a three-month-old issue of *Arizona Highways,* Gil scanned the vivid photographs. Some of the spots highlighted were typical of tourist Arizona, tall saguaro cacti, arms outstretched like ghostly sentinels welcoming the weary traveler. Other pages showed an Arizona rarely seen by outsiders—snow-covered mountain peaks, mile after mile of rich forest blanketed with ponderosa pine trees. He flipped back to the photograph of the snow-capped mountains and wondered if he knew how to ski.

Maybe, after all this was over, he and Valerie could head to those mountains this fall and test the bunny slopes.

Then he remembered. By fall, his case would be over and he would be dispatched to some other city, burying himself in some other horrific crime.

He tossed the magazine aside. What was keeping Valerie? And why did Sidney Weingold's name continue to set off Gil's silent alarm system?

A shadow falling across the commercial-grade carpeting that absorbed the sound of footsteps caused him to look up. Valerie and Dr. Weingold were approaching. She had her hand wrapped around Weingold's forearm and was laughing up at him, her ivory face radiant.

Raw jealousy slashed through Gil. Had the good doctor stepped in and offered more than a comforting shoulder when Gil had disappeared?

He bit off the sharp barb that hovered on his lips. Valerie deserved someone solid and dependable like Weingold. How could he resent her finding solace in another man's arms when he himself had nothing to offer her? No stability, no permanence—hell, he couldn't even share her memories of their brief past.

Forcing an amiable smile, he rose and stepped forward to meet them. "Ready to go?"

She tossed her braid over her shoulder. "Sid offered us a ride to a car-rental company."

"We don't need to bother a busy man like Dr. Weingold," Gil demurred. "We can just take a taxi."

"Nonsense." Weingold cast Valerie an affectionate gaze. "My car's right outside."

Unable to think of an excuse that didn't sound childish and petty—that *wasn't* childish and petty—Gil gave in as gracefully as possible and followed them out the wide glass doors to the staff parking lot. As he might have expected, Weingold drove a shiny gold Lexus coupe with a wine-colored leather interior.

Opening the passenger door, the doctor held the seat belt aside and motioned for Gil to climb into the rear. "Sorry, bucket seats," Weingold said with a trace of triumph.

With a growl of irritation, Gil threaded his way between the nylon strap and the leather seat and squeezed into the tiny space. Because Weingold was so long-legged, he'd set the driver's seat back as far as it would go, causing Gil to fold up his knees an inch from his chin.

Glaring into the rearview mirror, he caught Weingold's self-satisfied smirk as he solicitously helped Valerie into the front seat. With a jaunty whistle, he skipped around the front of the car and slipped behind the wheel. Then, reaching under his seat, Weingold retrieved a tweed Irish-wool driving cap and slapped it on his head.

The doctor, Gil decided, was a first-class putz.

He was also a skilled driver, weaving his way effortlessly through the heavy rush-hour traffic on Interstate 10.

In the dazzling Phoenix sunshine, it was hard to believe that only hours before, someone had tried to murder Valerie.

Gil stared at the back of Sidney Weingold's neck. He sure was Johnny-on-the-spot, concerned and helpful. It was more than possible that his jovial assistance had an ulterior motive. By giving Valerie a shoulder to confide on, he could gain her trust and deflect any suspicion.

The suave and oh-so-charming Dr. Weingold would bear close scrutiny, Gil decided. Very close.

Within moments they pulled into one of the rental agencies that ringed the airport. "Now, Valerie," Weingold said as he hurried around the Lexus to open the passenger door, "this really isn't necessary. You're more than welcome to borrow my car. Just pick me up this evening and take me back to my condo—"

"Thanks, Sidney," Gil cut in as he deftly removed Valerie's elbow from the physician's grasp. "But this is much more convenient. For all of us."

Weingold glanced questioningly at Valerie, who nodded and smiled brightly. "We wouldn't want to put you out, Sid, but I already have a car reserved."

"If you're sure? It's really no bother."

Yeah, right. No bother at all for Valerie to drop into his condo late at night. Gil had to hand it to the lanky doctor. Lending his prized Lexus was far more enticing than the promise of seeing his etchings.

Ignoring Gil's scowl, Valerie took Weingold's hand. "I truly appreciate everything you've done. Thanks again."

With a tip of his snazzy driving cap, Weingold winked and returned to the driver's seat. Then he revved his powerful engine and glided back into the traffic.

Gil couldn't figure out what Val saw in the jerk. The man was truly loathsome. He gave her a curious glance.

Her already pale complexion was the color of sunbleached bone. A raw scrape, painted bright red with antiseptic, marred her perfect cheek. Unlike her normally serene visage, she looked totally spent.

As they walked past the shiny windows, he caught a glimpse of himself in the reflective glass. Purple and yellow bruises, crimson abrasions and a couple of ugly black stitches. The two of them made a lovely couple—like refugees from a boxing ring.

With a firm grasp on her elbow, he hurried her out of the broiling sun into the cool car-rental facility. After taking a look at their banged-up features, the clerk first tried to talk them into a different agency down the street.

When Valerie presented her identification, backed up with several platinum credit cards, he softened.

After much discussion and several phone calls to Valerie's credit-card company to double-check her limit, they were on their way in a shiny new sports-utility vehicle.

With Valerie navigating, Gil eschewed the heavily traveled freeway system and stuck to the side streets as he drove them back to her house. He didn't say much during the short drive; it was obvious she hadn't reached the same conclusion he had regarding her failed brakes.

The primary reason he had lived through so many undercover operations was that he didn't believe in coincidences. Accepting that her brakes just *happened* to fail the day after a hired gun tried to kill them both was too great a coincidence to swallow.

"Oh! Take a left at that next corner." Valerie pointed toward a commercial thoroughfare.

"Why? I thought your place was straight ahead."

"Food."

"Ah." He flicked the turn signal and pulled into the left lane.

Leaning forward, she scanned the multitude of fast-food establishments, rejecting first one, then another. "No, I don't want a burger."

"How about the Colonel?"

"No. I had a sudden craving for— There! Paco's Tacos." She pointed to a disreputable-looking Mexican carryout stand with tired turquoise paint covered by hand-painted signs.

"I want to see their health-department rating," he groused as he pulled into a parking space. To his surprise, about a dozen people waited in line at the window.

Barely waiting until the vehicle came to a complete stop before climbing out, Valerie licked her lips in anticipation. "Don't be such a wimp, Branton. This place is authentic."

"Yeah, so's Montezuma's revenge, but that doesn't mean I want it." Nonetheless he took his place behind her in the long line.

When they finally reached the order window, she insisted Gil let her do the ordering. "I know just what I want. Two guacamole tacos, an order of *carnitas* and oh, one of those *carne asada* burritos, with extra sour cream, and a huge order of refried beans."

"Good grief, are you planning on feeding all of Scottsdale?"

She frowned. "I'm hungry. Should I order for you, too?"

Ten minutes later, arms laden with fragrant packages, Valerie led the way into her house. Walking directly to the kitchen, she opened bags and sampled tidbits while she walked. "Hurry up, Branton. I'm starving."

Dumping the entire contents onto the table, she rustled through the cupboards for plates and napkins. "Sit, sit," she directed, parking herself close to the pile of mouthwatering delicacies.

Gil had to admit the food smelled delicious.

After they had sated their initial hunger, Gil hesitantly brought up what was certain to be a sore subject.

"After we finish, I want you to pack a suitcase."

She raised a quizzical eyebrow. "Where are we going?"

"To a motel."

Her eyebrows rose. "Isn't that a little presumptuous on your part?"

"A motel for sleeping. And safety."

Now her eyebrows dipped into a frown. "Safety?"

He set aside a half-eaten burrito and met her gaze directly. She had to understand how serious this was; her life depended on her listening to him now. "I'm far from convinced that your brake failure was an accident. And until I'm proved wrong, I think you'd be much safer in a motel. Unless I can talk you into leaving the city entirely until this is over?''

''Not a chance.''

''I didn't think so. So the next best thing is for us to check into a motel. Some plain little out-of-the-way cheapie where no one will think to look for you.''

Her own half-eaten taco dropped from her fingers. ''You…you think someone arranged for that accident? That someone wants to kill me?''

He felt a strong urge to gather her into his arms, to reassure her—and himself—that she was safe and that this nightmare would soon be over. But they would only be fooling themselves. Until this case was resolved and the kidnappers safely tucked behind bars, they were both in grave danger.

Obviously he represented a law-enforcement agency that was creeping entirely too close for comfort. But why Valerie? Did the kidnapper believe he might have confided in her? Or did she know something that made her a danger?

It didn't really matter. If her brakes had been tampered with, it had happened last night while the Celica was parked right outside this house. The would-be killer obviously knew where she lived and wasn't afraid to act.

Cupping her trembling fingers with his palm, he sought to keep his voice calm, professional. ''I know it's hard to face that someone wants to kill you, but, Val, you have to believe that the danger is very real. I can get some men assigned to watch the house. But what about the hospital? Or the clinic? Whoever is behind this knows you and your routine. Only if we break that pattern do we have a chance of staying alive long enough to make an arrest.''

''Oh, Gil, I'm afraid.''

"Good. It's good to have a cautious fear of these people. But if we stay together and you do exactly as I tell you, we're going to defeat these bastards. I promise."

Her gaze held his for a very long time. Finally she nodded. "All right. I'll pack a suitcase. What else should I do?"

Before he could answer, the phone rang.

Pulling her hand from beneath his, she walked to the phone that was mounted on the wall. "Hello? Oh, yes, Detective Sanchez. What can I do for you?"

She listened for a moment, then replied, "Within ten days. Yes, I understand. Who? Oh, yes, he's right here."

Holding the receiver out, she waited until Gil took it from her hand.

"Gil Branton."

"Ferdy Sanchez here. Understand your lady friend had a bit of trouble this morning."

"Yes, that's right." Gil glanced at Valerie, who was watching him intently. "You have any news on that front?"

"'Fraid so," Sanchez replied. "The accident reconstruction boys went over what's left of the Celica with tweezers and a magnifying glass. Like you suspected, the brake line was cut almost all the way through. The fluid was long gone by the time she made that overpass. If I was you, I'd get my girlfriend outta that house. Somewhere safe."

"That's exactly what I intend to do."

"Good. Oh, and Branton?"

"Yeah?"

"Make sure to let me know where you folks go to ground. Nobody else but me, understand?"

"You got it. And...and thanks, Ferdy."

"Don't mention it. Just keep a good eye on the doc.

And make sure she gets that accident report filed within ten days.''

"Sure thing.'' Gil dropped the phone back on the hook and turned to face Valerie.

"Well?''

"Get your suitcase, Doc.''

HE DROVE AIMLESSLY down the urban streets, looking for a motel. He passed by dozens of places. Too ritzy, exposed parking lot, too near the freeway. If anybody was going to ferret out their hiding place, they were damned well going to have to work at it.

A bright pink neon sign caught his attention. The Tepee Motel. Arranged in a courtyard style like motels of the fifties, the Tepee was perfect. The office sat square in the middle and was housed in a giant plaster tepee, the fake beams of which rose more than twenty feet in the air. The entire front of the motel was littered with touristy props: a Conestoga wagon, a couple of smaller wickiups for the kids to play in and a gigantic plaster buffalo with immense horns. The cars parked in front of the units were effectively hidden by all the cheap special effects. The decor was so tacky no one would ever guess the sophisticated and respected doctor would be hiding out in such a place.

They checked in and carried their suitcases into the room. Although it was certainly not fancy, it was remarkably clean, the linen fresh and the carpets recently shampooed. Valerie dropped her suitcase on the floor and sat on one of the two double beds. She wrapped her arms around her knees and stared into space.

"You okay?''

"Do you have any idea how many times you've asked me that?''

"It would probably be less if you ever answered."

She waved an arm, then locked it back around her knees. "I'm fine. My professional reputation is in shreds, my car is totaled, someone—probably a friend—wants to kill me, and I'm living in Disney Does Dallas. What's not to like?"

He leaned down and ran a knuckle over her smooth cheek. "At least you still have your sense of humor."

"Oh, that's doing me a lot of good."

"You still have me."

She looked up abruptly and pinned him with that disconcerting azure gaze. "Do I, Gil?"

He drew in a deep steadying breath. He couldn't lie to her, not after all she'd been through. Sitting on the bed beside her, he returned her steady gaze. "Val, I can't make any promises about the future. Hell, I'm not even certain we'll both live through the night. But for what it's worth…yeah, I'm yours for as long as it lasts."

Her eyes held him in place as she studied his features. Finally she nodded. "Okay. I can believe that. And accept it."

Lowering his head, he cupped her chin and placed his lips on hers. Kissing Valerie was like eating a spoonful of honey. A remembered sweetness, light and not too cloying. A luscious taste that made him want only more.

He pulled her into his arms. Running his fingers along the soft downiness of her arms, his fingers found the edge of her shirt and his hand slipped beneath it. He stopped when he reached the constraining fabric binding her ribs.

"Does it hurt?" he asked, lightly touching the bandage.

"Only when I laugh."

Gil wanted nothing more than to hold her tightly

against him. When he'd been lying in the hospital bed in Los Angeles he'd had an almost constant sense of heart-rending emptiness. As if something precious had been lost, along with his memory. Now he understood. Even though he didn't recall her name or even her face, his heart still held onto the love he'd felt. The love he'd lost.

Now that he held her in his arms again, he didn't want anything to break this precious moment. He bent down and gently pressed his lips to the fine hair at her temple. She'd unloosened her braid and her hair fell about her shoulders like a golden cloud. He buried his face in its clean softness and drank in the essence of this woman who touched him so. The woman who held the key to his past.

Her hand touched his face and he lifted himself up. Gil looked into her eyes, seeking and finding the feverish emotion that mirrored his own. "Are you sure?" he whispered.

Valerie nodded, her eyes bright. "I've never been more sure of anything in my life."

He ran his fingertips down the smooth plane of her cheek, down her throat, lingering at the tiny pulse point at the base. He wanted to savor every inch of her being. Every inch of her heart.

His fingers raced downward. Although he had no memory of their shared intimacy, he felt as if his hand was following a well-known path. Gil knew without recalling that their past lovemaking had encompassed rousing passion, and tender gentleness as well.

He continued his quest. His need to know her as he knew himself was overpowering. A soft smile lit her face when Gil touched her gently rounded stomach, as if she were savoring a sweet secret.

Her fingertips laced through his hair, and pleasure

shuddered through him. As they found the old familiar rhythms, there were no utterances of love. As if they both understood that they were two shell-shocked victims, dazed by the frightening events of the war they'd been dragged into. Two embattled spirits finding solace in a single moment of calm before fresh fighting broke out.

Valerie touched and caressed him as if she knew the secrets of his body and was determined to give rather than receive.

As his desire built to a frightening crescendo, he finally lowered himself onto her. Her fingers tightened around his neck as he entered her and they moved together in a rhythm that was timeless and yet uniquely their own.

"Oh, Gil," she breathed against his neck. "Hold me. Tighter!"

He buried his face in her shoulder, pressing closer as though he could meld her body into his. He understood her need for closeness, for it was only when he was with Valerie that Gil felt safe. Needed. And he desperately needed her need to complete him as a man.

She cried out as she climaxed, and Gil felt a powerful surge of fulfillment in having given pleasure to a woman who so touched his soul. Free at last to luxuriate in the boundless gift of pleasure she offered him, Gil found his own release.

Later he held her softly rounded form in his arms while she slept. His senses still singing from their lovemaking, he fell into a deep sleep.

Just as his lovemaking with Valerie released the physical tension of the past weeks, their emotional closeness seemed to crack the carefully constructed wall around his memory. As he slept, he dreamed of swinging a powerful sledgehammer and shattering a stained-glass window.

Colorful fragments of memory bombarded him. A tiny piece of his past here, a sliver of awareness there.

He remembered running barefoot as a boy and cutting his foot on the tab of a soda can.

Then another memory covered that one, and he was laughing with Valerie as they goofed around washing her car.

Then that dream faded and another, more disturbing one took its place. He was following the paper trail that led to a pair of adoptions.

In this dream, Gil's hands grew clammy and his pulse quickened as he opened the adoption folders. In both cases, records were signed in blood-red ink by Dr. Valerie Murphy.

No! Not Valerie, not the woman he'd grown to love. The fear that she was involved sent him racing through the night. In his dream, he remembered speeding across the desert highway, but didn't know whether he was running to or away from the truth. After nearly four hundred miles, he arrived, physically and emotionally exhausted, on the outskirts of the asphalt jungle known as Los Angeles.

The dream memory stopped abruptly. Swirls of images flitted through his mind. His pulse raced and his breath huffed painfully when a new and disturbing picture filled his mind. He was driving again, this time on a winding, almost deserted road. A green truck—why did he see the color clearly?—was behind him. Too close. Pushing. Pressing. Tapping his bumper.

Pushing him to the edge of the highway. Hundreds of feet below he could see the flashing lights of the city. Then his little rented car was airborne and Gil was flying toward those twinkling lights.

Gil awoke and sat bolt upright in bed, sweat pouring

over his face. The dream had been too real. Almost a photographic image of the actual events of that night, he realized, as a precise memory of the events shoved through his conscious. It had been that very night when the green truck ran him off the edge of Mulholland Drive. The night he was almost killed.

The same night when every piece of evidence pointed to the woman he was sleeping with, the woman he thought he loved, as the ringleader of this dreadful racket.

Valerie moaned in her sleep and snuggled closer to the warmth of his body.

Had his faith in her been shaken by the overwhelming mountain of evidence?

Gil couldn't remember.

Was he, in fact, sleeping with the enemy?

The facts certainly pointed to that conclusion.

But facts, he knew, didn't always point to the truth.

He was willing to bet his very life that Valerie Murphy was innocent. Hell, he thought as sleep finally claimed him. That was a wager he'd already made.

Chapter Ten

Valerie peeked out the blinds in the motel window for the fourteenth time in the past hour. When Gil had left to check in with his office shortly after nine that morning, he'd promised to be gone only an hour. Two max. Now the noon news broadcast was almost over and still no word from him.

She picked up the bed pillow and slammed it on the newly made bed. Why was she always setting herself up like this? Time and again Gil Branton had proved himself to be the most unreliable, most conniving, person she'd ever met. Still, after a single night wrapped in his arms, she'd fallen for the same old stories. The same old lies.

Was she so love-starved, so desperate, that this man was worth swallowing her pride and choking on her self-respect?

Fortunately a noise at the door saved her from having to answer that question.

"Valerie? Unfasten the chain. It's me."

Her earlier misgivings temporarily shelved, she raced for the door and fumbled with the brass chain. "Gil! What took you so long? I've been a nervous wreck. I was almost ready to call out the troops when you—"

She broke off and stared at him. His jaw was set and

his eyes were hard. "What's wrong? Has something happened?"

"You could say that." He tossed a thick manila folder, bound with a rubber band, onto the bed. "Another infant disappeared. Last night."

"Oh, no! This baby wasn't delivered at Parker Memorial, was it?"

"'Fraid so. Day before yesterday."

Valerie's hand rose to her throat. "Not...not another of *my* babies? Please say I didn't deliver this child."

Gil turned his head and stared at the framed poster of a desert scene in ubiquitous pastel hues. "Sorry, Doc."

She sank onto the edge of the bed and dropped her face into her hands. Sadness, bone-deep and penetrating, settled in her very soul. This wasn't happening. Couldn't be happening. Not again. Not to her.

A spark of shame burned her cheeks. Some noble compassionate healer *she* was, worrying about her professional reputation when a mother—a woman she'd helped bring an infant into the world—had just lost her most precious possession.

She'd had four deliveries the day before yesterday. Valerie was fairly certain the Diaz baby was safe; both parents were dark-skinned Hispanics. Besides, it had been a difficult delivery, and mother and baby weren't scheduled for release until later this afternoon.

She brushed a strand of hair from her face and looked up. "Who? Whose baby was kidnapped?"

"A woman named Lundquist. Karen Lundquist."

"Oh, no!" Karen Lundquist was a particular favorite of Valerie's. Barely eighteen, but a sparkling ray of sunshine whenever she'd come into the clinic. Karen's boyfriend, Brent, the baby's father, had been killed in a tragic auto accident coming home for Thanksgiving last fall.

Karen later confided that she hadn't told Brent about the pregnancy. She hadn't wanted the news to obstruct his studies. She'd been going to tell him that fateful Thanksgiving weekend.

For a long time Valerie had thought Karen might give up the child—she was so young, after all. But Karen said her baby was the second chance she and Brent never had. So, with the help and support of both families, she'd opted to bear and raise the child. It had been a boy, Valerie recalled. She'd named him Brent.

"Oh, poor Karen," she breathed at last. "That baby meant the world to her. How did it happen?"

Gil shrugged. "I don't have any details. It was just phoned in this morning. I thought we might go out to her house this afternoon and talk to her. Since you're her doctor, she might respond better with you there."

Glad to finally have something to do, Valerie jumped up from the bed. She stopped at the dresser long enough to twist her hair into a loose ponytail and dab on fresh lipstick. "Let's go."

"I thought we might stop for lunch first, since we skipped dinner last night and I only had an apple for breakfast. I've had enough Mexican to last a good long while. I need some good old American food. How about a nice bacon cheeseburger?"

Bile rose in Valerie's throat and she dashed for the bathroom. Five minutes later she came out, her face still damp from the cool water she'd splashed on it. She was supposed to be past morning sickness, according to all the journals, but apparently this baby didn't know that.

"Are you all right?" Gil asked, his voice husky with concern.

This was the opening she'd been waiting for. The perfect time to tell Gil about the baby. And she had to tell him. Soon. But still she hesitated. No, she wouldn't tell him yet, not until she could fully trust him. If he was going to pull another disappearing act, then she'd rather he'd never be involved at all.

With a wan smile, she reached for her purse. "Guess I OD'd on those guacamole tacos last night. I'm fine now. Really," she insisted, seeing his furrowed brow. "Let's go."

He reached for her elbow as if he wasn't fully reassured by her explanation. "Okay, but you've been through a lot the past few days. If you start feeling ill, just give me the high sign and we'll come right back here so you can rest. Got it?"

"Got it."

She waited while he unlocked the passenger door of the rented Blazer and helped her up the high step. When he had taken his place behind the wheel and was strapping on his seat belt, she asked, "When was the Lundquist baby taken, do you know?"

"Yeah, about seven, seven-thirty last night. Why?"

She felt as if a three-ton weight had been lifted from her shoulders. "Because that proves beyond a doubt that I'm not involved."

"What do you mean?"

"Some detective you are, Branton. I was right here in this motel with you when the kidnapping took place. So you don't have to worry any more about my possible involvement."

"Mmm," he responded noncommittally as he backed the Blazer out of the parking space.

"What? You don't sound convinced."

"Oh, I am," he said, looking both ways before entering the stream of traffic. "That's what I told my boss—

that the timing of this latest disappearance proved your innocence.''

She sensed he'd only related part of the conversation. The part he was telling her might be the truth, but it wasn't all of it. ''Do I have to pull this out of you word by word? And your boss said what?''

Stopping for a red light, Gil turned to her and grimaced. ''My boss said it seemed pretty convenient to him that you managed to get me all by yourself at the exact moment the kidnapping took place. He suggested you might have engineered getting me out of the way and conveniently setting up an alibi for yourself, while your confederates pulled off the actual abduction.''

''Humph. Well, your boss is an idiot.''

''That's what I told him,'' Gil murmured as they passed Camelback Mountain and headed for Tempe, from where the Lundquist infant had vanished.

Having moved out of the family home in her quest for independence, Karen Lundquist moved into the Casa del Prado apartments a few weeks before little Brent's birth. Typical of many apartment complexes in the Phoenix valley, Casa del Prado was a low-rise, mock-Spanish building stuccoed to look like adobe.

The deep-set doors were painted a vivid teal blue and fake *viga* beams protruded over the arched entrance to the apartments. Set in a two-story horseshoe configuration, and ringed with lacy paloverde trees, Casa del Prado was a ''starter'' complex. The Southwestern adornments were only for show; inside were just the standard boxy rooms. The only amenities one might expect were clean carpeting and an air conditioner that actually worked.

Apartment six was a few steps away from a tired-looking swimming pool where a handful of youngsters frolicked, oblivious to the near hundred-degree temperature.

Taking the lead, Valerie knocked softly.

As if she'd been standing just inside awaiting their arrival, a tearful Karen Lundquist opened the door. "Oh, Dr. Murphy!" Throwing her arms around Valerie's neck, Karen vented her grief in a torrent of wrenching sobs.

Leading the heartbroken girl back inside, Valerie held her in her arms until the tears subsided. Gil, who'd remained in the background, nudged Valerie's shoulder and passed her a handful of tissues he'd apparently appropriated from the bathroom.

"Come on, honey." Valerie handed Karen the tissues and guided her to the sofa. "Can I get you something to drink? Some water?"

"N-no. No thanks." Karen hiccupped. "Every time I try to eat or drink, I start throwing up."

"You can't let yourself get dehydrated and sick."

"Why not?" Karen wailed. "What have I got to live for? Somebody took my baby!"

A fresh deluge of tears followed her pronouncement.

Gil fetched a glass of water from the tiny kitchen, and while Valerie tried to convince the distraught young woman to drink, he brought a cool damp washcloth from the bathroom. A good man to have around in a crisis, Valerie reflected, while she waited for Karen to regain her composure.

"I—I'm sorry," Karen said at last. "I know it doesn't do any good to keep on crying but...but I can't seem to stop."

Valerie nestled close to her on the stiff sofa and wiped her face with the cool cloth. "That's all right, honey. Sometimes you just have to cry it out."

"Who would do such a thing, Dr. Murphy?"

"I don't know, Karen. Can you tell us what happened?"

Karen raised her head. "I told you. They took Brent!"

Glancing at Gil helplessly, Valerie signaled for him to take over. Her interrogation skills, she'd quickly learned, were nil. All she wanted to do was hold Karen until her pain receded.

Hunkering down in front of the stricken young woman, Gil tried to get details out of her. "Karen, I'm Special Agent Branton, from the FBI. I'm trying to find out who might have abducted your baby. I know it's hard, but if you can pull yourself together long enough to answer my questions, it might help us find Brent."

Karen dabbed at her wide blue eyes with the soggy tissue. "I—I'll try, but I don't know anything. I...I just went into the bedroom and he was gone!"

Gil rose and pulled a straight-backed kitchen chair into the already crowded living room. Sitting directly across from Karen, he patted her shoulder. "I know it's hard, but you have to stay strong. For Brent."

Miraculously Karen's shoulders straightened and she pushed a tangled sheaf of pale hair out of her eyes. "I can be strong for Brent. What do you want to know?"

"That's my girl." Gil smiled encouragingly. "Now, when was the last time you saw Brent?"

"Just before seven. I'd fed him earlier and put him in his crib and was waiting for Mrs. Horton, and I just wanted to make sure he was dry. In case she checked."

"Mrs. Horton?"

"Yes, she's my caseworker. She was coming over last night to make sure Brent and I were doing all right. It...it was our first night alone. My mom stayed with us most of the day." Her voice caught again and Valerie feared there'd be a new wave of tears.

"That's fine," Gil said. "Just take it easy. Have some more water."

Karen obediently lifted the glass and swallowed. A moment later she nodded, ready to go on.

"So Brent was asleep in his crib at seven. In the bedroom?" He pointed to the half-open door beside the bathroom.

"Yes. Brent's folks, the baby's grandparents, brought over a brand-new crib yesterday and some pretty blankets."

"What time did Mrs. Horton arrive?" Gil asked in an obvious attempt to keep her focused.

"Six minutes after seven."

Valerie and Gil exchanged looks. "Six minutes after? How can you be so certain?" Valerie asked.

Karen pointed to a clock radio on top of the television set. "Mrs. Horton was due at seven and I kept watching the clock. I was afraid she'd be real late and Brent would wake up and start crying and…and she'd think I didn't know what I was doing, and—"

"But she showed up while he was still asleep, is that right?" Once more Gil effectively stemmed the flow of her digression.

"Yes. At six minutes after. We talked for a while and she looked at the kitchen, checked out the food and high chair, although he's way too little to use it yet. She said I was a real good housekeeper and would be a great mother," Karen ended proudly.

"When did you first discover Brent was missing?" he asked.

Karen's blue eyes pooled again. "It was almost eight o'clock and he still hadn't cried or anything. Mrs. Horton was ready to leave, but I wanted her to see him. See how clean I was keeping him. We went into the bedroom and...and he was gone!''

Valerie glanced around the minuscule space. "And you hadn't heard him cry since you put him down?"

"No." Karen gestured to the wall behind the sofa with her thumb. "The people next door play their TV real loud at night. I was afraid it would wake Brent, but Mrs. Horton said babies adapt to almost anything. She said...she said it wouldn't bother him."

Placing a calming hand on her shoulder, Gil continued, "So at eight o'clock you and Mrs. Horton went into the bedroom and found Brent's crib empty, is that right?"

"Y-yes."

"Is there a back door into the apartment?"

"Yes, but it was still locked. Th-the police said the kidnappers pried open the screen in the bedroom window. It was real hot last night and the air conditioner wasn't working in the bedroom, so I left the window unlocked and...oh, it's all my fault!''

Valerie gathered the young woman into her arms again. "No, sweetie, it isn't your fault. It's the fault of the people who took Brent. Now you've got to stop worrying and get some rest. Brent's going to need his mother to be alert and in good health when we find him."

Karen blew her nose and looked up hopefully. "Do you really think you'll be able to find him?"

"Sure—" Valerie started to reassure her when Gil smoothly interrupted.

"We'll give it our best shot, Karen. And you've been a real big help."

"I have?"

"Of course. Because you were so attentive you've narrowed down the actual time to a very fine margin. Once we have definite suspects, we know exactly what time frame they'll have to account for.''

''I have helped, haven't I?''

''You betcha.'' He rose to his feet.

''Is there someone who can come stay with you?'' Valerie asked, also rising.

''My folks will be over later. My mom wanted me to come home but...but I can't leave. What if the police find Brent and I'm not home?''

Gil handed her a card with his office and pager numbers. ''I can be reached twenty-four hours a day at one of these numbers. If you think of anything else, any detail that might seem insignificant to you, just give me a call.''

''Okay.'' She took the card with trembling fingers. ''And thank you.'' Karen smiled at Valerie to include her in her expression of gratitude. ''Thank you both.''

As they walked to the Blazer, they mulled over Karen's story. Gil started the engine immediately to get the air conditioner going to combat the blistering heat. After pulling out of the small complex, he said, ''What did you think? About her story.''

''I think Karen was telling the truth, but...but something bothered me.''

''A little too pat?''

''What do you mean?'' She gave him a sharp glance. Could the man read her mind? How could the kidnappers know that Karen would be occupied during that hour?

''Think about it. That was one small apartment. I don't care how loud the television was next door, if you were sitting on that couch you could hear a cricket burp in the bedroom.''

She considered his logic. ''The walls *are* thin. But if the baby didn't cry and she was intent on her conversation with the social worker, I can see how they could take Brent without Karen hearing anything.''

''Exactly.''

''So the question is…''

''How did the kidnappers know Mrs. Horton would be there to distract the mother between seven and eight?''

Valerie shook her head, confused. ''It's too farfetched to think they tapped her phone line, isn't it?''

''Yeah.'' He glanced both ways before turning right on the red light. ''Tapping a phone is done a whole lot more frequently in movies than in real life. Even a government phone tap is a rare event, except in big cases like a drug cartel or organized crime. The average Joe Criminal certainly doesn't have the technical skills to pull off a phone tap.''

''One thing occurs to me,'' Valerie said. ''Most of these cases involved mothers who are under the guidance of social services. Maybe we've been looking in the wrong place. Maybe the criminal isn't an employee of the hospital, but someone who has access to the social-services computer.''

''That's a thought,'' he agreed. ''You know where the social-services office is located?''

She looked out the window to get her bearings. ''I don't know if it's the main office or not, but there's a branch just a few blocks from here. Why?''

''Nobody's going to answer any questions on the phone. I thought we might drop by and see exactly what their procedures are. Find out how easy it would be to tap into their information system. Unless you have any other ideas?''

''Fresh out.''

After only a couple of wrong turns, they were at the Valley Office of Social Services. The receptionist was dumbfounded by their request and quickly referred them to Marsha Ainslee, the manager of the branch.

After carefully inspecting their credentials, Ainslee, a plump motherly-looking woman with eyes that darted back and forth between them, glanced at her watch. "I can only give you fifteen minutes, I'm afraid. Another interminable staff meeting. If you work for the government," she said to Gil, "you know how many of those I attend every week."

She led the way into her office, a sterile cubicle painted blinding white, the only adornments a few black-framed photographs and certificates. Taking a seat behind a clunky wooden desk, she gestured to a pair of chairs opposite. "Now, what can I do for you folks?"

Gil filled her in on the stolen-baby ring operating in the area.

"Gracious! You know, I've heard rumors of that kind of thing happening in Mexico and South America. Stealing tiny babies to sell to folks here in the States. But I never imagined such a thing could happen here. What about the legalities, birth certificates and such?"

"In this computerized age," Gil explained, "a person with fair skills can hack into almost any system. Alter whatever data they need to change and, presto!, official documents are instantly available."

Ainslee gave her own desktop monitor a suspicious glance. "It's all a muddle to me, I'm afraid. My computer skills are taxed just filling out the reports somebody somewhere is always wanting. But what does all this have to do with our department?"

"Maybe nothing," he responded. "But when we were talking with the latest victim of this scam and discovered her social worker had been visiting at the actual time of the abduction, we wondered if someone hadn't managed to hack into social-services files.''

Marsha Ainslee went on the defensive. ''Applicants for positions in our department are rigorously screened.''

''So are hospital employees,'' Valerie said. ''But someone is accessing confidential records, either at the hospital or in your department. One unscrupulous person doesn't mean the entire institution should be faulted.''

Nodding as if somewhat appeased, the social worker swiveled in her chair, donned a pair of gold-rimmed glasses and clicked a few keys on her computer. ''If we have a bad apple smelling up our organization, I want him or her out of here as much as you do. Now, what was the mother's name?''

''Karen Lundquist.'' Valerie spelled the last name.

Marsha's fingers tapped the keyboard with astonishing speed. ''When did you say that baby was born?''

''Two days ago.''

The social worker frowned and typed in a new sequence of commands. ''That's too soon, unless... No, Karen Lundquist wasn't receiving any benefits prior to the baby's birth. Her medical expenses were covered by her father's insurance and she was living at home. She'll start receiving aid for the infant of course, but she isn't even scheduled for her first appointment until next week.''

Gil leaned forward. ''I don't understand what you mean. A social worker, a Mrs. Horton, visited the Lundquist home last night. Was she doing some sort of preliminary site investigation?''

''Who? Horton?'' Marsha shook her head. Her mouse-brown hair, curled into chubby little sausage rolls, jiggled.

''That's right,'' Gil replied. ''I don't have a first name,

but Karen Lundquist said the welfare worker's name was Mrs. Horton.''

"I thought I knew every field investigator in the Valley," Marsha said thoughtfully. "Let me make a phone call."

Gil and Valerie sat back in their seats while she made not one, but three phone calls to different governmental entities. When she finally hung up, Marsha Ainslee took off her glasses, carefully folded them and set them on her desk blotter. "Something appears to be wrong, Agent Branton. As I feared, no one with that surname is employed by the social-services system in Maricopa County."

Gil jumped up and leaned forward, his knuckles grinding on the desktop as he carefully watched Ainslee's face. "What! Are you certain?"

"Absolutely. I called in every favor that's due to me in Human Resources. There is no one, male or female, named Horton working in any capacity in social services in this county."

Gil turned slowly and made eye contact with Valerie. Marsha Ainslee's disturbing news exploded into discordant possibilities. Either Karen Lundquist was lying or someone had posed as a welfare worker to gain entrance to her home.

Since she'd come to know Karen well over the past few months, Valerie leaned toward the second option. Until proved wrong, she would never believe Karen guilty of a crime concerning the disappearance of her own baby, or any crime, for that matter. Why would the girl manufacture a nonexistent social worker when it was so simple for the authorities to double-check her story?

No, Karen wasn't at fault here.

The truth chilled her. No one person was responsible

for these kidnappings. A team of at least two people was
working in tandem, setting up the mothers, stealing their
babies, then selling them to the highest bidders.

These criminals, these reprehensible heartless ghouls,
were as coldly efficient as a surgical team.

With their limited knowledge, would she and Gil be
able to stop them?

Chapter Eleven

All afternoon Gil pondered the ramifications of what they'd learned. He'd had plenty of time to dwell on the case. After their intimacy of the night before, Valerie had withdrawn again. Offering no explanation, she'd simply retreated into her shell like a frightened turtle.

Just as well. In fact, he ought to be happy. Most women wanted to jabber incessantly about the "relationship" the moment they moved into the sexual arena. As a loner with no ties, Gil generally dreaded these verbal ordeals.

With Valerie, though, he *wanted* to talk. He was sure she could help him recover some of his past. And for the first time in his life, he wanted to take those initiated tentative steps toward a future. Apparently Valerie wasn't interested.

So he threw his energy and concentration into the case. So far he'd determined that no caseworker had called on Karen Lundquist yesterday. He'd stake his professional reputation on the distraught young mother's truthfulness.

That meant the operators of the phony adoption ring understood the system a lot more fully than he'd first believed. But was the ringleader a medic or someone in the welfare office?

A doctor, nurse or other medical technician might well know how the social-services department was structured, he reflected. Hospital personnel were often instrumental in guiding their patients to the appropriate social services. But did it necessarily follow that a welfare caseworker would be as familiar with the internal workings of Parker Memorial?

Until these infants were actually under the social-services umbrella of protection, how would a caseworker even know of their existence? Much less know which doctor delivered each infant. No, the "caseworker" who had called on Karen Lundquist was only a diversion, a ploy utilized by the gang to gain her confidence.

Someone at Parker Memorial Hospital was the mastermind of this well-organized team.

Despite what Gil felt were compelling arguments, his immediate supervisor still held on to his suspicions that Valerie was involved. Granted, she was intelligent enough to pull off such a complicated scheme, but she was no villain. Gil would bet his life on it.

Still, his instincts, his years of observing and interpreting human body language, warned him that she was keeping something back. Perhaps she was fearful of incriminating a friend or colleague, but she was definitely withholding information. He could smell it, the way a dog could sniff out a morsel of prime rib at sixty paces.

Somehow he had to convince her to trust him with whatever knowledge she was concealing.

The bedside phone rang, interrupting his troubling thoughts.

He snatched up the receiver. "Yeah?"

Out of the corner of his eye, he saw Valerie emerge from the bathroom dressed in jeans and a sleeveless cotton top, toweling dry a long length of golden hair. "Hi, Nick. What do you have for me?"

Gil grabbed his pen and notebook. After ten minutes of frantic scribbling, he replaced the receiver.

Valerie crossed the room to sit on the opposite bed. "What is it?"

"I asked the local field office to run background checks on your pals at the hospital."

"And?"

"And mostly they're clean." He looked at his notes. "Dr. Bender owes the national debt in student loans, which is natural for a doctor at his stage. Weingold makes decent money but has extravagant tastes. He currently has five credit cards maxed out and two more on the way. He hasn't missed a payment, though, so he's not in real trouble. He also has some money stockpiled in an account in the Cayman Islands. Your administrator, Martin Abel, is above reproach. Of course, power can be as big a motivator as money, and there's no doubt Abel is a power monger."

"True, but I don't know how stealing and selling babies can enhance anyone's power," she argued.

"Money *is* power. Rumor has it that Abel has political ambitions. It takes a great deal of money, and power, to take even a tiny step into the political arena."

Valerie began rubbing her hair again. "I suppose that's true. But it was a woman who pretended to be the social worker, so maybe we'd have better luck working from that angle."

They'd stopped at Karen Lunquist's apartment on the way home to obtain a description of the mysterious "Mrs. Horton." Karen's description didn't fit anyone in the case. Medium height, medium build, medium brown hair, glasses, whoever she was, the false social worker had made sure to disguise her identity.

He flipped a page in the spiral notebook. "I did check out a few women. First, that Nazi who works in the ER—Pierce? I saw her name in at least one of the missing babies' files."

She chuckled at his description of Fierce Pierce. The no-nonsense nursing supervisor had been called far worse by her own staff from time to time. "Emily Pierce might be lacking in charm, but she's certainly a dedicated caregiver. She volunteers one of her days off each week at the WomanCare clinic." Valerie paused in her hair-drying routine. "Surely you didn't uncover any detrimental information about her, did you?"

Gil consulted his notes again. "She's frugal to a fault. Probably has more money salted away than Manuel Noriega. No known sexual partners, male or female. No gambling or drug problems that we could discover. The woman's a paragon of virtue."

"Doesn't surprise me at all," Valerie declared.

"Yeah, well, I never met a paragon yet who didn't have *some* skeleton rattling around in the closet just like everyone else. We just haven't found it yet."

"Did you check out anyone else? Like me?" She averted her eyes and Gil knew she was obliquely asking if he had done a background check on her, as well.

To keep from telling her an outright lie, he replied, "Yeah, we checked out that physician's assistant you have running the WomanCare clinic—Monica Giesen."

Valerie laughed and stood up. Strolling to the dresser, she picked up a soft-bristled brush and ran it through her hair. "Monica is a saint. Everyone loves Monica."

"Everybody but her ex-husband. He called her a cold-blooded snake."

"That's because she threw him out for cheating with their next-door neighbor," Valerie said in staunch defense of her working partner.

"Not according to the next-door neighbor. She said Monica was crazy jealous and always screaming at him. According to both the ex and the neighbor, the husband left Monica quite voluntarily—she didn't throw him out."

Valerie set the brush back on the dresser and turned to face him. "Okay, maybe she told us that story to save face. That doesn't mean she'd be involved in such a despicable crime. What would be her motivation?"

With a dry chuckle, he closed the notebook and stuck it in his laptop case. "You've seen too many Columbo reruns. Motivation? Greed, power, lust, money, revenge, ambition, hate…" He dropped his voice and intoned in the dramatic voice of an old-time radio announcer, "Who knows what evil lurks in the hearts of men? Only the Shadow knows."

He crossed the room and stood in front of Valerie. His voice reverting to normal, he said, "And I'm going to turn into a shadow if you don't take me out and feed me. I'm hungry, woman. You sapped my strength. I need nourishment. Energy." He waggled his eyebrows suggestively and leaned forward to nibble on her earlobe.

Laughing, she pushed him away. "Not so fast, Shadow. You never finished answering my question. Did you have my background checked?"

Trying to keep the mood lighthearted, he grinned. "But of course. If I'm going to take you home to Mom, I needed to know exactly what kind of temptress I was dealing with."

"That's kind of creepy, you know? Someone having

the ability—and the right—to delve into my personal affairs."

"I *am* your personal affair," he said.

"You know what I mean. It...it makes me feel violated. I know there's nothing...shocking in my background. I'm basically a very boring person. I go to work, pay my bills—"

"You're not completely lily-white," he interrupted. "There *was* that vicious sit-in during college when you were involved with that human-rights group. As I recall, you were in the pokey for several hours before you were sprung."

"That's exactly what I mean! You shouldn't know that. Not unless I wanted to tell you. My life is...well, my life should be my business."

He reached out and took her chin between his fingers. "First, I hope you realize that I would never violate my authority by doing a background check without excellent cause."

"I know that, but—"

"You should also know that these investigations don't tell us about the real you. We get raw data, hard facts. I know how long you've been a doctor, where you went to school, how much money you make and how much you spend. But I don't know what you love, what you dislike. What makes you laugh or brings you to tears. Although I intend to find out."

He raised two fingers and gently pressed her lips when she started to interrupt. "No, let me finish. The real you, the intrinsic Valerie Murphy, is a complex and special human being, who holds the keys to her own privacy. I'm not saying I don't want to know all those secrets. Not because I'm on a case, though, but because I want to know everything I can about the most fascinating woman I've ever met.''

She stared at him. Then her gaze softened, the corners of her eyes crinkled, and she laughed aloud. ''You must have been a snake-oil salesman in a former life. So let's go get a pizza.''

FINDING A FREE TABLE at Bits 'n' Pizzas on Saturday night was no easy task. Finally Gil spotted a free table and grabbed her arm. ''Hurry, let's stake our claim before somebody else does.''

Valerie trailed behind him through the crowded restaurant until they reached the empty spot. It quickly became apparent why the table was still empty. On one side was the swinging kitchen door; on the left, a noisy birthday party for a dozen preteen boys livened up the atmosphere.

''I think I see why this one is still free,'' she commented as he held out a chair for her.

''What?'' he shouted over the din. ''You think people would be bothered by a few rowdy kids? Nah.''

He took the chair beside her and they scanned the menus. Miraculously a harried waitress appeared almost immediately. ''Hi, folks, can I get you something to drink while you're deciding?''

A sudden clear flash of memory shot to the forefront of his mind. They'd eaten here before. Pepperoni and pineapple, thin crust, was Valerie's favorite. Accompanied by a light beer. ''Two beers,'' he ordered. ''Whatever light beer you have on—''

''Actually,'' Valerie interrupted, shooting him a confused look. ''I'll have a soft drink. Any diet cola.''

''You got it.'' The waitress nodded and hurried off.

Gil sighed in exasperation. ''Just when I thought I had it right.''

"What do you mean?"

"I had a memory of us pigging out here once before. Guess I was wrong."

She looked away, studying the table of boys who were now blowing the paper off their straws at one another. "You weren't wrong. We've eaten here a couple of times."

"But I remember your saying that only uncivilized peasants ate pizza without beer."

She ducked a flying paper, and his implied question. "Hand me a napkin, please."

Making a large show of wiping the already clean table, she managed to avoid his eyes until the waitress set their drinks down.

"You decided, folks?"

Gil nodded. "We'll have a medium pepperoni and pineapple, thin crust, extra cheese." He glanced at Valerie. "Unless I got that wrong, too?"

"No, that's fine." She smiled at the waitress and carefully stripped the paper from her straw.

When the woman walked away, he reached across the table and clasped Val's hand in his. "So what am I missing?"

"Missing?"

"Yeah. A dedicated beer-and-pizza woman suddenly chooses diet cola, instead. Are you sure you're feeling okay?"

Feeling trapped, she yanked her hand away. Pregnant women weren't supposed to drink, but she couldn't just blurt that out. "For Pete's sake, Gil, I simply decided not to have a beer. Let's not make a federal case out of it, all right?"

His shoulders raised in an exaggerated shrug and he lifted his hands, as if they could ward off her sudden fit of temper. "Sorry I mentioned it. Look at that kid, the one in the red hat."

She peeked at the table of raucous youngsters. The dark-haired boy in the red baseball cap had found a rubber band and was taking careful aim at the back of the boy seated beside him. Waiting to make certain he had the attention of his peer, he pulled the rubber band taut and let it go.

"Yeow!" The other youngster clutched his back and turned around, his fists at the ready. "I'm gonna tell Mom!"

Valerie grimaced as if she'd been the victim. "Charming child," she muttered.

"I can't stand a whiner, either," he said.

"I meant the other one, the instigator. He's a brat."

"Nah. Just being a boy. Reminds me a bit of myself at that age. And my brother, Geoff, was always tattling to my Mom. I think I spent more time restricted to my room than I did out of it."

"I'm sorry to say it doesn't seem to have done much good. You're still a brat. You never told me you had a brother. He's younger than you?"

Gil shook his head. He'd been wondering exactly how much he and Valerie had shared besides a bed. Apparently they hadn't gotten past the hot and hurried stage to the point of exchanging personal histories. In a way that was kind of nice. Now he wanted to know every detail of her life. He wanted her back in his bed, too, but was willing to let that happen in its own time. "Geoff was older. Two years, but somehow I always felt like the older one. He was…sickly."

"I'm sorry. Is he…?"

He lifted his tankard and swallowed deeply. Wiping the foam from his mouth with the back of his hand, he closed his eyes and leaned back in his chair. He was the one, after all, who wanted to share their histories. "No," he said at last. "He died two months after I graduated from high school. Cystic fibrosis."

"Oh, Gil, I'm so sorry. And your folks, are you close?"

"It's just my mom. My dad left when I was real little. We had a few letters here and there, once in a while a birthday card or a Christmas present, but he was pretty much out of our lives from the time I was four or five. How about you? What's your family like?"

"Big and rowdy. Five kids, three boys and my sister and I. My folks just had their fortieth anniversary. They live in Tucson. I try to get down to see them every couple of months. The others are scattered around the country."

"How about your sister? Are you close?"

She batted a runaway balloon back toward the birthday celebration. "Gail and I are closer since we've grown up. I was the family anomaly. The only reader, lousy in sports and kind of a wimpy kid. She coaches junior-high girls in Sacramento. Married, two boys."

"Watch it, folks, this is hot." The frazzled waitress elbowed her way around the table of boys and set the steaming pizza on a rack. "Can I get you anything else?"

"No, that'll do it for now," Gil said after casting Valerie an inquiring glance.

As soon as the waitress put down their napkins and shaker of Parmesan, they dove into the pizza.

They munched happily until the edge was off their hunger. Valerie stretched a strand of mozzarella around her finger and nibbled at the gooey cheese. "So what's next on our agenda?"

"What do you mean?" Gil asked in between bites.

"I never got to the hospital to do any research. Think I should go back this evening?"

Wiping his mouth with a paper napkin, he shook his head decisively. "No way. You are officially off the case, Doc. A civilian from here on out."

She dropped the uneaten portion of her third slice on her plate. "What do you mean, 'off the case'? You were glad enough of my help this morning."

"That was before somebody tried to kill you. It's too dangerous, Doc. Your involvement is finished."

"I seem to remember patching you up in the ER just a couple of days ago. We're both in danger until these criminals are behind bars where they belong."

"Taking risks is part of my job. Not yours."

"Are you kidding me? This is *my* life, my career hanging by a thread here, Gil. Besides, without me, you don't have any way to access those records."

"Then I'll find another way. I'm not letting you put yourself in any more danger."

She swallowed the last of her soft drink and leaned back, arms crossed over her chest. "That's not your decision to make."

For the first time Gil glimpsed a bit of that steel core that ran through her. He knew it wasn't easy to get through medical school, much less earn a position as head of the obstetrical unit in a large metropolitan hospital at such a young age. He considered his options. Either accept her help or muddle along blindly.

If this were any other woman, any other person, his decision would be simple—let them in on the case at their own peril. But not Valerie. He couldn't risk losing her. Not again.

The gorgeous Dr. Murphy might have a stubborn streak, but she'd never come up against someone as single-minded and hardheaded as he was when he made up his mind.

Polishing off his beer, he set the mug solidly on the table. He leaned forward and intoned in his most severe agent-to-suspect manner, "You're off the case, Doc. I don't want to hear any arguments. That's my final word on the subject."

Chapter Twelve

An hour later they pulled into the parking lot at Parker Memorial.

"Having the last word didn't do me a helluva lot of good, did it?"

"Nope," she said. "Wait here while I go get a temporary parking permit for the Blazer. Then I'll sneak you in through the WomanCare clinic so no one will know you're here."

"Since when did you start giving the orders?"

"Since you finally wised up and started listening to me." She climbed out of the SUV and dashed across the asphalt lot. Planting a confident smile on her face, she strolled through the double glass doors into the front lobby.

"Evening, Mabel. Any messages?"

Mabel, a sprightly older woman, a volunteer who spent untold hours manning the information desk, looked up. "Oh, hi, Dr. Murphy. My goodness, what happened to you?"

Valerie touched the swollen area just below her left eye. "A fender-bender on my way in this morning."

"Gracious! No one was badly hurt, I hope."

"Just my pride," Val replied as she started toward the elevators.

Mabel's voice rose. "We didn't expect you in at all this weekend. As a matter of fact I just told someone…" She thumbed through a jumble of message slips on her desk. "Now where did I put that note? It was right here a minute ago."

"Someone was asking for me?"

"Yes, a call. I checked the schedule and told him you wouldn't be back on duty until Monday."

"Him? Did one of my patients go into labor?"

"I don't think so. He didn't have that panicky edge to his voice, if you know what I mean. No, this sounded more like one of the other doctors, although— I remember!"

Val turned around and walked back toward the reception desk to retrieve the message. Mabel, however, wasn't fumbling through her stack of pink slips. She was shaking her head in a rather befuddled manner.

"What is it?" Val asked.

"He wouldn't give me his name, was quite rude about it. That's why it stuck in my mind so."

Curious, Valerie leaned on the counter. Mabel had worked at Parker Memorial longer than anyone could recall, and she always took the most contentious of callers in her stride. Now, though, she seemed vaguely upset by the incident. "Do you remember what he said?"

"Like it was branded in my brain. He asked me to page Valerie Murphy. Not Dr. Murphy, mind, but Valerie, like he knew you. So I checked the schedule and told him you weren't expected in until Monday and asked if I could take a message. That's when he got testy."

"Testy?"

"Yes. He said, 'Listen to me, you gray-haired old

crone, I didn't ask you for a recitation of her movements. I merely asked that you page her. Immediately.'''

"He actually called you an old crone?"

"He did." She puffed up indignantly. "Imagine the nerve. And he was dead wrong of course. Everyone knows a crone is skinny." She laughed at her witticism.

"What did you do then?" Valerie couldn't imagine who among her friends and colleagues would be so disrespectful to the woman.

"I paged you of course. I left the nasty fella on hold for a good five minutes before I got back on to tell him you hadn't answered your page, but he'd already hung up."

"What time was that, do you remember?"

Mabel cocked her head and studied the large clock over her desk. "About an hour ago, maybe a little longer. Say six or six-thirty. Visiting hours were just starting and things were kind of hectic."

"Well, I'm sorry he was so rude."

Mabel sniffed. "He was the worst of the week, that's for sure. But don't you worry, Dr. Murphy, it'd take a lot worse than that to ruffle these old feathers."

The two shared a chuckle at the vagaries of human nature, and Valerie once more headed toward the elevators. Before she fetched Gil, she wanted to make certain the Human Resources office was empty. It was housed in the left wing of the administrative floor, just a few doors from Martin Abel's office. The carpeting was thicker up on "mahogany row," masking her footsteps as she moved down the deserted corridor.

It occurred to her that she'd rarely been to this sanctified floor during regular working hours. Babies had a peculiar habit of choosing the wee hours before dawn to make their entrance into the world, so the few hours she was in the hospital during the day were generally devoted to keeping the WomanCare clinic running.

The murmur of voices from the hospital administrator's office told her that Abel was working late, as usual. Otherwise the entire floor had an eerily empty feeling.

Like the administrator's office, the Human Resources Department had an anteroom outside with a desk for the secretary and a handful of hardback chairs upholstered in aqua corduroy. Stepping past the secretary's desk, Valerie paused outside the Human Resources door. She was reaching into her pocket for her key card, when a sudden metallic noise made her jump.

The door knob to the HR office was slowly turning.

Acting from instinct more than fear, she dashed behind a huge rubber-tree plant that stood next to an institutional gray four-drawer filing cabinet.

Heart thudding in her chest, Valerie watched as a dark figure eased the door open and peeped into the hallway. The stealthy motion raised her hackles. The furtive person obviously didn't want to be seen.

Holding her breath lest the faint movement of air give her away, Valerie watched as the intruder stole into the anteroom and paused a scant two feet from where she was crouched behind the planter.

The person was so close she could hear the heavy exhalation of breath, smell the soft perfume that identified the interloper as a woman.

Of course, one of the clerks must have worked late. Relieved and a little abashed at having jumped to such a sinister conclusion, Valerie almost stepped out from behind the rubber tree. Only the knowledge that she would frighten the poor clerk with her sudden appearance kept her hidden.

At that moment the woman stepped out of the shadowy

area into the dim light cast by the overhead fixtures in the corridor. Valerie's hand flew to her mouth to stop the gasp of surprise and dismay that hovered there. Monica Giesen!

What possible business could her assistant have in the personnel office hours after closing?

She stayed behind the rubber tree another few moments before easing out. Stepping up to the door, she tried the handle. Locked. Hoping against hope that an authorized employee had stayed late to meet with Monica for some legitimate reason, Valerie tapped on the wooden panel.

No answer.

Using her key card, she entered the room.

As she had feared, the department was deserted. Stepping farther into the fairly large room that held four desks, she decided to check the only other possibility. The interior door that led to the personnel manager's office was closed.

But her persistent knock wasn't answered. So what was Monica Giesen doing here, alone, well after the staff had closed shop for the night?

Then she remembered it was Saturday. Like most of the other administrative functions, the Human Resources Department only operated Monday through Friday. Monica would know that.

Chagrined by the unpalatable possibilities that kept worrying her mind, Valerie decided to go back to the car and fetch Gil. Maybe he could offer an explanation that wouldn't paint her trusted assistant with such a broad black insinuation.

GIL DIDN'T HAVE any explanations to offer. At least none that would assume Monica Giesen's innocence. Still, the

woman could have been doing something as blameless
as turning in a late time card, so he decided to withhold
judgment until they had more facts.

Their own mission wasn't nearly so virtuous.

With full knowledge of the possible consequences,
they were going to illegally enter a classified area of the
hospital and snoop through confidential employee files.
If they were caught, it would mean both their jobs and
possibly criminal prosecution. Nor would any evidence
they found be admissible in a court of law.

This was a fool's mission, he conceded, but his back
was to the wall. Five babies had been stolen from their
cribs. Five mothers lay awake nights, frightened and bro-
kenhearted. These monsters had to be stopped before another infant disappeared. No matter the cost.

"Ready?" he whispered.

She held up her key card.

Gil stood watch while Valerie slipped her card into the
slot and punched in the numbered sequence. In seconds
the green light blinked on and the door lock clicked open.
They were in.

"No!" he whispered urgently as she reached for the
overhead-light switch. "Use a small one, on that desk."

He pulled a penlight from his hip pocket while Valerie
turned on the small desk lamp. "Do you know where
they keep the employee files?"

She pointed to three matching filing cabinets, each se-
cured with a long bar through the handles and fastened
with a padlock. "Now what?"

"Now we see if those lessons from Jimmy-the-Grip
paid off."

"I don't think I want to know." She held up her hands
in mock horror.

"You don't." He extracted a set of stainless-steel lock

picks. Holding the penlight between his teeth, he flicked through them, looking for the right size. "Jimmy's currently a guest of the federal government for the next eight to fourteen years. He gave me a few...practical lessons and I spoke to the prosecutor. Otherwise he'd be doing life."

"Gives quid pro quo a whole new meaning."

He shrugged as he tried the second pick. "Far more common than you'd imagine. Bingo!"

The padlock snapped open and he tugged out the iron bar holding the drawers closed. "Okay, who's first on our list?"

"B is for Bender. The ever-charming Dr. Carl Bender."

Gil opened the top drawer and rifled through the manila folders. "Banks, Beam, Bender. Here we go."

He carried the file to the desk where Valerie had switched on the small lamp. She was seated in the chair, and he dropped the folder in front of her and leaned over her shoulder.

Bender's personnel file was skimpy. Original job application form, letters of recommendation, copies of degrees and medical license, health-insurance questionnaires, W-2 form for payroll taxes, a computer printout showing vacation and sick leave taken and a single sheet of personal information. The data neatly typed on the form was also scant. Bender was single, originally from Omaha, Nebraska, hired just over a year earlier and was under the direct supervision of Valerie Murphy, MD.

"He works for you?"

She shrugged. "Only in the most general sense. At his level of training, he's supposed to be receiving more responsibility. Making more decisions and diagnoses on his own. Once a week I go on rounds with him, and the entire staff has weekly meetings to rehash various cases. And, of course, any of the senior OBs, including myself, are on call to give him assistance.''

He flipped the manila folder shut. "Not much here."

"I don't know what you expected to find."

"Me, neither. Just hoping for a golden needle in the haystack."

Walking back to the filing cabinets, he asked, "Who's next?"

"Andrea Carter, RN."

One by one they went through the entire list: three physicians, two nurse-practitioners, four RNs, two orderlies and three clerical workers, who made up the staff of the WomanCare clinic. Also a few, such as Emily Pierce, who volunteered at the clinic.

An hour later, his eyes burning with fatigue, Gil dropped the last folder onto the stack. "Nothing."

Valerie leaned back in the chair, clasped her hands in the air above her head and stretched. "I don't know what you were looking for in the first place," she said, yawning.

"Anything out of the ordinary. A pattern of absences. A patient complaint, some minor infraction that might have nudged our antennae a little. Something. Anything."

"Martin Abel runs a pretty tight ship," Valerie said. "Employees who might be accepted elsewhere, such as recovered alcoholics, aren't tolerated around here."

"Old Marty's a man of compassion, eh?"

"It isn't that. It's just that he feels the stakes are too high. If a guy who used to have a drinking problem falls off the wagon even once, lives are put at risk."

"I see your point," he said. "But where do we go from here?"

He didn't want to admit how much hope he'd been placing on gaining access to these records. Drawing up another hardback chair, he sat and laced his fingers behind his neck. "I feel so damned helpless. One of these people, maybe more than one, is involved. I know it. You know it."

"No! I don't know it. The only reason I agreed to help you with this wild-goose chase is to prove once and for all that you're wrong. None of these people would ever be involved in something as atrocious as this. I work with these people every day. I'd know if any of them were criminals."

"You would?"

"Of course."

"No, you wouldn't. The Boston Strangler was a married man whose wife had no idea about his extramarital activities. Jeffrey Dahmer's parents didn't have a clue their son was a sicko. At least a dozen times a year we arrest someone, a child pornographer or drug dealer, and their co-workers and best friends are utterly shocked. If a criminal wore his guilt like a scarlet letter, then we wouldn't have much need for a police force."

"All right, you've made your point." She grimaced and rose to her feet. Grabbing a stack of folders, she stalked to the filing cabinets. "Let's get these files put away before the janitor comes in and catches us with our pants down."

He waggled his eyebrows. "Interesting image, Doc."

He came up behind her and blew gently on the skin at the back of her neck. Pressing his lips there, he nuzzled until he felt her squirm beneath him.

"Gil," she whispered, her voice urgent, "I have to get these folders put away."

"Here, let me help you." He flicked his tongue along

the slender length of her neck and lifted his fingers to her shoulders. Slowly, almost lazily, he traced his fingertips down her bare arms until his hands encircled her wrists. Breathing hotly against her nape, he whispered, "Bender goes in the top drawer."

He leaned forward to "help" replace the folder, thrusting his hardened groin against the small of her back.

"Stop it!" She giggled. "Someone might come in."

"How could anyone object to an employee so dedicated she comes in to do a little filing at night? Uh, Carter goes in the second drawer. You'll have to bend over."

With another nervous titter, she bent slightly to replace the folder. Gil bent with her, grinding against her tantalizing fanny.

With a small moan, she slammed the filing cabinet drawer shut. Leaning back, she rested the full length of her body against his. "You're a rogue, you know that?"

Twisting an errant lock of golden hair around his finger, he breathed in her ear. "That's an awful thing to say, Doc. Just for that, you need to be punished." Tilting his head to the hollow between her neck and shoulder, he nibbled gently.

Valerie shivered in response and turned in his arms. Facing him now, her blue eyes dark with desire, she murmured, "It's true." She dipped her head forward and nipped his lower lip with her teeth. "You're one of those twisted men who are turned on by danger, aren't you, by the fear of exposure."

"You're wrong, Doc. I'm turned on by *you*. Are you going to expose something?"

"You're crazy," she breathed, and found his mouth with hers.

Then reality returned and she pushed firmly against his chest. "Martin Abel's already less than enchanted with me. If I was caught in flagrante delicto it could mean my job.''

''That sounds like the medical term for mad-cow disease.'' He made another lunge for that tender spot right behind her ear.

She laughed, keeping him at arm's length with her splayed fingertips. ''It means getting caught with one's panties down on someone else's desk.''

''Mmm. Kinky. I like it.''

''Later, Gil. Right now help me get these records refiled.''

Wanting nothing more than to get back to the motel and its huge cushy bed, Gil took the stack of manila folders from her hands. The image of the reward he'd receive at the end of his labors caused him to work at warp speed. Five minutes later he slammed the last padlock closed. ''Turn out that lamp and let's get outta here before I have my way with you on the photocopy machine.''

''Don't tempt me, Branton. Hanging out with you has—''

She broke off at a noise from the outer room. Although the sound was small, muted, in the sudden silence it rang like a cathedral bell.

''Quick! Someone's coming,'' he whispered. Grabbing her arm, he tugged her toward the nearest desk. Switching off the small lamp, he pulled Valerie with him and they hunkered in the desk well just as the door opened.

Another soft click, a switch being thrown, and the room was bathed in harsh fluorescent light.

Chapter Thirteen

Strong masculine footsteps marched across the room in a determined manner. A pause, then a loud clang reverberated just above their heads, sounding for all the world like a gunshot in an echo chamber. Valerie clapped a hand to her mouth to keep from shouting.

Had they been discovered?

A disconcerting thought occurred to her. She'd forgotten all about the closed-circuit television, a hospital security system. Hidden cameras peered down from the dropped ceilings throughout the hallways, elevators and other public spaces. But she'd never considered that the administrative offices might also be armed with the silent sentries.

Her mind started spinning frantically, conceiving and discarding "explanations" for their presence in a clearly out-of-bounds space. Maybe she could say that she'd come into the Human Resources Department to leave a note about her car accident and requesting her shift be redistributed among the other physicians for the next few days. That would work, wouldn't it?

Except it only took a few moments, at most, to leave such a missive for the personnel director. If those camera sequences were timed, and she believed they were, how could she explain their rifling through the filing cabinets for nearly an hour?

Her face reddened as another, even more embarrassing memory came to the fore. Gil coming up behind her, touching her, her wanton reaction...

Suddenly the astringent scent of a powerful cleaning solution wafted through the air. A swishing sound, like liquid being stirred in a metal container, followed by off-key whistling.

Valerie tapped Gil's shoulder. When he twisted his head in the confined space to face her, she gave him a thumbs-up sign. The newcomer was Henry Ortiz, a custodian who had worked at Parker Memorial for more than twenty years.

Good old Henry. He might be surprised to discover the head of obstetrics huddled under a battered desk, but he was discretion itself. During his tenure, Henry had happened upon dozens of overworked medical students and interns finding...solace in each other's arms. And in the damnedest locations, too. Valerie had heard of one young couple caught in a huge hamper in the laundry room.

So, although hospital liaisons were legendary, no one had ever heard of them from Henry Ortiz.

She was just about to rise and make her presence known when a deep male voice spoke from the open doorway. "Henry, could I interrupt you for a moment?"

"*Sí*, Mr. Abel, sir. What can I do for you?"

"I'm afraid I just spilled coffee all over my desk and onto the carpet. I tried to mop up as best I could but—"

"No *problemo*, Mr. Abel. I am coming right now."

More clanks and rattles as Henry retrieved his cleaning supplies.

"Here, let me help you carry that stuff."

"Oh, no sir, is not necessary."

"I insist. So how's Yolanda doing, Henry? Still busy with that new grandbaby?"

Their voices trailed off as they left the office.

Like marionettes being controlled by the same string, Valerie and Gil popped up from behind the desk. She wiped her forehead, surprised at the sheen of perspiration. "That was a close one. Let's get out of here."

"I'm right behind you, Doc."

Renouncing the elevators in favor of the fire stairs, lest the ping of their arrival alert Martin Abel to their presence, they hurried down to the next floor. Pausing at the landing, she asked, "What now? That was certainly a waste of time."

Gil's finger skimmed her upper lip. "I wouldn't say a *total* waste."

She brushed his finger aside. How had he snuck back under her defenses so easily? After all her promises to herself to keep him at arm's length, the first time he touched her she'd melted like hot butter in his very hot hands.

"As far as the *case* is concerned, that got us exactly nowhere."

He shrugged. "That's the way investigative work is sometimes. A dozen dead ends before you find a trail that leads somewhere."

"I've been thinking. We've been going about this records check from the wrong angle."

"What do you mean?"

"We need to find a common denominator in each disappearance."

"I thought that's what we were trying to do." Exasperation tinged his voice.

She knew how he felt. This entire ugly business was as tangled as a ball of yarn after a litter of kittens had finished with it. If they could just find a loose end, surely they could unravel the mess.

"Look, I'm still not conceding that one of the WomanCare staff is involved. I know and like all of them and can't believe any of them would take part in something like this. However—" she raised her hand when he started to interrupt "—just for the moment, let's accept your scenario and someone at the WomanCare clinic *is* involved. Maybe he or she targets the prospective mothers who fit the profile they're looking for."

"Exactly my premise, my dear Watson."

"Well, Sherlock, we need to be looking at the medical records of those mothers. That's where we'll find the common denominator—if there is one."

"Oh, there is," he assured her. "So let's boogie over to the clinic and see what we find."

She shook her head. "Not so easy, Sherlock. After the mothers give birth, their records are moved out of the clinic and into Central Files. I have to fill out a written request to have someone pull them for me."

"How long does that take?"

"I usually have them brought to my office the day before a patient's appointment. But since it's the weekend, no one will think anything if I go down to Central Files and have them pulled while I wait."

"Might look a little strange if I'm tagging along."

"Good point. Why don't you grab us some coffee from the cafeteria before it closes and meet me back at the clinic in, say, twenty minutes?"

"You got it, Doc." He touched her cheek as if unwilling to let her go even for that short a time.

Again Valerie's secret knowledge tore at her like a hungry shark, tearing and biting at her conscience. She

had to tell Gil about the baby. Had to. But how? And
when? The timing never seemed quite right.

Besides, if he knew about her pregnancy, he'd never
allow her to be involved in this investigation. What he
wouldn't understand was that she was *already* involved.
Her patients' lives were being destroyed; her professional
reputation was on the line. No way was she going to sit
idly by and let these thugs get away with their heinous
crimes.

Okay, she thought. After this was over, she'd tell him.

GIL HELD TWO STEAMING CUPS, one disgustingly tainted
with double cream and double sugar, and waited for Valerie's return. Working with her had rekindled his interest
in his work, got his juices flowing for the first time in
years.

As suddenly as he had the thought, a coherent crys-
talline memory came to him. He was sitting behind a gray
metal desk in a cramped cubicle. A heavy black govern-
ment-issue telephone receiver was propped on his shoulder, as if he'd been on the phone a very long time.

On the desk was a calendar with the date September
first circled in red. The image was vivid. He recalled
being on hold, and while he was waiting, he kept circling
that date with a broad-tipped felt pen. As if watching that
recollection like a scene from a movie, Gil could see a
tiny smile encroaching on his weary expression as he
circled.

Why, he wondered now, had that date held such importance to him? More importantly, was the memory a
distant recollection, or was the September first *this* year?

Valerie came around the corner, distracting him from
his thoughts, a thick stack of multicolored patient folders
in her arms. Juggling the unwieldy stack against her

chest, held in place with her left hand, she inserted her key card and tapped in the now familiar code.

He'd never paid particular attention to the numbers she punched in for clearance, but he suddenly realized the first two digits were 9 and 1. September first? Surely just a coincidence.

Pointing to the key pad, he asked nonchalantly, "How often are you supposed to change your code?"

She shrugged. "They recommend every month. The reality is that most of us resist change and are doing well if we come up with a new code number once a year. Why do you ask?"

"I don't know." He tried to balance the coffee containers in one hand so he could help her with the files, but almost dropped the whole works.

"I've got it," she said. "I'm used to opening doors with my arms full." She balanced the edge of the door with her hip and motioned for Gil to precede her into the clinic.

When they were inside, he strolled directly to her office as if he'd walked that route a thousand times before. Again, stopping for her to unlock the door, they went inside and he flicked on the overhead light while she dropped the bundle of folders onto her desk.

"That code number," he continued, striving for a diffident tone, "seems familiar."

She arched an eyebrow. Those eyes, the color of the Arizona sky, looked intently at him as if seeking a hidden meaning in his words. "It ought to. It's your birthday."

"Oh. Of course."

He couldn't think of a thing to say to break the awkward silence that followed her pronouncement. The whole puzzle of his past shifted suddenly, and pieces he thought were firmly in place skewed crazily off center.

Funny how some bits of his life were readily accessible, but he'd forget other things. Like his own birthday.

The urge to pound his empty head with his fists washed over him. Why the hell couldn't he just remember? He thought through the order their relationship must have taken. First she was a suspect, then, apparently, a trusted ally, then lover. But Gil knew his history as well as he knew the confusion flooding him at this very moment. He had never been a hang-around kind of guy. His job wouldn't allow it.

Yet he sensed his alliance with Valerie had been far more meaningful than a casual affair. Her choosing his birthday as a code she would use hundreds of times a week seemed to confirm it.

He remembered that image of the calendar with that same date circled in red. What significance, other than another birthday, did September first hold?

Instinct warned this wasn't the time to pose the question to Valerie.

Later, after the case was over, there would be plenty of time to wrestle with the complexities of their past relationship. As well as their present one.

Handing her the cup of sweetened coffee, he took the chair across from her. "Okay, Doc, let's get a system going. One of us needs to pore through the data while the other makes notes."

Automatically he held out his hand for the files.

"You play secretary," she said archly. "I'm not breaking my patients' confidentiality by allowing anyone to go through their medical files. That's not negotiable."

He reached for a steno pad and pen, and crossed his legs in a coquettish manner. "Ready, boss."

Ignoring his attempt at humor, she opened the first file. "Okay. What, exactly, are we looking for?"

"I don't know without seeing the information myself. I know, I know," he said when she started to protest. "Doctor-patient privilege. What's in that envelope inside the front cover?"

"This?" She extracted a stiff white card. "It's a history of who checked a file out."

"That seems kind of odd."

"Not at all. If a patient comes in to see me and I notice Dr. Gehren, for example, in internal medicine last pulled her file, I'd want to know what the trouble was."

"Aren't his notes inside?"

"Eventually everything makes its way to the file. But, still using Dr. Gehren as an example, if he saw her a few days ago, he would release her file right away, but he might not get around to dictating his notes until the next day. Then they have to go to the steno pool to be transcribed, then back to Central Files to be replaced in the patient jacket. Sometimes a week or more can elapse between the actual visit and all the accompanying lab reports and notes ending up in the file."

"Seems like a lot of trouble for such a slim possibility."

"Oh, there are more reasons than delayed filing. Although these records are relatively thin, except for Natalie Brewer's, because of her infertility treatment, sometimes a patient's file can be several inches thick. Doctors don't always have the time to flip through page after page of notes, but they still want to know who's treated her in the recent past. This little card makes it simple."

Gil grinned and tapped his pen on the steno pad. "I think we just found the perfect starting point, Doc. Let's see if one person checked out every one of those files."

"Makes as much sense as anything, I guess. Okay, these are in no particular order. Let's start with Karen

Lundquist's file. It's been checked out by me, Carl Bender, Sidney Weingold—''

"Why so many doctors? I thought women generally saw the same doctor while she was pregnant."

"Patients with their own OB usually do. The WomanCare clinic is different. Remember, the vast percentage of our patients are indigent or uninsured, so they kind of have to take potluck. In addition to the few people actually on full-time staff, we have part-timers and volunteers, which makes scheduling a nightmare. Unless it's a special-needs pregnancy, in which case we try to keep the patient/physician relationship intact throughout the term."

"Okay, makes sense. Go on."

She picked the card back up. "In addition to the three physicians, this jacket was pulled by Monica, Mark Withers and—"

"Withers. Who's he?"

"One of the clerical staff."

"Why would he check out a file?"

"Any number of reasons. Maybe one of the doctors asked him to, or maybe the patient phoned in for a prescription and he knew the doctor wouldn't fill it over the phone without first checking the file. Perhaps he'd pull it in anticipation of an appointment."

"Okay, go on."

"Ed Grant—"

"That's another name I don't know."

Valerie tapped the folder with her fingernail, remembering suddenly the odd encounter she'd interrupted between Ed Grant and Martin Abel. "Ed's an orderly. He normally works in the ER, but volunteers here once in a while. Nothing formal, just whenever he has some free time he gives us a hand."

"Kind of peculiar, an orderly having access to a medical file, isn't it?"

"Yes and no. Theoretically patient files are accessed only on a need-to-know basis. But in reality, orderlies are often asked to pick up files, prescriptions, any number of odd jobs, if you will. And Ed's kind of special, anyway."

"How do you mean?"

"He has more…initiative than most of the other orderlies and technicians. A very caring man. As a matter of fact, I've been trying for some time to convince him to enroll in nursing school. I'd be happy to sponsor him—he'd be a wonderful asset to any nursing staff."

"Sounds like you're kind of sold on the guy."

"Why, Special Agent Branton, do I detect a note of jealousy?"

"Me? Jealous? Not a chance. Go on with the list."

She laughed at his unwillingness to even entertain the idea that he was discomfited by her interest in Ed Grant. "Next was Emily Pierce, Martin Abel—"

"Abel? The hospital administrator?"

"That's right."

Gil scratched his head. "Now I am at a loss. Why on earth would a big shot like Abel be looking at the records of a little welfare case like Karen Lundquist?"

"Precisely because she *is* a subsidized patient. Only part of our funds are from the federal government. A large portion is donated by Parker Memorial, including the actual facilities and most of our supplies. Because we were coming up for refunding a couple of months ago, Abel went over dozens of our files to make sure he was prepared for the board's questions."

"Oh. Nothing out of line in that, I guess."

"Nope." Going back to the beginning of Karen's

pregnancy, they listed all the people who had accessed
her medical file, then went on to the second folder.

It was well after midnight by the time they'd completely dissected the five patient portfolios. In addition to
listing the people who had actually checked the file out
of Central Files, they cross-referenced with lab technicians and other nursing and medical staff who'd had contact, no matter how slight, with the five pregnant women.

Gil tossed the steno pad onto the desk. "There, Doc.
Our perp's name is right there."

She picked up the notebook and studied the list of ten
names. Was he right? Was one of these trusted colleagues
guilty of such corruption?

Although, in her tenure as a medic, especially during
her emergency-trauma rotation, she'd come to understand
that human beings were capable of committing almost
any atrocity.

A shudder of pure horror nibbled up her backbone.

The frightening thing wasn't that a person was capable
of committing such an evil crime, but that she'd been
working side by side with that person for months. Without the slightest suspicion that she was trusting a monster.

Chapter Fourteen

Feeling tired and dissatisfied with their night's efforts, they climbed into the Blazer and headed back to the Tepee Motel.

Valerie leaned against Gil's shoulder as he opened the door. The solid heft of his shoulder felt safe, comforting. Even with his injuries, which had been dreadful, he'd been a rock these past few days. He'd changed somehow. Whether the difference was the result of his auto accident and the subsequent amnesia wasn't clear, but he *was* different. Oh, he had the same devil-may-care grin and irreverent attitude, but he was...softer. Gentler. More mature.

A nice change, she reflected. Although she hadn't thought he was too imperfect before. The added complexity and depth of character were more like a natural evolution of his growth, rather than a different Gil altogether.

Now would be the right time to tell him about the baby. She'd done all she could to help in the investigation, so if he booted her out now, it really wouldn't matter. Except she wanted to be in on the arrest. Wanted to see with her own eyes who of her confederates had violated their sacred trust. Who had abused her trust and her friendship.

Maybe she should keep her secret a while longer, after all.

Then, a gentle movement fluttered through her stomach. A smile of delight lit her from within. This was the first time she'd felt their baby kick. Her every instinct cried for her to take Gil's hand, to place it against the child he'd planted deep within her body.

The gentle movement rippled through her again, and she almost laughed aloud with joy. But still she kept quiet.

It wasn't right, she thought, to be so selfish. This moment should be shared with the father of her child, but...she couldn't tell him. Not yet. Tomorrow. If they hadn't made an arrest by the end of the day, she'd tell him then.

The quivering abruptly ceased, as if her unborn child was expressing his disapproval of her decision. A pain, sharp as the stab of a knife, slashed through her heart. She'd called Gil manipulative and deceitful. What she was doing, keeping this incredibly beautiful event from him, was far worse.

She'd almost decided to reverse her decision, even if that meant she would no longer have an active role in the investigation, when she felt a tiny buzzing at her hip. Her pager.

Valerie blew out a weary breath. "Oh, no. I don't have any babies due for another two weeks. Now who's early?" she muttered, reaching for her pager.

To her surprise Sidney Weingold's extension was displayed on the tiny screen.

"Who is it?" Gil asked. "Someone in labor?"

"No. At least, I don't think so. It's Dr. Weingold."

Gil glanced at his watch. "At one o'clock in the morning?"

Her shoulders inched upward in a half shrug. "Must be an emergency."

Dropping her purse on the bed, she picked up the phone and dialed Sid's extension at the hospital. He answered on the first ring, as if he'd been sitting by the telephone.

"Hello?"

"Sid? This is Valerie Murphy. What's up?"

"My God, Val, where are you? I tried your house, your service, your office. No one knew where to find you!"

"Well, you've got me now. What did you need?"

"Listen, I have to take a few days off. Something…personal has come up."

"But, Sid, this is my four-off rotation. There's no one to cover your shift."

"No, no," he said impatiently, "it's all arranged. Lee Jantz and Marta Kimball have agreed to cover my shifts. And I rearranged my appointments."

"This sounds important," she said.

"You know I wouldn't ask for the time off unless it was."

Reaching behind her back, she released her hair from its braid and ruffled it loose with her fingertips. "Of course. But…is something wrong? In your family, I mean?"

"No, my mother is fine. It's… Look, I want to confide in you, I truly do, but if I'm wrong, well, great damage could be done."

Her fingers, which had been fluffing her hair, stilled. "Sid, this all sounds very mysterious."

"I know. And I hate to be melodramatic, but there's

something I have to follow up on. Like I said, if I'm wrong, which I truly hope I am, then…listen, I'll let you know whatever happens. Thanks, Val.''

He abruptly broke the connection.

Dropping the receiver onto the cradle, she looked up at Gil. ''That was very strange.''

''So I gathered.''

''He…he needs a few days off. Says he has to follow up on something, but won't tell me what.''

Gil pulled off his shirt and tossed it on the opposite bed. ''As if I couldn't guess.''

''What do you mean?'' Despite the hour and her utter exhaustion, she couldn't pull her eyes from his lean upper body. Scrapes and bruises aside, she loved the way he looked. Not all buffed up and muscled as was the current fad, but finely honed, like a sleek jungle cat.

As if unaware of her hungry gaze, he dropped onto the other bed and pulled off his sneakers. ''Somewhere two people who think they've legitimately adopted the Lundquist baby are anxiously awaiting delivery of their newborn. Obviously that's Weingold's task.''

She tossed her head, causing waves of crimped flaxen hair to billow over her shoulder. ''That's not necessarily true. The adoptive parents could have come to Phoenix and might already have the baby.''

''Uh-uh. No way would they let recipients know where the infants come from. I'll bet the adoptive parents are as far flung as Boise and Seattle, maybe even the East Coast. That way, if anything ever goes wrong, no one would have a clue where to look for the doctor who handled the adoption. And I'd be willing to bet my next year's salary that Weingold uses a different name when he's in the adoption racket.''

''I still don't believe Sidney is involved.'' Valerie

stood up and stretched. Her lower back was aching from being on her feet for so many hours. She dropped her hand to the crest of her rapidly blossoming stomach. Her pregnancy was starting to show now, evidenced by the little pouch she couldn't suck in any longer. The strain of pregnancy, her demanding full-time job, her complicated relationship with Gil and the traumatic events of the past few days were starting to take their toll. She wanted nothing more than to crawl into bed and sleep for the next fifteen hours, but this adoption scam had to take precedence over everything else. Even her health.

Although she would draw the line at the well-being of her unborn child.

She glanced down as Gil pulled the phone closer to him. "Who are you calling?"

"The local field office. This is the closest we've come to a break on this thing. Hello?" He broke off as the party he was phoning answered. "Who is this? This is Special Agent Branton. Has Nick filled you in on my operation? Good. Listen, get a team to Dr. Sidney Weingold's house and to his office." Gil read the addresses from his notebook. "Don't intercept him, but keep a tail on him. Get right back to me if he moves. Got it?"

He listened for a moment. "I don't care if it *is* the middle of the night—page me. Okay, and thanks."

Valerie sat on the side of the bed watching him. Gil Branton was such a comfort and such a thorny enigma at the same time. One moment warm, tender, even playful. The next an unyielding guardian of the law, determined to bring the perpetrator to justice no matter how high the stakes.

She only wished it wasn't her friend he was so intent on bringing down.

The shrill ring of the bedside phone startled her. Gil reached across the nightstand to pick up the receiver.

"Yeah."

He listened intently. "Damn! Okay, check all the airlines. Have them flag their computers in case he buys a ticket. You did. Okay, then, thanks for the help. I owe you, buddy."

He dropped the phone back on the hook. "They lost him. He'd already left the hospital before the surveillance team arrived.

"We're checking the airlines but he could have decided it was safer to drive to, say, San Diego or L.A. Catch a plane from there. We can't monitor every airport in the country."

"So there's nothing else we can do until morning?"

His dark eyes flashed and instantly his mood changed, as if quicksilver ran through his veins. "Oh, I can think of something we can do to while away the dark hours before dawn."

Crossing the few feet that separated the beds, he drew her into his arms.

A moment ago even her bones felt bruised and weary. Nothing, she had thought, could keep her from dropping into slumber. Until Gil touched her.

FAINT GOLDEN DAWN burnished the shabby interior of the small motel room. Gil had been awake for hours, struggling with the demons that had so recently and thoroughly taken possession of his soul.

Born and raised in a small northern Minnesota farming community, he had always hated the parched, sundrenched Southwestern states. Too much heat, too much brown. His soul yearned for clean snowy winters and brief hot summers. A standing joke in his hometown had been that they only had two seasons—winter and the Fourth of July.

So why did he feel so torn about leaving Phoenix at the end of the case? And the end *was* rapidly approaching; he could feel the tingle of the impending arrest in his very bones. The pressure was on. Sooner or later someone would make a mistake.

Valerie stirred beside him and he turned to watch her sleep. What was it that drew, and held, him to this woman like a powerful magnet?

Beauty? She was too…deliciously curved to fit the current mode, yet her blond good looks would turn heads at any Hollywood party. But it wasn't her softly rounded beauty that held him captive. Valerie Murphy was an anomaly in his experience. Caring little for her own looks and comfort, she was a constant source of nourishment for those who drank at the well of her compassion.

No matter how many hours she put in at Parker Memorial, she always had time to counsel and often console patients, underlings and co-workers. And the woman was a wellspring of integrity. Her inherent sense of honor made Gil feel ashamed of the shenanigans he'd pulled in the past—all in the name of furthering justice of course.

If Valerie were running the world, he reflected, the world would have to get used to unbending honesty.

But the truth was, she made him feel soft inside. Mushy and silly. Although at the same time, she had a way of making him feel like a giant among men. Not to mention constantly horny.

Intelligent and aware, she was the only woman he'd ever been involved with who kept his mind sharp, kept him on his intellectual toes. And she was the only woman he instinctively knew he could trust with his life.

Trust was a major deal to Gil. If an agent couldn't

trust his partner, he stood the chance of living a very short life.

Valerie was the best partner, in every sense of the word, he'd ever had.

When she stirred again and opened her eyes, he said, "I have a plan. Kind of."

Her eyes widened. "Great! What can I do to help?"

"I'd like you to set up appointments with each of our major suspects. Bender, Weingold, Abel—"

"Surely you don't consider the hospital administrator a suspect? That's…absurd."

"Why? Because he's too high on the hospital food chain? Don't you remember Watergate, where the criminal activity went all the way to the Oval Office? Not to mention a few dozen bank presidents who are serving time for their financial peccadilloes."

"I guess," she said doubtfully. "Just those three?"

"No. That orderly, Ed Grant. Strikes me odd that an ER orderly would do so much volunteer work at the clinic."

Valerie laughed. "He says it's a great place to meet chicks."

"Yeah, pregnant ones. Anyway, him, and the two nurses, Monica Giesen and that mean one—Pierce. Anyway, I want you to call and arrange for us to meet with them."

"I don't know, Gil. What are we going to say?"

"Let me worry about that. Anyway, the attempt on your life means our cover is blown, anyway. It's time to come out of hiding. Time to take a hard look at their alibis."

"But these are my friends!" she protested. "I don't want to set a trap. Why don't you just arrange your own interviews?"

He shook his head. "These kidnappers aren't your run-of-the-mill gutter criminals. Your friends have money and influence. If I call them, guilty or not, they're going to have expensive lawyers sitting at their sides telling them not to answer a single question. But if *you* ask to meet with them, it won't raise their suspicions."

"And once we're there asking our questions, they won't call their lawyers?"

"I doubt it. Common sense says they'll try to bluff their way through. Most people have the mistaken belief that only the guilty should have a lawyer present during police questioning."

She sighed. "I sure hope this works."

Knowing Sid Weingold was currently unavailable, they decided to start their interrogations with Monica Giesen. She, Gil reasoned, had the most contact with the patients. It would have been a cinch for her to screen the expectant mothers for the ones that fit the needs of the adoption scam.

Since it was Sunday, the WomanCare clinic was closed and Monica would be at home. "I have her address in my book," Valerie volunteered. She rummaged through her backpack until she fetched a tattered address book. "Here it is! 4050 Via Saguaro Avenue, in Scottsdale."

Gil raised his eyebrows. "Isn't Scottsdale a pricey neighborhood for a nurse?"

"Parts of it are expensive. I remember when she bought her condo right after her divorce. She probably got a settlement from her ex."

They piled into the Blazer and headed for Scottsdale. Gil had opted not to phone first. He'd rather they caught her off guard.

While he drove, Valerie served as navigator through the plushly landscaped residential community. Via Saguaro was a broad avenue, lined with towering palm trees. None of the residents parked on the street; probably the homeowners' association wanted to keep this affluent neighborhood looking its best.

Monica Giesen's condominium complex was a far cry from the shabby little apartments where Karen Lundquist lived. Hidden from the casual observer by palms and lush palo verdes, the complex sat at least a hundred feet from the road behind a high wall and ornate gates with a uniformed security guard.

Gil whistled as they presented their identification to the guard. "I had no idea nursing paid so well."

"It doesn't." Valerie looked around, her eyes wide with amazement. "I doubt even Martin Abel, with his high six-figure salary, could afford a place here."

"Just a minute, folks, and I'll call Ms. Giesen and announce you."

Gil knew that was a fancy way of saying they had to be approved by the resident before they would be granted admittance. He fished in his pants pocket and took out his shield. "Listen, I'd just as soon you didn't let Ms. Giesen know we were coming."

The man shook his head. "That could mean my job, sir."

Pulling a business card out of his shirt pocket, Gil scribbled his pager number on the back. "Here. If anyone gives you any static, you let me know. I'm sure your boss wouldn't want you interfering with a federal criminal investigation."

"No, sir, I'm sure he wouldn't."

While the guard was making a notation on his clipboard, Gil casually asked, "How much do these units go for?"

The guard laughed wryly. "If ya have to ask, ya can't

afford 'em. Ain't none for sale right now, but when they was being built, me and the missus came and looked at a couple models. The small unit went for four hundred grand. I've heard they've appreciated since then.''

He gave them directions to Monica's unit and told them where to park. As Gil threaded through the winding road through the complex, he commented, ''It sure doesn't look good for Monica.''

Valerie looked up, her eyes dark and troubled. ''You mean because she lives in an expensive condominium? Maybe she has an independent source of income we know nothing about.''

''You mean like rich parents?''

''Yes, or investments or a trust fund or something.''

''Nothing like that turned up on her BI—background investigation,'' he clarified.

They found Monica's unit and parked in the visitors' lot under a huge acacia tree. Gil lowered the windows a fraction to let the blistering air escape. With the early-morning temperature already hovering in the nineties, he knew the inside of a closed car could reach 120 degrees within half an hour.

He took Valerie's arm, and they headed for the corner unit. She rang the doorbell while Gil stayed in the shadows. After a brief wait, Monica opened the door.

''Dr. Murphy! What a surprise.'' Monica was still in her dressing gown, a luscious creation in ivory silk that Gil was willing to bet cost a week's salary.

''We're sorry to disturb you at home, but you remember Gil, don't you?''

He stepped out of the shadows.

''Of course. Hi, Gil.'' She didn't invite them in, but continued to stare as if bewildered by their presence.

He moved forward, surreptitiously placing the front of

his shoe inside the doorway. "If we could come in, we'd like to ask you a few questions. Won't take but a few minutes."

Monica hesitated. "Questions? About what? I thought they had terminated whatever accounting you were doing at the hospital."

Again reaching for his badge, he presented it for her inspection. "That was an undercover assignment. I'm here on a far more serious matter."

She dropped his shield back into his palm as if it were molten metal. "You're an FBI agent? This is a joke, right?"

"No joke, Monica. Now can we come inside?" When she still hesitated, he said, "Or we can conduct this interview out here where all your neighbors can get an earful. Your choice."

Giving Valerie a sharp venomous glance, Monica opened the carved wooden door. "Come in."

Said the spider to the fly, he thought with a sudden burst of insight into her too-sweet personality.

Monica's spacious condominium was a shrine to gilt-and-white minimalism. Twenty-foot vaulted ceilings were seemingly held aloft by a pair of thick white Doric columns. Wide expanses of white marble floor were topped by the occasional sofa, upholstered in nubby ivory silk. Glass tables with golden accessories and the occasional towering green plant were the only embellishments. Not a single personal item, photo or memento, marred the spartan beauty.

Still, he thought as she led them to a pair of ivory love seats separated by a small glass table, the milky surroundings were the perfect foil for Monica's striking dark looks.

"Nice place," he commented after they were seated.

"Meeting the mortgage must cut into the kids' milk money."

She smiled. "Maybe that's why I never had children—so I could have nice things."

As if unable to contain herself any longer, Valerie leaned across the table. "Monica, what do you know about—"

"—Dr. Weingold's needing some personal leave over the next few days?" Gil smoothly interjected.

For the first time Monica's composed shell cracked just a fraction. "Wh-what do you mean?"

"Just that. Dr. Weingold had some pressing personal business. Do you know what it's about?"

"No." She glanced at Valerie, the overt hostility on her face replaced by confusion. "And I truly fail to see what business it is of mine. Or the FBI's."

Deliberately baiting her, Gil said, "Let me be the judge of what is and what isn't our business, okay? You just answer my questions."

She drew a deep breath and leaned back, chin tilted high. For a moment he thought she was going to toss them out, but after a long unpleasant pause she nodded. "All right, what do you want to know?"

"Where were you between five and eight on Friday evening?"

"This week?"

"Yes."

She tapped a manicured fingernail against her cheek. "Hmm. Got off work right at five, I believe, then ran some errands. Bank, post office, stopped at the mall. Then the grocery store. Guess it was after eight by the time I got home."

"The bank and the post office both close at five," he said.

Her poise unruffled, Monica didn't miss a beat. "True, but the bank has an automatic teller and the post office has stamp machines and mailing slots in the lobby."

"Where do you bank?"

"Pardon?"

He shrugged. "Simple enough question. What branch did you stop at to use the automatic teller?"

After another hesitation, during which he was certain she would refuse to answer his question, she finally divulged the name of her bank, adding that she couldn't recall which branch she'd stopped at that particular evening.

"But you must have the receipt."

Monica raised her elegant shoulders and let them drop. "I'm hopelessly disorganized. I doubt I still have the receipt."

"No matter." Gil noted the name of her bank in his spiral pad. "We can check the bank records."

"What is this all about?" Monica asked suspiciously. "This isn't about Dr. Weingold's taking personal leave."

Time to show a couple more held cards.

"Are you aware that the newborn infant of one of the WomanCare patients was kidnapped from its crib on Friday evening?"

"No! That's terrible! What can I do to help?"

The words were right. Even her tone held the perfect tinge of shocked horror. But no emotion reached those pitch-dark eyes. Nor did she ask the identity of the patient. A strange omission.

Gil intercepted an impatient glance from Valerie. He gave her a warning shake of his head, but she plunged ahead, anyway.

"Monica, we have reason to believe that Sid Weingold is somehow involved. Anything you can tell us might help. Any small thing he might have said or done that you felt wasn't...well, wasn't right.''

Tapping a finger on her sculpted cheekbone again, Monica appeared to consider the question. ''He *has* been...crabby lately. Preoccupied. And...and I didn't want to mention this because it seemed so silly, really, but the past few weeks he's been hanging around the hospital nursery. Several nurses have complained that he was interfering with their duties.''

''Now that *is* odd.'' Valerie turned to Gil, her eyes bright with excitement. ''Sid isn't a pediatrician. His responsibility toward the newborn pretty much ends with a healthy birth.''

They stayed another half hour, with Gil asking questions and Monica dodging them. Almost every query brought a sudden recollection of some unusual behavior on Sid Weingold's part.

Finally he stood up, along with Valerie, and handed her a business card. ''Well, I thank you for your cooperation, Monica. As Dr. Murphy told me before we came, you've certainly been open with us. Wish everyone was so cooperative.''

Rising gracefully to her feet, she swirled her silk lounging jacket around her generous chest and reached to take his hand. ''The WomanCare clinic is the most important thing in my life. I'll do anything I can to help you learn what happened to that baby.''

''Does that mean I can come back if I have more questions? Since you probably know the skinny on everyone who works there,'' he added when her brow furrowed.

''Oh. Well, yes. Of course. Anytime.''

She walked them to the front door, and Valerie led the way into the bright sunlight. Standing between the two women, Gil touched the locking mechanism on the door.

"Thanks again for your help," he said.

"Yes." Valerie smiled over his shoulder at her assistant. "You've been a big help."

With a brief wave of her manicured fingertips, Monica shut the door behind them as they strolled down the tree-lined sidewalk.

They were halfway to the car when Valerie looked up at him. "What did you think? She certainly seemed willing to help."

"Yeah, right. She was willing to help us right down the garden path. That woman is up to her plucked eyebrows in this scheme."

"How can you be so certain?"

Stopping under the dappled shade of a weeping acacia tree, he enumerated the reasons on his fingers. "The first red flag is the fact that that woman's living way above her means. I know, I know—" he held up a hand to block her ready objection "—we'll check out the private income angle."

"I'm sure she'll be completely exonerated."

He flicked the tip of her nose with his fingertip. "Point number two, Pollyanna—she didn't throw us out or even demand her lawyer to be present when I played hardball at the beginning of the interview."

"But a lot of people have an instinctive…fear of the authorities. That doesn't mean she's guilty of anything."

"True, but most innocent people won't be bullied in their own homes. Point three—she couldn't remember which branch of her bank she stopped at two nights ago? Come on!"

Val, still playing devil's advocate, tossed her head in frustration. "We took her by surprise, dropping in like that. Maybe we woke her up. Maybe she was too rattled to recall."

"Possibly. Except I've never seen a woman wake up in full face paint. Point four—why didn't she ask whose baby is missing?"

For the first time Valerie's confidence in her assistant seemed shaken. "You know, I wondered that myself. Maybe she didn't think she was allowed to ask questions."

"Maybe. And my last warning signal was the way she kept piling everything on Sidney Weingold's head. If she'd been that suspicious of the man, wouldn't she have at least mentioned it to you before now? Since you're her immediate supervisor, that would seem the proper course."

"I would think so," she agreed. "Except that taken one by one, those odd episodes she attributed to Sid wouldn't mean much. It's the accumulation of all this strange behavior that has me concerned."

"Exactly. And she's the one who recounted every incident."

"Oh!"

He looked up at Valerie's suddenly pale face. "What is it?"

"I just remembered something."

He stopped and leaned against the pale green trunk of a paloverde tree. "So tell me."

"Nothing really." She waved her hand like she was swatting at a pesky mosquito. "It...it's just an odd incident. While you were gone, I think. Yes, I'm sure. In fact, it was shortly after you disappeared. I'd had a difficult delivery, a preemie. We were concerned about the baby's lungs, so I went to the nursery to see if I could catch the neonatologist. The nursery's kept very dim and quiet, so I didn't see them at first."

"Who?"

"Monica and Sidney. They were having a terrible fight."

"Over what?"

"I'm not sure. I could only catch a few words and I didn't want to interfere unless one of them asked me to, so I left them to sort it out."

"But something about that encounter bothered you, made your subconscious associate the incident with these kidnappings."

"I just can't remember." She rubbed her temples with her fingertips. "I remember thinking how unlike Sidney it was to be shouting at a nurse. He was so angry I could see the veins throbbing in his forehead."

"Sounds like mellow old Sidney has a temper. And you don't have any idea what they were fighting about?"

"No. Like I said, I couldn't hear clearly but— Oh! I just remembered. It...it was about Natalie Brewer's baby. He was screaming at her about the 'Brewer infant.' I remember wondering what Monica could possibly have to do with that child."

Gil thought about the possible impact of the incident. The Brewer child was one of the victims. Neither Weingold nor Monica were regular nursery employees. So what had happened to cause such an argument? A falling-out among thieves?

Something else bothered him. He turned to Valerie. "And you forgot about this fight?"

She shook her head. "Not really. I was thinking about it yesterday, but I couldn't imagine it had any bearing on this case. Then this morning, something Monica said reminded me and I decided to mention it. Why, do you think it's significant?"

He scowled in disbelief. Was she putting him on or what? "Of course it's significant! It's the first clear link between them. And you weren't even going to mention it?''

"I'm sorry. I just didn't want to involve my friends in something this awful based on a half-heard argument."

Gil's brow furrowed unhappily. "And you didn't trust me to make that judgment?" He sighed. "It's not looking too good for your pals, I'm afraid."

Sadness darkened Valerie's eyes. "I know."

She stepped toward him and sagged against his chest, seeming so vulnerable he was almost diverted. She'd known something of major importance and hadn't confided in him. Hadn't trusted him to maintain his objectivity regarding her co-workers.

Valerie lifted her head, her eyes shimmering with guilty tears. "One thing doesn't make sense, though. If Monica and Weingold are partners in this thing, why was she so quick to point the finger at him this morning?"

"To deflect suspicion from herself?"

"I guess you're right."

With his arm draped loosely around her waist, they continued walking toward the car. "She was pretty eager to foist him off as the sacrificial lamb," Gil said, "so I'd say she has an escape plan in mind for herself."

He stopped and released Valerie. Then he turned and started strolling back the way they'd come.

"Where are you going?" Valerie demanded.

His head jerked toward Monica's condo. "I just discovered that I must have left the car keys at Monica's. Guess we'll have to go back and check."

"What are you up to?" she groused as she hurried to catch up with him.

He didn't respond as she obediently tagged along. A few seconds later they were back at Monica's doorstep.

Chapter Fifteen

"Oops!" Gil whispered as he nudged the door open with his knuckle. "Guess I forgot to shut it all the way when we left."

One look at his smug expression told her there was nothing accidental about the unlatched door.

"You still have to knock," she hissed in his ear.

"Okeydoke." Delicately tapping his index finger on the heavy wooden surface he made a pretext of knocking.

"Guess she can't hear us." He led the way into the spacious foyer.

Because they were both wearing rubber-soled athletic shoes, their steps were silent as they moved down the marble corridor. At the sound of Monica's muted voice, Gil stopped and held his fingertip to his lips. After waiting a long moment to make sure she wasn't aware of their presence, they inched farther down the hall, pausing by the entry to the living room.

With her back to the foyer, Monica was talking in a frantic voice on a white-and-gold French-style telephone. "Don't panic! I'll get Earl to take care of them. You just come up with five thousand cash to pay for the outside help," she added, malice dripping from her lips. "Since you don't have the guts to do it yourself."

She paused, listening. "Don't screw this up. They're close, too damned close. We need to handle this today."

Stepping closer to the window, she raised her wrist and peered at her slim gold watch. "I'll meet you in the hospital cafeteria at noon. Have the money."

She stalked back to the glass-and-brass console table and slammed the phone back on the receiver. "Idiot," she muttered.

By mutual accord, Gil and Valerie quickly retraced their steps and slipped back outside. Gil removed the wad of gum that held the lock open and gently closed the door behind them.

"Come on!" He grabbed her wrist as they dashed down the sidewalk. "We don't have much time."

The visitors' parking lot was a couple of blocks from Monica's condo, and Gil led a charging pace the entire distance. By the time they reached the Blazer, sweat was pouring down Valerie's face.

She leaned against the hot vehicle to catch her breath while Gil used her cell phone to have a surveillance team set up a stakeout at Monica's condo. If she didn't start going to the gym and getting in better shape, she was going to be in for a rough time when her labor started.

"What's the matter, Doc? I think you need more frequent...exercise."

She glanced up at Gil. The jerk hadn't even broken a sweat. "Guess what, Sherlock? We didn't get the car keys back."

He made a theatrical show of patting down his pockets. "Oops, again. Guess I had them all along."

"You're such a fraud, Branton. Good thing you chose this side of the law to be on," she grumbled as he helped her into the Blazer.

By now, he pretty much knew the route between

Scottsdale and the Tepee Motel, leaving Valerie free to ponder what they'd overheard at Monica's.

The nurse's sinister words kept digging into her mind, refusing to let go. A week ago the only crimes in Valerie's life were the clever plots in her favorite Agatha Christie mystery movies. Now she feared she was the intended victim in a very real, very earnest, plan to commit murder.

Seeking reassurance that she was being melodramatic, that her life wasn't in jeopardy, she turned to Gil. "I keep thinking about what Monica said. About 'taking care of them.' For some reason, I don't think she was referring to her nursing skills."

"No, I think she had a more permanent 'cure' in mind," he said grimly as he negotiated a complicated freeway interchange. "Sounded to me like she was the brains of the operation and whoever she was talking to— Weingold, probably—was following her orders, not the other way around."

Valerie turned away and looked out the window, for once not seeing the hauntingly beautiful desert surrounding them. She could no longer deny the growing evidence that Sid Weingold and Monica Giesen were accomplices in the kidnappings. A sick feeling settled in her stomach. She couldn't believe that someone she'd admired and trusted as much as Sid could be involved in a plot to kill her.

The truth, however, was as undeniable as the new life growing inside her. Until yesterday, only Sid Weingold knew about her unborn child and that Gil was the father. Unfortunately he must have also known about Gil's undercover assignment.

By confiding in Sidney, she was the inadvertent cause

of Gil's accident, as well as her own. It was a chilling thought.

Remembering the bitter fight she'd witnessed between Sid and Monica, she realized now that Sid must have been afraid she would report that encounter. So he had decided to protect himself by killing Gil.

But why the attempt on *her* life? What did Sidney Weingold have to fear from *her?*

Back at the Tepee Motel, she was so lost in her troubling thoughts it was a while before she noticed that Gil was very quiet. Almost morose.

Throwing the keys on the battered dresser, he flopped onto the bed—the one they hadn't been sleeping in—and leaned against the headboard.

"Is something wrong?" she asked.

His eyebrow arched but he scarcely glanced up. "Five children have been stolen from loving parents in the past year, and I've failed miserably at getting any of them back. My prime suspect, your buddy Sidney, has apparently fled the jurisdiction."

"And?"

"And what? Isn't that enough?"

"No. Not for a foul mood like you've been in since we left Monica's. You knew all that last night and weren't irritable and defeated. What's changed?"

"Last night I thought we were in this together. Last night I didn't know you were holding back. Keeping secrets."

Valerie's heart leaped into her throat. Somehow, he'd guessed the truth. She couldn't blame him for being angry. If the situation were reversed, she'd be furious at his duplicity. She had intended to tell him about the baby, regardless of how he would have reacted to the news.

Even if he blamed her, hated her, she had still planned to share her secret with him. But would he believe her?

"Gil, I was going to tell you. Truly."

"When? After I was pulled off the case for incompetence and shipped back to D.C.?"

"No. Later this evening. I swear!" His response was a bitter glare. Her eyes pleaded for understanding. "When you first came back, I was angry. Hurt. I couldn't trust you."

He waved an impatient hand. "I'll give you that. You had every reason to be ticked off—even though I had a rational explanation for disappearing. But what about later, Val? Why didn't you tell me later?"

Because I was selfish. Because I knew you wouldn't keep me involved. Because... Because she was still hurt, still bitter. If he'd really loved her as much as he said before he left for Los Angeles, wouldn't he remember her? Remember all they'd shared?

"You didn't trust me, either," she reminded him. "Before the accident in Los Angeles, you didn't tell me why you were really at Parker Memorial. You took advantage of my friendship. My feelings. You used me."

"Ah. The best defense is a good offense. I see. So is that the way you want to play it, Val? Quid pro quo? I made a mistake last year, so you get to make one now?"

"No, of course not. That's childish..."

"And really beneath you."

"Okay, okay. Let's not degenerate into name-calling. I said I was sorry."

"No, you didn't. You just told me what a bastard I'd been for not confiding in you when every shred of evidence I uncovered pointed to you as the perp. In spite of a damning mountain of evidence, I went out on a very skinny limb with my bosses in Washington. On your behalf.''

She dropped her gaze as shame filled her. ''I didn't know that.''

''I know.'' He dragged his fingers through his hair, his voice calmer now. As if the anger that filled him like an incendiary device had finally fizzled out. ''I should have told you what was going on before I went to L.A. I'm sorry.''

''Me, too.''

Fists clenched tightly at her sides, she crossed the narrow space between them. Unfurling her taut fingertips, she reached to smooth an outlaw strand of hair that was always falling into his eyes. ''Can we start over? Now?''

A deep sigh shuddered through him as he pulled her down onto the bed and gathered her into his arms.

''I'm sorry I've been such a jerk about Sid Weingold. I do admire you for being so loyal. I'm just a little jealous, I guess.''

Sid? What did Sid have to do with any of this?

''Even if I'd known about his fight with Monica,'' Gil went on, ''it wouldn't have made much difference. I mean, I was already suspicious of the guy. Besides, that wasn't any real proof, just more circumstantial evidence.''

''You...you're talking about their fight in the nursery?''

''Of course.'' He frowned at her. ''You must be tired. What did you think we were talking about?''

Now! Now was the time.

But she couldn't speak. He'd been so enraged over a simple oversight. If she revealed that she'd been deliberately concealing information that would affect the rest of his life…well, she wouldn't be surprised if he walked off and never spoke to her again.

That wasn't true, she immediately refuted. He'd talk. He'd be polite and so very, very cold when he inquired about her plans for the baby. Knowing Gil and his strong sense of duty, he would always be a part of their child's life. Would acknowledge his familial and financial responsibility. But would *she* be included in his life?

Not likely.

Unless…

He was too overwrought right now. The pressure of this case had been building within him and threatening to burst for months. It would be insensitive to add to his burden right now.

If, however, she could help him gather enough evidence for an indictment, even at the price of Sid Weingold's freedom, then he'd have to listen to her. He'd have to understand that circumstances forced her to keep her secret.

Yes, once the pressure of this case eased, he'd be more willing to listen to reason.

Relief poured over her. She didn't have to tell him today. For at least another twenty-four-hour period she could go on pretending that all was right with her world.

"Valerie? Is everything okay? You're very quiet."

"I'm fine." Even to her own ears, her voice sounded weak. Stressed to its limit.

"Oh, Val," he groaned taking her into his arms, pressing his lips against her hair. "I'm sorry. I shouldn't have blown up like that. It…it's just that I hated thinking you'd deliberately held back vital information. To protect Sid Weingold."

She raised her head from his shoulders, her eyes starred with tears. "I'd never do that, Gil. The incident was so long ago and seemed so unimportant, that I truly just plain forgot to mention it to you.''

He propped extra pillows behind them and nestled her into the crook of his shoulder. ''Let's just forget the whole thing. I won't mention it again. Promise.''

''It's okay, Gil. Really. Right now, the important thing is closing down this kidnapping ring. We need to concentrate on getting enough evidence to convict them.''

''Convict!'' he snorted. ''We couldn't even get a search warrant with as little hard evidence as we've got. Everything is circumstantial. But you're right. We need to come up with a plan.''

While relief and guilt waged a battle in her heart, Valerie wondered if their relationship was going to be a casualty of her emotional war. How could a relationship built on a foundation of deceit ever survive? Ever grow into maturity?

''A plan,'' she repeated, determined to get her mind off the heavy burden she carried. Closing her eyes, she willed her mind to come up with a strategy, some way to garner the hard evidence that would stand up in court. And rebuild her own tarnished self-image.

Since she knew nothing about real-life criminal procedure, she thought back over the hundreds of plots of her favorite mystery movies. Miss Marple would have called upon her experience in her tiny, but deadly, community of St. Mary Mead. But Valerie didn't have any experience with cold-blooded criminals. Poirot, the intellectual, would have exercised the little gray cells, but her brain cells were apparently on vacation.

Jessica Fletcher, the bane of Cabot Cove, Maine, never worried about accruing evidence. She always just set a trap. The killer would take the bait and, just before plugging Jessica, he'd brag about the details of his crime.

Then, from their hiding place in the next room, the cops would spring forward and nab the blackguard before he could make good on his threat.

"Too bad I'm not Jessica Fletcher," she murmured.

Gil stared at her blankly.

She felt slightly chagrined by her half-joking suggestion, but plunged on. "I meant, just try and get him to confide in me, since he's always seemed to trust me. Then we could just trick him into admitting the truth."

A slow smile began on Gil's face that grew into a beaming grin. "That's it!"

"What?"

"We'll set a trap. You're right, he *does* trust you. We'll set something up in a public place, so you'll be safe. I'll stay hidden while you let it slip to Sidney that I have the evidence that will put him away."

"What evidence?"

"How should I know?" He held out his hands, palms up. "Besides, it doesn't matter."

Valerie sat upright and stared at him in disbelief. "Evidence...doesn't...matter?"

"No. We'll put a voice-activated recorder in your backpack. Since you're a civilian, he can't even plead entrapment if he says something incriminating. It's a long shot, but right now, it's the only shot we have."

"But what will I say to him? I don't want to lie to a friend."

"Even if that friend is guilty of kidnapping and attempted murder?"

She sighed. "Not if you put it that way. So how do I entice him to incriminate himself?"

Gil tapped his chin while he thought through the scenario, trying to decide on an approach that would work with Sidney Weingold's personality. "Tell him I'm ready to arrest him. Just say you're letting him know because you think I've trumped up the evidence. I think he's willing to believe the worst about me."

"And this is supposed to help? How?"

"If he takes the bait he'll either say something on tape that incriminates himself and the recorder will pick it up, or he'll make a run for it. In which case, I'll come out of hiding and nab him."

Lips compressed, she slowly shook his head. "You still won't have any evidence."

"But he won't know that! Then I'll have something to work with when I interrogate him. If he runs, I can build a good bluff. Get him to confess."

"I don't know...."

He was starting to get irritated about her negativity. He wished he knew for certain if her unwillingness to get involved was based on her belief that the plan wouldn't work, or if she was still harboring some soft feelings for Weingold. Without examining his own motives too closely, Gil was nonetheless aware that it was very important to him that Valerie side with him now. Stand by him. To draw out her motivation, he forced a joking tone. "Give me three good reasons why it won't work."

She rolled her eyes. "Reason number one: This is real life, not a television show."

"Life imitates art. Happens all the time," he retorted.

"Reason number two: Someone could get hurt."

"That's why you have to meet him in a public place."

"Reason number three: I, uh, can't exactly think of a reason but I'm sure there are dozens if you give me a minute."

"Nope." He jumped out of bed and reached for the telephone. "This is foolproof. Trust me."

She threw up her hands in surrender. "Okay, you've convinced me. How about if I meet him at the hospital cafeteria? That's fairly public and he should feel comfortable enough in a familiar environment to take the bait."

"Good idea." He handed her the cell phone. "But how are we going to reach him? My men are watching the hospital and his house, but he hasn't shown up."

Valerie dug through her backpack for her address book. "I have his beeper number. Maybe he'll answer my page."

She punched in his number. "I hope this works," she said, still obviously uncomfortable about tricking a friend.

Gil had no doubt Weingold would return the call; he'd seen the adoring way the man stared at Valerie. Well, after all this was over then she'd certainly see that her trust in the rich, handsome doctor had been misplaced.

They didn't have long to wait to find out if their ploy worked. Less than an hour later, the telephone rang, shattering the tense silence in the small motel room.

Gil reached for the receiver, then stopped. "You'd better get it. In case it's Weingold."

Nodding, she pushed a strand of hair from her eyes and stared at the ringing phone. Gil knew she was feeling lower than a snake's belly for lying to her friend, but she had to get over it. Her so-called friends weren't worth the powder it would take to blow themselves to hell.

Finally, she picked up the phone on the fifth ring. "Dr. Murphy speaking. Oh, hi, Sid."

Gil gave a satisfied nod and leaned back against the headboard. His gut feeling had been right all along. Weingold and the nurse were in this together. What a cozy little game they'd worked out. Monica played the

mature, caring counselor. Getting the confused young
girls to pour their hearts out. Getting them to listen to
her supposedly well-intentioned "advice."

Her real job, however, was to cull through the dozens
of expectant mothers who came through the clinic until
she found those select few who met their criteria. Then
she would pour on her professional charm and coerce the
young women into continuing their pregnancies to term.
Convince them they were doing the right thing by keeping their babies, no matter what their social or economic
circumstances.

Then, shortly after the birth, she and her accomplice
would arrange the kidnapping. Gil doubted the nurse and
good doctor were personally involved in many of the
actual kidnappings. Too risky. No doubt the hired hit man
who'd stalked him in the hospital was dispatched to do
their dirty work.

Weingold's job was handling the actual "adoption."
No doubt he submitted phony birth certificates to the state
and collected the huge sums of money from the over-
joyed, and unsuspecting, adoptive parents.

A quick trip to the Cayman Islands to filter the money
through his account there, and, presto, the deed was done.
Without a trace of evidence that could be tracked back
to the miscreants.

Gil was brought back to the present when Valerie hung
up the phone.

Pale and shaking, she chewed on her lower lip in an
obvious effort to stop the trembling. "Well, I guess that's
it, then. We're meeting at the hospital cafeteria tonight
between six and seven."

Valerie slowly dropped back onto the bed. From the
troubled look on her face Gil knew she was still only
half-convinced of Sid Weingold's complicity in the kid-

nappings. She obviously felt like a louse for manipulating someone she'd always considered a friend.

In an effort to cheer her up, Gil dropped on the opposite bed and smiled broadly. "Good job!" His delicate sensibilities weren't beset with guilt over their charade. "You missed your calling, Doc. If you'd chosen acting, you'd have a mantle loaded with Oscars before you were through."

Her eyebrows dipped in chagrin. "Great. Wonderful. My folks will be so proud. Their daughter is an accomplished liar."

She wondered if Gil would be so impressed if he knew she was still lying to him—with every word she *didn't* say.

He moved over to sit beside her. "I know it's hard when someone you trusted turns out to be a jerk. And, who knows? Maybe he's innocent."

She knuckled away a tear. "No, he's not. I'm convinced now."

"Why? What did he say?"

"He seemed almost anxious to meet me," she said "But that's not the worst part. He was calling from Monica's."

"What! He told you that?"

Valerie nodded. "Didn't even try to conceal it. No doubt she was listening to every word. I used to think he was one of the nicest, most ethical men I'd ever met. Boy, that sure says something about my ability to judge character."

"Don't beat yourself up. You had no way of knowing he was a psychopath."

She looked up and gave him a wry smile. "That's funny. People use the term *psychopath* to describe any kind of mental disorder. Psychopathic killer, psychopathic liar. A true psychopath is exceedingly rare. They're convinced they're above the rules because they don't have the same feelings as other people. They don't, you know. They don't share our emotional foundations. I think that's how Sid was able to fool me and so many others for so long. So he must be a true psychopath.''

Gil reached over and took her hand. It lay limply in his as she tried valiantly to stem the tears that shimmered in her blue eyes. "I'm really sorry, honey."

"Oh well," she said in a show of false bravado, "he agreed to meet me as we planned. It should all be over tonight."

Chapter Sixteen

The cafeteria was less crowded than Gil had expected, so he hung back while Valerie grabbed an orange juice from an ice-packed bin and headed for the cashier.

The food service was at the far end, and a conveyor belt for dirty dishware was at the opposite. The open middle space was freckled with oblong tables, sparsely occupied on this quiet Sunday evening.

Valerie took a table in the center of the room and sat down facing the door. Glancing around for a location where he could remain concealed, while keeping Valerie in sight, Gil finally settled for a small table half-hidden by one of the four wide columns that supported the ceiling.

She was about half-finished with her juice when the tall and too-damned-good-looking Sid Weingold entered the cafeteria. He cast an anxious glance around the room. Spying Val, he rushed to her table.

Gil did a double take. The doctor's tanned face was wan, and his thick hair was no longer stylishly coiffed but sticking up at odd angles as if he hadn't combed it since he'd gotten out of bed. Gil smiled in satisfaction; the doctor was definitely rattled.

Valerie and Weingold were too far away for Gil to

overhear their conversation, but foreseeing such a possibility, they had rehearsed simple signals to convey necessary information. She drained her plastic juice glass and rubbed the tip of her nose with her index finger—the sign that everything was under control.

Weingold leaned across the table, speaking earnestly. Pushing her empty container aside, Valerie leaned forward, too, as if she didn't want to miss a single word.

Sensing that they'd be engaged in their intense conversation for a while, Gil allowed his gaze to stray. Even on a peaceful Sunday night, there was still something forebidding about the hospital environment, he thought. Red-eyed visitors sipped their coffee, their fearful gazes darting constantly to the entrance as if they expected every newcomer to be the bearer of bad tidings.

Gil's eyes followed their gazes to the entrance and he jumped in surprise.

Monica Giesen, flanked by two white-coated men, stepped through the double doors. He gave her companions scant attention, his focus being Monica. What was she doing here? She'd told Valerie that she was only coming into the clinic to finish some paperwork in the afternoon. Were she and Weingold planning a sinister surprise for Valerie?

Laughing up at one of her companions, the coldly beautiful woman entered the cafeteria line. But not, Gil noticed, before she cast a hard glance in the general direction of the table where Valerie and Weingold were seated.

What was she up to?

Still laughing flirtatiously with her companions, Monica continued down the line, stopping for a yogurt and diet soda. When the threesome reached the cashier, she reached into her purse. One of the men stayed her hand

with his and paid for her purchases. Gil grinned wryly.
Like a deadly black-widow spider, Monica knew how to
lure men in and bind them tightly with her silken web.

He realized with a jolt that sweet Valerie was no match
for the ruthless nurse.

He turned back to Val's table to see how she was far-
ing with Weingold.

The empty juice carton lay on its side. Otherwise, the
table was deserted.

They were gone.

His heart knocking in his chest like a frenzied drum-
beat, he anxiously scanned the cafeteria. No sign of them.
He jumped up to look around the column, knocking his
chair over. The clatter drew the attention of the other
patrons, including, he noted, Monica Giesen.

Fine undercover operative he'd turned out to be. With
a single motion he'd lost the subjects of his surveillance
and managed to tip off one of the suspects to his presence.

Thoroughly disgusted with his unprofessional behavior, he stalked toward the door.

Where could they have gone? Why hadn't Valerie gotten his attention, given him a sign before she allowed
herself to be lured out of the safety of the public space?

*Because she trusted you were watching and would
keep her safe.*

Reaching the deserted hallway outside the cafeteria, he
glanced left and right. Then left again. Completely
empty. No sign that anyone had passed this way.

What did you expect? A trail of bread crumbs?

Not knowing what other course to take, he headed toward the main lobby.

Eight or ten people wandered about, none Valerie or
her colleague. Where did they disappear to so quickly?

The open area served as a hub, with five corridors angling away from the center like spokes on a wheel. They could have gone down any of those hallways, he reflected with a grim sense of foreboding. Or into the elevators. By now she could be anywhere in the vast hospital structure. And as far from his help as if she were stranded on the moon.

Where did Weingold take her? And why?

Obviously the man had been aware of his presence. He'd lured Valerie away from the relative safety of the cafeteria, knowing that Gil would follow.

Weingold was shrewd; take the chicken from the henhouse and the fox is sure to follow. Gil set his jaw in determination. When he caught up to them—and he would—Weingold was going to be one sorry bastard.

Spotting a familiar face at the information desk, he hurried over.

A well-padded older woman, whom her name tag identified as Mabel, smiled up at him. "Good evening, sir. How can I help you?"

"Do you know Valerie, I mean, Dr. Murphy?"

A wary look came into her eyes. "Yes, of course. Would you like me to page her?"

He considered. Would Weingold let her answer a page?

Maybe. But he didn't want to draw attention to himself on the odd chance that Weingold wasn't aware of his presence in the hospital.

Leaning on the counter, he dropped his voice, hoping to sound like an abashed boyfriend. "No, that's okay. We were going to meet here this evening, but to be honest—" he shrugged and grinned "—I forgot where I was supposed to meet her. She'll have my hide if I don't show up, but I don't want to interrupt her by paging her—in case she's with a patient.''

The older woman gave him a conspiratorial smile and patted his hand. ''I doubt she'd skin a foxy dude like you!'' She winked broadly.

Gil felt the surprising heat of a flush creep into his cheeks. The feisty old gal had taken him by surprise.

''Oh, sugar,'' she said with a deep laugh, ''don't be so shocked. A woman don't ever get too old to dream! Why don't you check over at the WomanCare clinic? I saw her headed that way a few minutes ago.''

''Was she with Dr. Weingold?''

The gray-haired volunteer frowned. ''You know, I'm not sure. I was on the phone when she passed. I know *someone* was with her but...I just couldn't say for sure who it was, sugar.''

''That's okay. But they were definitely headed for the clinic?''

''Unless she had a strange yen to have some blood drawn. Nothing else down that corridor except the laboratory facilities.''

The relief washing through him felt sweeter than a spring rain. ''Thanks, Mabel, you're a peach.''

''Ah,'' she said, waving away his compliment. ''But if you ever find yourself craving some *mature* companionship...''

''It's a deal!'' he called as he raced down the corridor.

He passed through the breezeway that connected the WomanCare clinic to the main hospital structure. When he reached the clinic itself, he was startled to find the door unlocked. Had Valerie deliberately turned off the time-lock device? He hoped she still had that much latitude. That by now she wasn't being held prisoner—or worse—by the corrupt doctor.

He slowly made his way through the empty spaces. The unoccupied clinic had a ghostly feel. The main lighting was still off, the only illumination being the dim reflection of the red exit sign over the door and the luminous glow that surrounded the tiny emergency lights spaced throughout the area.

He passed the main reception area, then Monica's office. Rest rooms were next, followed by the counseling center, and finally, a half-dozen tiny examining rooms. The doctors' private offices, he knew, were located down the short hallways on either side of the main area.

Suddenly he glanced to the left. Reflected light, almost blinding in the darkness, poured into the hallway. Keeping his back flat against the wall, he edged toward the illuminated area.

A wide glass window separating the corridor from another room was the source of the light. Taking a long five-count, he dropped onto his haunches and peeked up over the sill of the window.

The other room was some sort of laboratory, evidenced by the long expanses of stainless-steel countertops and assorted beakers and vials. A single goose-neck lamp illuminated an expensive-looking microscope, shedding ambient light on the surrounding white-tiled room.

To his surprise, the room wasn't as harshly lit as he'd expected. In fact, it was dim, shadowy. The contrast between the lab with its single lamp and the much darker hall had led to that impression.

Something moved suddenly within his peripheral vision. Gil shifted his position so he could get a better view.

Two shadowy figures stirred at the far end of the laboratory. He inched forward, praying that one of the figures was Valerie.

The hesitant hum of muted voices reached his ears. Gil strained, but couldn't catch their words. However, enough sound filtered through so he could tell the speakers were a man and a woman. Valerie?

At that moment the woman turned and walked directly into the narrow beam of light cast by the small lamp.

Monica Giesen!

After spotting him in the cafeteria, she must have rushed over here, passing him while he was talking with Mabel at the information counter.

Monica turned and gesticulated to the other figure, motioning wildly. Then, with a growl of anger, she stalked forward, disappearing from Gil's view.

A moment later she returned, pulling something behind her.

From his vantage point below the window, Gil couldn't get a glimpse of what Monica had dragged into the lab. Hoping that her more brightly lit environment would shadow him from view, he rose slightly to get a better look. Any moment he expected to hear Monica shriek an alarm, alerting her partner to his presence.

But for once, his luck held and Monica turned away, affording Gil a look at what she'd tugged into the lab.

Sterile gauze bound a frantic-looking Valerie to a black padded hospital gurney. Wide strips of adhesive bandage were taped over her mouth in a makeshift gag. Her luminous blue eyes darted around the room in obvious fright.

For the first time in his life, Gil was terrified.

Not for his own safety, but for someone whose well-being, he realized, meant more to him than his own life.

He reached into his jacket pocket, savoring the heft of his service revolver. As Monica moved into view once more, he suddenly wondered about the thickness of the glass panel separating them. Safety was so important in a hospital setting that the window was no doubt fashioned of safety glass. But would it also be shatterproof? Certain kinds of glass-acrylic compounds, he knew, would deflect the bullets from a small-caliber weapon.

Valerie's safety was paramount.

If only there was some way of knowing exactly what was going on in there. What they were talking about. He had to find out if Valerie was in immediate danger, or whether he could bide his time and wait for a better opportunity to attempt a rescue.

Dropping again to his haunches, he duck-walked beneath the window and approached the door on the other side. The red light on the electronic panel told him the door was securely locked. No way in.

While he was deciding whether or not to sneak back into the front of the clinic and phone for backup, he noticed a steel control panel on the wall beside the window. Curious, he opened the small door. Several switches and dials controlled the air-conditioning, lighting and other physical aspects of the confined laboratory. Then he noticed a small toggle switch.

The light in the hall was so dim he had to squint to make out the tiny letters etched beneath the switch. "Microphone."

Was it possible that throwing the switch would allow him to hear what was transpiring in the impregnable lab? Glancing up, he spotted what looked like a small speaker mounted on the wall just above the window panel.

Gil flipped the switch.

Immediately Monica's strident voice could be plainly heard in the corridor.

"For once in your life, be a man!" she fumed at the male figure who was still hidden from Gil's sight. "There

are no options here. Unless you want to spend the next
fifty years making license plates!''

The murmur of a masculine voice filtered out. Gil still
couldn't catch his actual words, but his tone was suppli-
cating.

"Listen to me." Monica waved her manicured fingers
in the air. "Let me clarify our situation for you. We have
to end our operation tonight." She hooked a thumb at
Valerie. "Her boyfriend has probably already reported
his suspicions. He doesn't have any hard evidence yet or
we'd already be in jail. So we have to mop up all the
loose ends tonight. Including the nosy Dr. Murphy here."

Again the man spoke, but his words were still unclear.

Monica rolled her eyes, then punched her fists onto her
slender hips. "It's all worked out. You don't have to do
a thing." Again she gestured toward Valerie. "As soon
as she's out of the way, I can start on the computer work.
A few quick changes and Dr. Murphy's name is going
to appear as physician of record on all five births. Should
have done that all along. An oversight on my part."

A groan from the gurney attracted her attention, and
she bent over and hissed in Valerie's ear. "Stop whining.
You're giving me a headache."

Straightening, she once more addressed her associate.
"A careful leak to the media about the kidnappings will
start a public panic. No one will think about the missing
doctor for a few days. Once her 'suicide' is discovered,
the police—and the hospital—will be so happy to have
a scapegoat they won't dig very deeply into her death.
That's a given."

Her companion must have moved closer to the microphone. For the first time his voice clearly filtered through
the speaker. "What about that FBI boyfriend of hers?
He's not going to believe she committed suicide."

Monica laughed. A vile chortle that caused goose bumps to ripple along Gil's flesh.

"Oh, he'll believe it all right. Remember, our darling Dr. Murphy has been keeping a gigantic secret from him. When he finds out she was pregnant, he'll be so stunned at her deception he'll believe anything. And when the cops find out our little doctor had a bun in the oven, they'll think that's more motive. After stealing everyone else's babies, she turns up preggers and her guilty conscience drives her to suicide."

Monica's accomplice responded, but his words were lost on Gil.

His ears were roaring. With all-consuming rage. With utter confusion.

Valerie pregnant?

With his baby?

He wanted to break through the glass and grab her with his hands, shake her until the truth rattled from her lips. Why hadn't she told him? Why?

Sinking to the floor, Gil buried his face in his hands as he tried to swim above the bewildering feelings that were threatening to drown him.

Something had driven him to rush off in the middle of the night to Los Angeles. Something he'd found out. But it wasn't about Weingold or Monica, he was sure of it. Something was wrong, out of kilter. Slowly but steadily bits and fragments of his shattered memory were returning. If only those memory chunks would arrive in an orderly fashion, instead of a jumbled mess.

Out of the confusing chaos of his mind, a single truth crystallized. All of these bewildering thoughts could wait. Valerie's explanation—if she had one—could wait.

Right now he had to get a grip on himself. Had to don

the cold professional detachment that had cloaked his feelings for the past twenty years.

These people were going to kill Valerie.

Going to murder his unborn child unless he did something.

He didn't know exactly what the fiends had planned, some sort of lethal injection, probably. There was no time to summon backup officers.

He himself was the only barrier between the woman he loved and her death.

HORROR BUILT in Valerie's mind with every evil word that Monica uttered.

How could she ever have considered the woman a trusted friend? A valued colleague?

How could Monica have hidden this wellspring of hatred and greed for so long?

Not that it mattered. According to the terrifying plan she had just outlined, Valerie would be dead within the next few minutes unless she could find a way out of her predicament.

Turning her head, the only freedom of movement she still possessed, she spied the metal cart of supplies a few feet away. She tried to ignore the gleaming hypodermic needle and the vial lying beside it. A sickening feeling deep in the pit of her stomach warned that those items would be Monica's instruments of death.

But other medical paraphernalia was on the cart, as well. Encased in sterile paper and plastic liners were tongue depressors, tweezers, forceps and scalpels. If she could just reach one of those scalpels…

The cart was only a few feet away, but it might as well have been miles. She was so tightly bound that even wiggling her fingers caused excruciating pain in her wrists.

Monica had taken no chances when she'd trussed her hostage.

Tears wetting her lashes, Valerie turned her head from her former friend's mocking glare. If she and her baby had to die tonight, at least she wouldn't give Monica the satisfaction of seeing her heartache and fear.

Glancing at the observation window directly beside her, Valerie's pulse jumped at a sudden faint movement.

Was someone out there or was it merely wishful thinking?

As she watched a shadow moved. Gil? *Oh, God, please let it be Gil. Please.*

A strangled sob escaped her throat.

"What?" Monica screamed. "I told you to stop whining."

"No, look at her face. She looks…relieved. Like she saw something. I'll bet that FBI agent is here!" Monica's accomplice stepped forward, a gun in his hand.

With his other hand he grabbed the gurney and hauled Valerie away from the window.

Panic welled in her chest. She'd given Gil away! She had to do something, anything, to take their minds off him long enough for him to get away.

Frantic, she cast her eyes around the small space, looking for something to create a diversion. Then she noticed that she'd been pulled right against the cart of medical supplies.

Using every last fiber of her strength, Valerie lunged upward and forward at the same time, jerking the gurney a few more inches. But the small movement was enough to jar the cart.

Monica leaped forward, but before she could reach her side, Valerie hooked the tip of her toe under the lip of the cart. Once more mustering her strength, she kicked. The cart overturned with a satisfying crash.

Suddenly the room erupted in chaos.

Something battered the door. Monica was shrieking like a fishwife. Her accomplice raced for the door just as the lock finally gave and Gil burst into the room.

He didn't waste a second surveying the situation. As Monica's confederate raised the gun, Gil heaved the fire extinguisher he'd used as a battering ram.

At that moment Monica shoved the gurney into Gil's knees in a mad race for the door. Valerie could see Monica's hand slap the small lamp off the counter. Then the woman leaped at the flailing men, got tangled somehow and all three of them fell to the ground in a thrashing heap at the exact moment the only light went out.

Hearing a mad scramble at the door as the threesome fought to extricate themselves from the pile, Valerie closed her eyes and prayed.

Then the deafening report of a gunshot filled the air.

Chapter Seventeen

The acrid tang of cordite filled his mouth and lungs.

A hard ringing noise, like cymbals crashing, resonated in his ears as the reverberation of the gunshot went on and on.

He couldn't hear, couldn't think. Yet somehow, Gil's instincts, born from years of experience, kicked in. He wrenched the revolver from the other man's hands and pressed it into the small of his back. With all his heart, Gil wanted to pull the trigger. Wanted to eradicate from the earth this plague of a human who wrought such destruction after taking a sacred oath to nurture and heal.

But Gil had taken an oath, as well. He'd vowed to protect his country, its constitution and its law. He couldn't take that precious law into his own hands, no matter how justified it might seem.

Suddenly the man kicked backward, landing a solid blow on Gil's shin. Cursing with pain, he doubled over. Another sharp pain, like a karate chop, slammed into his wrist, and the gun went flying.

Ignoring the paralyzing pain, he dove for the floor in a mad scramble to recover the gun. Time stood still as he grappled with his foe. Before either could find the elusive weapon, Gil became aware of another sound. A sound more piercing, more urgent, than gunfire.

A woman's scream.

Valerie!

He struggled to his feet. Vaguely aware of a movement near the door, he knew one, if not both, of the criminals was escaping, but he didn't care. He had to reach Valerie. Had to help her.

Fumbling for the overhead-light switch, he winced as the brilliant blue-white fluorescent fixture came on. Then, he glanced down and saw Monica still lying in a crumpled heap at his feet.

She must have been knocked unconscious in the struggle, he thought with little concern. He nudged her inert body aside with his foot to clear a path to Valerie's side.

Her eyes were clenched shut against the harsh light, but she was alive and battling against her bonds like a woman possessed. Reaching into his pocket for his penknife, he cut the gauze bandages holding her prisoner, then tore the adhesive that was wrapped tightly around her head and mouth.

"Ouch!" she yelped.

He gathered her into his arms. "Did that creep hit you? Where are you shot?"

"I'm not," she said in a shaky voice as she struggled to sit upright.

"But I heard you scream," he said in disbelief. She must be in shock, he thought, as he scanned her body for signs of injury.

She finally made it to a sitting position, even though the trembling in her limbs was testimony to her fright. "It wasn't me. I…I think it was Monica. Help me."

Knowing better than to argue, he wrapped an arm around her waist and helped her off the table and onto her feet. She took a couple of wobbly steps then shrugged off his arm.

She had just knelt beside the injured woman when noise erupted all around them. Several armed security officers raced into the room.

"Someone reported gunshots!" the leader shouted, pointing a gun at Gil.

Knowing the men were operating on adrenaline, making a serious mistake a distinct possibility, Gil slowly raised his hands. "I'm Special Agent Branton from the Federal Bureau of Investigation. My identification is in my hip pocket."

He made a motion as if to retrieve his wallet.

"Don't move, fella!" the leader warned. "Keep those hands nice and high."

"This woman needs help!" Valerie shouted, gesturing to the fallen Monica. "I need a trauma team in here, now! Hurry, dammit," she insisted when no one responded.

Finally, as if recognizing the authority in her tone, the leader nodded his head. "Call for help. Get the Phoenix PD too. Tell 'em there's been another shooting."

BY THE TIME Detective Ferdy Sanchez strolled in, Valerie and the ER trauma team had fled with an unconscious Monica Giesen. The prognosis, Valerie said with a grim shake of her head, wasn't good. Accidentally wounded by her partner's gunfire, she had been rushed to surgery with life-threatening injuries—a .38 caliber bullet was lodged in her chest. The same caliber weapon as Gil's service revolver, which the officers promptly liberated.

IMMEDIATELY AFTER the medical team rushed the unconscious woman out of the WomanCare clinic, a hospital security officer ushered Gil out of the lab. To protect the crime scene, he stationed an officer by the door and herded Gil into the main reception area.

In the confusion surrounding the gunshot, Monica's accomplice had fled the scene.

Detective Sanchez pulled out his battered notebook. "We gotta stop meeting like this, Mr. Branton. It's bad for my reputation."

Gil twisted in the uncomfortable chair. "I know it looks bad, Detective, but you've got to listen to me."

"You have my complete attention."

Pulling his FBI identification from his pocket, Gil handed it to him. "I wasn't entirely on the level with you when we spoke before."

"Fancy that," Sanchez said as he examined the credentials. He tossed the wallet back. "'Course, I already knew you were a feebie."

"You did?"

The detective scowled. "You didn't think I swallowed your last story hook, line and sinker, did ya? Of course I checked you out. Matter of fact, if you hadn't volunteered this information by tomorrow, I'd already decided to have you picked up for obstructing justice. Figured an overnighter in the county jail might loosen your tongue."

Gil grinned at the sly cop. He'd been completely taken in by the man's "aw shucks" manner. Sanchez was nobody's fool.

Licking his index finger, Gil raised it in the air and chalked an invisible mark near the cop's head. "Score one for the local fuzz. Sorry about the deception, Ferdy. I just didn't know who I could trust."

Abandoning his good ol' boy routine, Sanchez leaned forward. "Why don't we start over, Special Agent Branton? I'd like to hear the whole story—from the start."

"All right. But first, you should start a search for Dr. Sidney Weingold. He might still be in the hospital."

His brow furrowed, Sanchez leaned back and studied Gil. "Now why should I look for Dr. Weingold?"

"Because he's behind this entire scam. And he shot Monica Giesen."

"You're sure?"

Gil hesitated. He wasn't one hundred percent certain, because he'd never gotten a clear look at his opponent in the dimly lit laboratory. But every sign pointed to the man. "It was Weingold."

The detective got up and stepped out of Gil's hearing to confer with one of his officers. The man nodded briefly and left.

Sanchez took his place back in the hard plastic chair. "We'll see what Dr. Weingold has to say about all this. Now, you were telling me about some scam?"

Closing his eyes to will the details into his memory-deficient brain, Gil slowly began his story.

FORTY MINUTES LATER, Gil was just finishing his tale when an exhausted Valerie slumped into a vacant chair beside the detective.

The two men glanced up. "How's Monica?" Gil asked.

"Still in surgery. If she survives that, it will still be touch and go for the next forty-eight hours."

"You know, I wondered what she was up to. One of the orderlies." Sanchez flipped through his notepad. "Ed Grant." He tapped the page with his fingertip. "Anyway Mr. Grant tried to tell your hospital administrator that he'd seen her searching patient files when she was supposed to be off-duty. But Abel wouldn't listen to him."

"I wish he'd come to me," Valerie said.

"Might have saved us all some trouble," the detective agreed.

Ferdy Sanchez rose to his feet and stretched. "Well, folks, looks like you have this situation pretty well under control. Won't be long until we have Dr. Weingold in custody and we can wrap this whole thing up. Good job, Agent."

Valerie stepped between the two men. "What did you say about taking Sid Weingold into custody? Why?"

Gil shot her a curious look. "Because of his role in kidnapping you tonight for starters."

She shook her head. "You've got it all wrong! Sidney wasn't involved."

"I don't understand," Gil said. "You were sitting with him in the cafeteria when Monica came in and drew my attention. Then you both disappeared. Are you saying that *wasn't* Weingold helping Monica in the lab?"

Valerie could see how he'd reached his conclusion, but Sidney Weingold was as much an innocent victim in this scam as she was. "We were talking about why Sidney needed the time off when Carl Bender, Dr. Bender," she said in an aside to Detective Sanchez, "came into the cafeteria. He said there was an emergency in the WomanCare clinic. But when we got there, he…he hit Sid on the back of the head then grabbed me. He was strapping me to a gurney when Monica showed up. I don't know what happened to Dr. Weingold."

Sanchez leaned forward, knuckles on the desk top. "Are you certain, Dr. Murphy?"

"Of course I'm certain! I know both men very well. Carl Bender is Monica's accomplice, not Sid."

While Sanchez left the room to modify the instructions to his team searching the hospital, Gil stood quietly, not even looking at her. Was he upset because he'd given misinformation to the police? Because he'd drawn the wrong conclusion?

Before she could ask, Detective Sanchez came back into the room. "Got that squared away. Now, there are a few minor points I'd like to clear up, Dr. Murphy."

Valerie wasn't sure she could summon the energy for another round of questions about Monica Geisen. Apparently taking her lack of enthusiasm for fatigue, the policeman smiled. "But I don't see any reason why those questions can't wait until tomorrow. Could you give me a buzz in the morning, Dr. Murphy? I'd like to arrange a convenient time to meet with you and get your statement."

"Of course." She took his proffered business card and slipped it into her jeans pocket.

Gil paused at the door. "Any chance I could have my service revolver back?"

"Nope. Need it for ballistics."

"But it wasn't fired."

"We still have to dot all the *i*s and cross all the *t*s. Especially with an officer-involved shooting. You know the routine."

"Yeah. Let me know when I can get it. I feel kind of naked without it."

"Will do."

Gil and Valerie left the WomanCare clinic, his hand on her elbow. The temperature had dropped dramatically, she noted as they crossed through the parking lot. With desert temperatures soaring to well over a hundred degrees during the day, a drop into the seventies at night was dramatic and soothing.

A soft breeze blew fine strands of hair into Valerie's eyes. She pushed them back and breathed deeply, savoring the scents of mesquite and night-blooming jasmine.

During the spring and summer, she spent most of her evenings on her patio, drinking in these very scents. Loving the fresh tranquility of her life on the edge of the vast desert.

Tonight, however, a troubling sense of doom weighed on her shoulders. Monica's betrayal had cut Valerie to the very core. How could she ever again trust her own judgment?

The unearthing of the kidnapping ring could have far-reaching consequences. Once Martin Abel got wind of the fact that WomanCare clinic employees were implicated in this scandal, he would no doubt withdraw his support for the clinic. Without the hospital behind her, the other funding would trickle away and the center would have to shut down.

Years of sweat, pleading and cajoling. All for nothing.

Valerie felt as if her heart were trapped between the jaws of a huge vise, and it was crushing the vitality and life from her soul.

One other burden weighed more heavily than the rest. Gil. The baby.

No more stalling, no more excuses. Tonight. As soon as they were settled back in her house, Valerie would tell him about the baby.

She must have rehearsed the moment a thousand times since she'd first discovered her condition. It was ironic, really. She, a doctor of obstetrics and gynecology, a woman who counseled others about birth control was going to have an unplanned baby.

Oh, she could explain *how* the accident had happened. That was the easy part. Her delicate body chemistry wouldn't allow her to take birth-control pills, so she had to rely on other less effective methods. A small laugh rippled up her throat, dying before it reached her mouth.

The manufacturer of her personal method of birth control crowed that its product was eighty-eight percent effective.

Great odds. Unless you fell in that twelve percent.

Oh, well, it was a done deal. She'd made her choice and she'd happily live with it.

But what about Gil? How would he take the news? Would he feel trapped? Would he hate her for her deceit over these past few days?

She realized with a start that he hadn't said a word since they'd left the clinic. Curious, she glanced over at him. His jaw was set, stoic. His dark eyes were focused dead ahead. She reached over to take his hand.

He allowed her grasp, but his hand was slack around hers.

She started to ask him what was wrong, but they'd almost reached the Blazer, and she decided to wait until they were home. Let him unleash all his fury at once. Get it over with.

Now that the urgent rush of adrenaline had finally faded, Gil was feeling let down. Almost dejected. Detective Sanchez said he'd smashed the kidnapping ring, and he guessed they had. So why didn't he feel victorious?

He knew it was only a matter of time until Weingold was found, safely he hoped, and Carl Bender was apprehended and tucked behind bars. For all practical purposes, the case was over.

In a few days he would be going back to Washington for a new assignment. For the first time Gil thought he might accept the training position they kept offering at Quantico. Fieldwork no longer offered the thrill it had in his youth. He was tired of living out of a suitcase. Tired of not having a life.

When Valerie reached for his hand, the core reason for

his sense of dissatisfaction came rushing back with the fury of a raging flood. She was pregnant. And she'd kept it from him.

Before Monica had blurted out the news, he'd half intended to put in his papers. Retire. Hell, Phoenix was a big city. He could get a job here. For the first time in his life, he'd thought he might have found the woman to grow old with. The woman he'd often thought didn't exist.

Until Valerie Murphy had snapped that blond braid over her shoulder and taken his heart captive.

Until she'd betrayed him with her lies and deceit.

Now, he just wanted it all over so he could get back to D.C. He'd see his lawyer, arrange for support payments to be taken out of his paychecks. That way he wouldn't have to deal with her.

He just wished running away from her gave him some sense of happiness. Peace. Instead, the thought of a life without Valerie Murphy felt like a prison sentence.

His troubled thoughts were interrupted when they reached the Blazer. Walking with Valerie to the passenger side first, he was about to unlock the door when a man's voice halted them.

"Just hold it right there!"

They whirled around.

Carl Bender was standing behind them with a gun carefully pointed at Valerie's midsection. His eyes were red-rimmed and his hair stuck out as if he'd received an electric shock. The man looked frightened to the point of desperation.

"I wondered when you'd show up," Gil said casually. If he could engage Bender in conversation he might have a chance to disarm him.

"Why couldn't you just stay out of it? Wasn't your accident in Los Angeles a strong enough warning?"

"Was that you?" Gil asked in mock surprise. "I didn't think you had the intestinal fortitude to come after me personally. I thought a hired assassin was more to your liking."

"Shut up before I shoot you right here," Bender said, waving the gun at Gil's head before refocusing on Valerie's stomach. On their baby. "Drop those keys and move away from the car."

Gil stepped in front of Valerie and placed a firm hand on her shoulder. Now that he was closer, he could smell the manic fear emanating from Bender's body. The man was a ticking bomb. Gil dangled the keys in the air and taunted, "You mean these keys?"

"Yeah, wise guy. Those keys. Now drop them."

He took another step forward, keeping his body between Valerie's and Bender's, and tossed the keys away from the car.

Instinctively Bender's head swiveled to follow their progress. "You son of a bi—"

Seizing the brief chance, Gil grabbed Valerie's wrist and pulled her to relative safety behind the car. "Stay down," he whispered, then rose slightly to peer over the Blazer.

Bender kept glancing over his shoulder, waving his gun at them while he searched the parking lot for the keys.

Gil ducked back down and again grabbed Valerie's arm. "Come on!"

They ran through the maze of parked vehicles, trying to stay low and out of sight while they made their way back to the safety of the hospital. Bender must have heard their running footsteps, though, because they'd only gone a short distance before they heard him shout. "Stop! Stop, dammit, or I'll shoot!"

Gil didn't know if they were within Bender's sights, but he knew their only hope was to get away from the crazed doctor. He kept his body between Valerie and the sound of Bender's approaching footsteps, as he urged her to keep moving.

Of all the times not to have his gun. Gil damned Sanchez for sticking to protocol and insisting that he surrender his weapon until the details were tied up.

But he had to protect Valerie. Had to protect his unborn child. The only weapon he had was his experience. And he had plenty of that.

On the other hand, this was no doubt Carl Bender's first real brush with the law. He would be terrified, almost insane with fear of exposure and jail. If Gil just stayed calm and kept out of shooting range, they could outwit him. He hoped. Their lives depended on it.

Crouching low, they darted between the parked cars until they were behind the last car, the last bit of cover. The brightly lit lobby beckoned like a welcoming beacon, but at least twenty yards of open ground stood between them and the hospital doors.

Suddenly he realized he could no longer hear Bender's footsteps. He counted silently to ten before inching up over the edge of his car.

Apparently having abandoned the chase, Bender was running back toward the Blazer. Gil could imagine the desperate man fumbling with the lock as he scrambled to make his escape.

Now was their chance. Maybe their only chance.

He grabbed Valerie's hand and they started racing across the remaining tarmac when they heard a car door slam. Bender was in the Blazer. Would he come after them? Try to run them down?

His heart pounding in fear, Gil pushed Valerie in front of him as they continued their frantic dash for safety.

They were still twenty feet from the hospital door when a force of immense magnitude thumped into his back and tossed him onto the scant lawn in front of the hospital. Then a loud boom threatened to burst his eardrums.

The explosion rocked the night. The noise was so loud, so penetrating, Gil had a momentary thought that a meteor had crashed through the atmosphere and was pulverizing the planet.

The blue-black night burst into sudden color.

A firestorm of white-hot flames shot a hundred feet into the air and rained down a clattering maelstrom of pieces of the Blazer. A huge chunk of flying metal landed only inches from his head.

As more debris crashed around them, he crawled on bloodied hands and knees and threw himself across Valerie's still form. *Oh, God, please let her be alive.* They could resolve the other problems. Everything would be okay. If she was still alive. Tears filled his eyes and his throat burned as if the fire from the bomb had invaded his very body. He hadn't cried since he was a small boy. Tears were for sissies. Still, the tears came as he dropped his head over Valerie's shoulder and whispered his love into her ear.

A soft movement caught at his heart.

"Val? Honey, are you all right?"

She laughed wryly as she struggled to sit up. "You gotta stop asking me that. I'm fine, I think. A few more bruises to add to the collection. What just happened? The end of the world?"

He pointed to the still-burning hulk of the Blazer.

"Oh, my God," she whispered.

Gil pulled her into the V between his legs and held on for dear life. "Guess that bomb is how Monica planned to take care of us."

"You mean when she told Carl she needed the money?"

"Yeah, when I had my mind made up that she was talking to Sid Weingold, not Carl Bender. I owe Weingold an apology. Guess I wanted him to be guilty, so I interpreted all the clues to fit my supposition."

She twisted in his arms. "Why *did* you want Sid to be guilty?"

He glanced back at the hospital, where a small horde of people poured out the door. They wouldn't be alone much longer. Dipping his head, he touched his lips to a skinned spot on her forehead. "I was jealous of him, plain and simple."

"But why?"

"Let's see…. He's rich, good-looking, a doctor and you think the sun rises off his salon-coiffed hair."

She laughed again. "Sid's pretty wonderful, but I always liked darker, more physical men." She reached up and touched the patchwork of stitches on his temple. "Rugged is good."

Embarrassed and oddly pleased, he took her fingertips and guided them to his lips. "Kind of ironic, don't you think?"

She swiveled to look up at him. "What is?"

The dark smudge on the tip of her nose was too irresistible. Gil kissed it away before responding. "Carl Bender provided the money to pay for the intended hit on us. So, in a manner of speaking, he paid for his own death. Poetic justice, if you ask me."

"Mmm. You know, he wasn't the nicest person in the world, but he was a fine physician. Could have had a great career, except he just didn't like people."

Gil nodded toward the smoldering heap. "No, I'd say the man was definitely lacking in people skills."

She nestled against his chest, seemingly oblivious to the sound of footsteps running toward them. "You know something, Branton? I don't think I'm cut out to be a cop."

"You know what, Doc? I don't think I am, either. At least, not any longer."

Twisting in his lap, she looked up at him, her face radiant in the orange-gold light shed by the burning vehicle. "What are you saying, Gil?"

Gil lowered his head until his lips were an inch from hers. At that moment the gang of doctors, nurses, technicians and police reached their side. The wail of a fire engine added to the cacophony.

He lifted his head. It was too late. The magical moment had vanished.

Ferdy Sanchez was the first to speak. "*Madre de Dios!* I can't leave you two alone for a single minute, can I?"

Without waiting for a reply, he turned and barked orders, and three men raced to direct the fire crew to the burning hulk. An ER nurse produced two blankets and draped them around the still-dazed pair. Valerie knew the nurse was anticipating the onset of shock, but she felt astonishingly calm. And relieved, now that the worst was finally over.

Emily Pierce pushed her way forward and knelt beside Valerie. After a somewhat brusque but thorough examination, she rocked back on her heels and scowled. "Doctor, I think you'll find there are easier ways to get a few days off than beating yourself half to death."

Her gruff demeanor was exactly what the doctor needed. Valerie grinned and held up a hand. Pierce pulled her to her feet. She moved to help Gil to his feet, too, but he waved her off. He hated to admit it, but the woman intimidated the hell out of him. He kept expecting her to yank a hypodermic out of her pocket and poke him in the rear.

Now that the fire crew had doused the smoldering Blazer, Ferdy Sanchez strode back and stood in front of them, hands on his hips. After asking a few questions about the events of the past half hour, he finally closed his notebook. "You two need another repair job in the ER?"

Valerie raked her eyes over Gil, as if assessing the damage. "I don't think so. I can clean these minor cuts and abrasions at home. And home is where I want to be right now."

Sanchez nodded. "Since you killed another car, I suppose you'll need a ride?"

She grinned broadly. "We'd appreciate it."

The detective barked out another order and tossed his keys to his assistant. The young man hurried off. Less than a minute later the detective's unmarked police unit squealed to a halt a dozen feet away.

Gil kept his arm around Valerie as they hobbled to the car. Every muscle and joint in his body ached. Tomorrow would be worse, he knew. Unless he could ward off some of the damage with a long, steaming shower.

Of course if they showered together, he wouldn't have to worry about saving enough water for her. He was nothing if not thrifty and mindful of the environment, he reflected as they slid into the front seat beside Sanchez.

With a short blast of his siren to clear the crowd, they finally left the hospital parking lot.

"Somebody said that crispy critter in the car is Dr. Carl Bender," Sanchez said. "Can either of you confirm that?"

"Yeah." Seated by the passenger door, Gil looked around Valerie to respond. "It was Bender, all right. I was so sure Sidney Weingold was Monica's partner."

"Nah," Sanchez replied. "Bender's guilt doesn't really surprise me. Dr. Weingold phoned me this afternoon with some crazy story about a phony adoption ring working out of the WomanCare clinic."

"He did?" Another surprising bit of news. "Weingold figured out what was going on?"

"Sort of. He thought *you* were behind it, Branton."

"Me?"

"Yeah. He'd sort of figured out that strange things started happening about the time you first showed up at Parker Memorial. That's why he was so desperate to reach Dr. M, here. To warn her."

Gil was so stunned he couldn't respond. No wonder Weingold acted so guilty whenever he was around. They'd had a real Mobius loop of distrust going, and neither of them had been willing or able to break it.

Valerie spoke for the first time. "Speaking of Sidney, have they found him yet? I'm so worried about him. I hope he isn't badly hurt."

Strangely enough Gil hoped the same thing. Pure juvenile jealousy had caused him to throw all his suspicions on the doctor. Now he had to meet the man face-to-face and apologize. He only hoped it wasn't too late.

While Gil was wallowing in guilt over his unprofessional treatment of Sid Weingold, Valerie was overcome with disturbing thoughts of her own.

As if sensing their need to sort out the details of the

past few hours, Sanchez kept his silence for the remainder of the ride to Scottsdale.

Now that it was safe to return to her little house, Valerie was filled with a yearning for home. For safety. But there was one more hurdle she had to face before the night was over. She had to tell Gil about the baby.

She felt sick to her stomach. Would he ever forgive her?

They had just pulled into the driveway when the car radio crackled. Sanchez picked up the microphone. After some arcane codes were exchanged amid a static jumble of competing messages, she was able to pick out the words of the young officer who had helped at the scene. "Just found Dr. Weingold."

"What's his condition?" Sanchez demanded.

More static. "Unconscious but alive. ER people said someone pistol-whipped him and left him for dead. He came to and crawled out of a utility closet. They got him in intensive care, but the doctor said his condition is stable."

Valerie and Gil exchanged a look of relief.

Sanchez signed off and put the cruiser in park. After thanking the detective for his help and promising to make themselves available for more questions the next day, Valerie and Gil climbed wearily out of the car. Valerie's anticipation of the secure feeling of home failed to materialize. She felt oddly discomfited now that they were alone in the house. No doubt her anxiety was only dread over the onerous task she still faced. "How about some coffee?" she asked, perhaps in a subconscious bid to stall for more time.

"Yeah. Just what the doctor ordered." Spreading the Santa Fe-style blanket over the upholstery to protect it from his filthy, sooty clothes, Gil collapsed into the arm-chair.

In Valerie's professional opinion, the man was emotionally and physically spent.

She returned a few moments later with a bamboo tray laden with coffee fixings. She added a double dose of cream and sugar to her mug, then sat on the edge of the sofa across from him. After a quick, fortifying sip she set the mug on the end table. "Gil, there's something I have to tell you."

"You're planning on eloping with Sid Weingold, after all."

She tossed her head. "This is serious."

His own mug rattled on the terra-cotta coaster as he pinned her with his dark gaze. "Okay, shoot."

"When…when you left for Los Angeles, I suspected but wasn't sure…. Anyway I found out for certain soon after that…that I'm going to have a baby."

He picked up his mug. "I know."

"You do?" She was speechless with shock.

"Yeah. Monica mentioned it in the lab tonight. I'd just found the switch for the speaker in the corridor."

"So you've known all this time and didn't tell me?"

His laugh was harsh. "Oh, that's rich. In the space of two hours, during which time I was in a fistfight, nearly shot, then mugged and finally almost blown up, gee, I guess I forgot to mention that your secret was out. Of course, you didn't happen to find the time, or think it worth mentioning, over the past what…three or four days?"

"I was going to. I even tried once."

"What stopped you?"

Valerie closed her eyes and sank back against the sofa

cushions. Her worst nightmare was coming true. Gil was furious. He would never forgive her. It was over.

She gave one half-hearted try at an explanation. "You'd disappeared without a word. Then showed up at the hospital with some crazy story. You didn't even come to see me when you got back to town! I felt I...I couldn't trust you at first."

He took a long swallow of coffee. When he spoke his voice was cold and emotionless. "You trusted me enough to sleep with me."

Valerie had no rebuttal. No words that could make him understand. In hindsight she wasn't sure she understood herself. Knowing Gil was quick to anger and just as quick to regain control, she waited.

Finally he looked up at her. His eyes were luminous, raw with pain. "I don't want to sound like a crybaby, but I have to tell you this past week has been a nightmare. And on top of it all, I never knew from one minute to the next where you stood, how you felt about anything. About me."

He held up a hand as she started to interrupt. "Ever worked jigsaw puzzles? That's what my memory feels like. A little piece here, that makes no sense on its own. Another piece over there—sometimes conflicting with what I thought I knew about the first piece. But as more and more of my memory has returned, I've started to get a glimpse of the whole picture."

Drawing a deep breath, as if he needed an infusion of courage, he continued, "Tonight I recognized one simple truth. How close I came to losing you for good. I wish you'd told me about the baby earlier, and I wish I'd taken you into my confidence before I went to Los Angeles. Since we can't have those opportunities back, I want us to start fresh. A child deserves two parents. So can we give ourselves a second chance?''

Her heart in her mouth, she said, ''Gil, I don't want to…force a relationship just for the sake of the baby.''

''The baby's important and probably sped up this process, but it's you I want to be with. You're the only woman I've ever said these words to.''

''What words, Gil?'' she asked.

When he finally uttered them, he wasn't quick or glib. Emotion wavered in his voice. ''I love you, Dr. Valerie Murphy, and want to spend the rest of my life with you. So what do you say? Care to settle down with a battered ex-FBI agent?''

Sliding off the sofa, she crossed the small space between them and knelt before him. ''Are you sure?''

''As sure as I've ever been of anything,'' he whispered, gently cupping her face with his hands.

''But there's so much to be worked out. Jobs, where we'll live, houses to sell.…''

''Details. Minor details,'' he assured her.

''Then I guess…what am I saying?'' Reaching up, she threw her arms around his neck and settled on his lap. ''Of course I want us to be together.''

''Good thing. While you were fixing the coffee I phoned D.C. and told my boss I was hanging it up. Now I'm an unemployed, homeless, battered ex-FBI agent.''

She trailed a finger down the maze of cuts and bruises marring his ruggedly handsome features. ''Definitely battered. But you're not homeless. And don't worry—we'll find you a job.''

He buried his fingers in her mass of hair. ''I could be a bouncer at a topless joint. Wonder if those bikers would give me a reference?''

Holding his precious face in her hands, she lowered her head until her lips hovered a scant whisper from his. "Shut up and kiss me. Doctor's orders."

And so he did.

Epilogue

After nine hours of labor, it was finally over.

They were back in Valerie's room, waiting while the pediatrician gave the baby a thorough examination. Of course, Gil had no doubts that they'd just delivered the healthiest, most beautiful infant on earth.

Valerie stirred and he leaned over the bed, brushing a strand of hair from her wan face. "You're the most beautiful woman on earth. I love you more than life."

"I hope you're not planning on a large family. Delivering babies is a whole lot easier than having them yourself," she groused.

"But you were wonderful. And our child is wonderful."

She touched his face. "The baby *is* beautiful. Perfect."

"Mmm. You know, before this case I'd never given much thought to kids. But seeing the faces of those five mothers when their babies were returned gave me a clue that there must be something special about children."

She laughed. "I thought Karen Lundquist was going to explode with joy. But no more than I felt when Sid first handed our baby to me."

As part of a plea agreement for a reduced prison sentence, Monica had provided authorities with the locations of the kidnapped children. Although Valerie was happy the babies were reunited with their families, she sympathized with the adoptive parents who were caught in the middle. She hoped they all found babies to adopt—through legitimate agencies.

They were interrupted by a soft tap on the door. Sid Weingold's tawny head peeked around the frame. "Safe to come in?"

Gil rose to his feet and went to shake the doctor's hand. "Sid, I have to hand it to you. You sure know how to deliver babies."

The doctor approached the bed and picked up Valerie's hand under the pretext of taking her pulse. Gil suspected the man was still harboring a crush.

"So you think you'll keep the baby?" he jested. "Decided on a name yet?"

Gil and Valerie exchanged a look. "Well, if it had been a boy, we'd considered naming him—"

Fierce Pierce chose that moment to erupt into the room, a tiny flannel-wrapped bundle tucked in her arms. "I don't care how grateful you are to Dr. Weingold," she announced as she laid the infant on her mother's breast. "You aren't naming this precious child Sidney. No offense, Doctor." She flashed him an unabashed look.

"Actually we have decided on a name," Valerie Murphy-Branton said as her husband reached down and knuckled the tiny perfect cheek. "You tell them, honey."

He looked up and fastened a wary stare on the nurse. "We've decided to call her Emily."

Emily Pierce's hand flew to her ample bosom. "After me?"

Gil raised a finger in warning. "Under one condition."

"What's that?"

"No one ever calls her 'Fierce.'"

Fierce Pierce swiped at a tear. "Oh, don't you worry about that, Mr. Branton. No one's going to call my darling little namesake by such an awful nickname."

Weingold patted Valerie's shoulder. "Well, I'd best be getting back to my rounds."

She grabbed his hand. "Her middle name, we decided, is going to be Sydney. With a *y*."

"Really?" He bent over to inspect the precious bundle a little more closely.

As four adults crowded around the bed, Emily Sydney Branton let out an authoritative yell.

Father, doctor and nurse exchanged a look, then turned their grinning faces to Valerie. "Yep," Gil declared, "she's already just like her mother."

*Get ready for heart-pounding romance
and white-knuckle suspense!*

HARLEQUIN®

I N T R I G U E®

raises the stakes in a new miniseries

★ THE McCORD ★

FAMILY

★ COUNTDOWN ★

*The McCord family of Texas is in a
desperate race against time!*

With a killer on the loose and the clock ticking toward
midnight, a daughter will indulge in her passion for her
bodyguard; a son will come to terms with his past and help a
woman with amnesia find hers; an outsider will do anything to
save his unborn child and the woman he loves.

With time as the enemy, only love can save them!

**#533 STOLEN MOMENTS
B.J. Daniels**
October 1999

**#537 MEMORIES AT MIDNIGHT
Joanna Wayne**
November 1999

**#541 EACH PRECIOUS HOUR
Gayle Wilson**
December 1999

Available at your favorite retail outlet.

HARLEQUIN®
Makes any time special ™

Visit us at www.romance.net   HICD

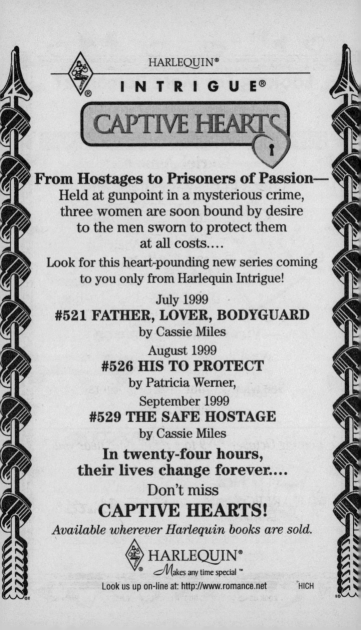

HARLEQUIN®
Makes any time special ™

WIN A
DREAM

In celebration of Harlequin®'s golden anniversary

Enter to win a *dream!* You could win:

- A luxurious trip for two to *The Renaissance Cottonwoods Resort* in Scottsdale, Arizona, or

- A bouquet of flowers once a week for a year from **FTD**, or

- A $500 shopping spree, or

- A fabulous bath & body gift basket, including **K-tel**'s *Candlelight and Romance* 5-CD set.

Look for **WIN A DREAM** flash on specially marked Harlequin® titles by Penny Jordan, Dallas Schulze, Anne Stuart and Kristine Rolofson in October 1999*.

FTD

RENAISSANCE.
COTTONWOODS RESORT
SCOTTSDALE, ARIZONA

K-TEL

COMING NEXT MONTH

#533 STOLEN MOMENTS by B.J. Daniels
The McCord Family Countdown

Sexy cowboy Seth Gantry "kidnapped" Olivia McCord to save her
life, but his reluctant hostage refused to believe him—until their safe
house exploded. Now, in a race against time, Seth's the only man she
can trust. Determined to resist her allure, Seth vowed to keep her—
and his heart—safe at all costs....

#534 MIDNIGHT CALLER by Ruth Glick writing as Rebecca York
43 Light St.

Meg Faulkner is on a mission—one she can't remember. Inside the
confines of Glenn Bridgman's military-like estate, unsure of who is
friend and who is foe, she must fight to evoke the memories that will
set her free—and resist the temptation of the intensely desirable
Glenn. But when the memories come, will Meg be able to escape with
her heart intact?

#535 HIS ONLY SON by Kelsey Roberts
The Landry Brothers

Born and raised in Montana as the oldest of seven sons, Sam Landry
knew the importance of family. He wanted nothing more than to keep
the son he had come to love as his own—until he discovered the boy's
real mother was alive. Finding the alluring Callie Walters proved
dangerous—someone would kill to keep the truth a secret. But Sam
was determined to keep his son—and the woman he had come to
love—safe....

#536 UNDERCOVER DAD by Charlotte Douglas
A Memory Away...

FBI agent Stephen Chandler knows he and his ex-partner,
Rachel Goforth, are in danger, but he can't remember who's trying to
kill them or why—though Stephen can vividly recall his attraction to
the sensual Rachel. But when Rachel's daughter is kidnapped, nothing
can stop him from tracking a killer—especially when he learns her
child is also his....

In October 1999,
Harlequin Intrigue®
delivers a month of our
best authors, best miniseries
and best romantic suspense
as we celebrate Harlequin's
50ᵗʰ Anniversary!

Look for these terrific
Harlequin Intrigue® books
at your favorite retail stores:

STOLEN MOMENTS (#533)
by B.J. Daniels

MIDNIGHT CALLER (#534)
by Rebecca York

HIS ONLY SON (#535)
by Kelsey Roberts

UNDERCOVER DAD (#536)
by Charlotte Douglas